THE ELUSIVE
LORD EVERHART

The Rakes of Fallow Hall Series

VIVIENNE LORRET

AVONIMPULSE
An Imprint of HarperCollinsPublishers

Excerpt from *The Devilish Mr. Danvers* copyright © 2015 by Vivienne Lorret.
Excerpt from *When Good Earls Go Bad* copyright © 2015 by Megan Frampton.
Excerpt from *The Wedding Band* copyright © 2015 by Lisa Connelly.
Excerpt from *Riot* copyright © 2015 by Jamie Shaw.
Excerpt from *Only In My Dreams* copyright © 2015 by Darcy Burke.
Excerpt from *Sinful Rewards 1* copyright © 2014 by Cynthia Sax.
Excerpt from *Tempt the Night* copyright © 2015 by Dixie Brown.

EPub Edition MARCH 2015 ISBN: 9780062380500

Print Edition ISBN: 9780062380494

AM 10 9 8 7 6 5 4 3

*To my grandparents, my dad,
my aunts and uncles, who shared stories
around a harvest table each Sunday
and taught me their craft.
I love you all.*

"Love is three-quarters curiosity."

GIACOMO CASANOVA

CHAPTER ONE

The end...

Those words never failed to captivate Calliope Croft with their power.

Holding back a sigh, she read the last page once more. *Oh, perhaps twice.* Then, she hugged the little book to her bosom, sending the story through the fur lining of her redingote and directly into her heart. The tale was over, and yet to her, *the end* signified a well-deserved beginning.

With the thought, her gaze drifted across the carriage, past the snowy rolling hills of Lincolnshire beyond the window, to where her brother and his wife napped. They'd been married nearly six months now. An arm around his bride, Griffin rested a cheek atop her head, while Delaney nestled against his shoulder.

If one ignored the fact that her brother snored like a bear and that her sister-in-law's open mouth had formed a spot of drool on his greatcoat, the image they created was actually quite romantic.

Calliope took complete credit for her brother's state of matrimonial bliss. A smug grin flitted across her lips as she looked down to the couple's joined hands.

One day Griffin might even thank Calliope for having abandoned Delaney during a summer storm in an effort to hurry along their endless courtship. After all, some trials must be borne for the sake of a perfect ending—as every great romantic novel had taught her.

Unfortunately, real-life happily ever afters were far too rare.

After a final quixotic squeeze, Calliope placed the book inside her satchel. Somehow, her gloved finger caught against the hidden pouch she'd sewn into the lining. For a moment, she went still. Did she dare reach inside?

Just once more, she promised.

Then again, Calliope *always* told herself it would only be once more. After five years of keeping this secret, she was ashamed of how many *once mores* there had been.

Her heart quickened. The rapid pounding in her ears was loud enough to awaken Endymion from eternal slumber. Worried her brother and his wife could hear it too, she cast a surreptitious glance across the carriage.

Still asleep. Good. It was safe to indulge just once more…

Taking a sip of air, she quietly lifted her treasure out of the satchel. Then carefully, she unfolded the thin, yellowed parchment that was so well loved it resembled a square of tea-stained linen.

My love,
    I am wrecked!

How can a single glance wield such power? Oh, but not even a glance—for you were turned away at first and all I saw were dark honey tresses spilling down the elegant curve of your neck. They pressed the barest of kisses to your shoulders. My own lips tingled.

Even though I did not know your name, there I stood, transfixed by a foreign sensation. In that moment, I was a voyager witnessing land after a lifetime at sea, and blind to the rocks jutting up between us. My only desire was to breech any distance in order to stand by your side. I longed to see you turn, lift your gaze to mine, and recognize the soul that had inexplicably crashed into yours.

Alas, before the tide could draw me in, you bestowed your smile upon another. The beauty of your face, alight with gaiety, speared through me with the green saber of jealousy. And yet, as I drew ever closer, the sight anchored me as well. For in your gaze, I saw no passionate glow from within. Instead, standing before me was a creature who yearned for something more but kept her wish carefully concealed.

We are the same, my love.

And this is love—I am certain. Nothing less dare swim through my veins at the thought of you. I feel at once as an anchor would—solid and unyielding—but also tethered to your hand. You are the line, the vessel, the sea, and the light that guides me to the shore. Your name is now a song that lives inside my heart—the siren call that compels me to dash myself upon the rocks of matrimony. Yes, matrimony!

This is no easy declaration. It would mean the end of this life. But to begin another with you—only you—would calm the churning sea within me.

> *Look for me, dear siren. My love. Call me to your shores and we will be united forever.*
>
>   *Yours irrevocably,*

Calliope let out a breath. Her heart always paused for two full beats when she reached the bottom of the page.

In the place of his signature, the parchment had been ripped—either by accident or by design, she did not know. Frayed and browning from years of her fingers tracing that jagged crescent-shaped edge, she still wished she knew the name that had once been there.

Oh, but what was the point of wishing? She could cover a meadow with the falling stars to which she'd whispered in the dark.

In the end, wishing had not given her back the last five years of her life.

When she'd first received the letter, she'd cast aside *everything* for him. She'd fallen in love with him—whoever he was—and all because of these words. They'd opened something inside her. It was as if the cover of her own book had lifted for the first time, rousing a story from the depths of her dreams.

Tempted by the kind of passion she'd only read about in novels, she'd wanted to experience that kind of love with a desperation she still didn't understand. Even now, her hands trembled as she refolded the letter and replaced it to the hidden pocket.

In the same moment, Griffin stirred. His snore cut off abruptly.

Calliope jerked her hand out of the satchel. Thankfully, her brother wasn't paying attention to her and did not see.

He shifted his hold on Delaney to peer out the window and rubbed a hand over the glass.

"We are almost to Stampton," he said quietly, without removing his gaze from the landscape. "Perhaps we should visit our cousin as we travel northward to Scotland. I received a letter from Aunt Augusta before we departed London, informing me that Pamela and Brightwell are at Fallow Hall."

Brightwell—her cousin's new husband *and* the man that Calliope had refused five years ago because of that letter.

Griffin waited. His gaze turned to Calliope. He was the only other person who'd known about the letter. Amongst tears and blubbering, she'd confided in him, confessing that she couldn't possibly marry Brightwell when she loved someone else.

And look how splendidly that turned out, Calliope's inner narrator mocked.

Offering a nod, Calliope encouraged Griffin to continue. She hoped it appeared as if she wasn't bothered at all by the mention of Brightwell.

"Apparently, Brightwell's friends have recently taken up residence at Fallow Hall and offered the quietude of the country for Pamela's...*recuperation*," Griffin said with the arch of a speculative brow.

Calliope remembered how Pamela had stayed in bed for over a fortnight because of a thistle in her finger. She hadn't been able to lift a thing on her own, even with her uninjured hand. Often, Calliope imagined that Pamela believed herself born to be queen. Yet when no princes had courted her— or dukes, marquesses, earls, or viscounts—she'd settled for being the wife of a baron. Brightwell was of a nature to accommodate her every whim, so it truly was a perfect match. At least, for Pamela.

Calliope's lips pursed. "The carriage accident was over a month ago. Aunt Augusta assured mother that Pamela wasn't injured."

"True. I have corresponded with her physician as well." A curious smirk hid beneath Griffin's stern expression. "And he states that she is well enough to return home once her mental faculties have returned."

Ah, now she understood the reason behind the smirk. Not only was Pamela used to being pampered, but she also was a bit scatterbrained.

Calliope tried not to grin. "Had the physician been acquainted with our cousin *before* the accident?"

"No." His deadpan expression caused a giggle to bubble up her throat.

"With enough inducement, I'm certain our cousin could remain wherever she was treated well…for a very long time."

"Yes," Griffin said with a nod. "However, Aunt Augusta can no longer stay with her. According to her letter, there was a horrendous beast of a dog who abused her prized Pekinese abominably, forcing a hasty retreat to Springwood House."

Aunt Augusta had been known to exaggerate on occasion for the sake of spoiling all creatures in her charge. Therefore, Calliope wasn't entirely certain this news warranted alarm. In fact, her aunt had once accused Calliope of abusing both Poppet and Lambkin when she'd refused to feed them the first bite of her tart.

"Without her mother's attention, it stands to reason that Pamela won't stay much longer in Lincolnshire. There can be little amusement for her in a house with her husband and his friends."

"I'd come to the same conclusion," Griffin said but with a trace of wariness in his tone.

Unfortunately, Calliope understood the source. Her brother watched over every limb of their family tree. Even before it was assumed he would inherit the earldom from their great-uncle, Griffin had possessed an innate sense of protectiveness. Right now, if Calliope's intuition was correct, he was battling between his duty to look in after their cousin and his desire to avoid causing Calliope distress.

Even though Brightwell was likely an excellent spouse for her cousin, Calliope couldn't help but think that he'd almost been her very own husband. Until that day in Bath five years ago when she'd said *I cannot* instead of *I will*.

She often wondered if she'd made the right decision.

Calliope drew in a breath and answered her brother's unspoken question. "I haven't seen Pamela since her wedding. It would only be right if we stopped by Fallow Hall while we are in Lincolnshire."

"If you are certain," he said. When she gave him a firm nod, he continued. "Then we shall make our journey on the morrow and remain for only a few hours."

With that settled, he turned to press a kiss into Delaney's auburn curls. "It is time to wake up, Mrs. Croft."

He whispered the words with such affection that Calliope blushed.

Feeling like a voyeur, she pretended a sudden desire to check the state of the coals inside the brass foot warmer. No rise of warmth penetrated her Limerick gloves. Regardless, she lifted the lid only to find a bed of finely sifted ash. Closing the lid, she sat back. Then, adjusting the heavy woolen blanket over her lap, she reached for the fur muff on the seat beside her.

Beyond the fogged carriage windows, heavy gray clouds shrouded the snow-covered countryside. The scenery should have appeared picturesque. Not bleak and desolate. But suddenly that was how she felt. Bleak, desolate…*alone*. In fact, if she were the lead character in one of the novels she read, she might expect castle ruins looming in the distance. Although, much the same, barren trees and scraggily shrubs marked the rutted landscape like scars along the Great North Road.

Since the clusters of evergreens did not suit a bout of melancholy, she chose to ignore their beauty and wallow for a moment longer. Because if one thought about snow-laden boughs, one naturally thought of sleigh rides. And no one could be unhappy while whisking through the brisk winter air with snowflakes kissing one's cheeks.

Calliope's sigh fogged up the glass, obscuring her view completely. Perhaps she never should have refused Brightwell's proposal. She'd genuinely liked his company. When he'd begun to court her all those years ago, she'd known the likely outcome.

Calliope blamed the letter. And *perhaps* her own somewhat overly romantic nature.

She could have made a life with Brightwell. Instead, she'd let him slip through her fingers. She could have had a sleigh ride partner for the rest of her life.

If she were the lead character in her own novel, she would have found the man who'd stolen her heart in a letter, married him posthaste, and lived happily ever after.

But sadly, her life hadn't turned out that way. She never found the man who'd written the most beautiful letter in existence. She'd spent years looking for him, compiling a series of lists in a journal on every gentleman of the *ton* who fit the criteria, and even those who did not.

In her opinion, her love-letter lover would possess:

1. *A poet's soul.*
2. *A passionate nature.*
3. *An undisguised yearning in his gaze.*
4. *An inclination to marry*

Or in the very least…

5. *Ink on his fingertips.*

She'd conducted surreptitious interviews with every dance partner, every sister, every maiden aunt and mother. Oddly enough, there had been numerous candidates, likely because she possessed a rather idealistic view of the world. Or at least, she *had*.

Until her love-letter lover had written to someone else.

When the first of the infamous Casanova letters appeared, her heart had broken. Other debutantes began receiving letters as well, six in all. While Calliope had kept hers a secret, the others had not. Their letters had been recited during calling hours with a great deal of sighs, fanning, and even a few swoons.

Yet while the other letters lacked the transformative intensity that hers possessed, she knew—after seeing them with her own eyes and noting the distinctive lettering—they were all written by the same hand.

That was when Calliope had realized that the *ton*'s Casanova was a glutton. A heart collector. Soon, it had become all too obvious that Calliope had been a fool for refusing Brightwell.

She'd often wondered if—upon his closer inspection— the anonymous author had found her nose too wide, her brows too straight, her lips too plump, and her brown eyes too plain. To each of those flaws she would concede. She believed, however, that her forehead sloped nicely to the edge of her blonde hair, and her ears were not too small. Those self-redeeming qualities notwithstanding, the result had been the same.

She'd been nothing special to him.

After the soul-crushing realization took hold, she no longer entertained the notion of having a Season. The love in her heart had turned from sweet to bitter. Afraid of breaking that fragile organ again, she gave up on marriage.

Now, five years later and on the shelf—a veritable spinster— she still wished to discover his identity. But not to marry him.

Absolutely not.

Instead, she wanted to expose this cad to the entire *ton* and make him pay for all the hearts and promises he'd broken.

Perhaps, one day, she would have the chance.

Gabriel Ludlow, Viscount Everhart, collapsed against the cushions of the sofa and gritted his teeth. The splint around his lower leg was a damnable nuisance. A month had passed since he'd broken the bone above his ankle, and he wasn't certain which bothered him more—the steady ache from the injury or the constant pinching from the cure.

Damn, he needed another drink.

Reaching forward to massage his leg between the slats of wood, Gabriel answered the challenge his friend had issued a moment ago. "Forget it, Montwood. Only a fool would wager against you. You have a peculiar way of winning when it suits you."

"Aye." Rafe Danvers nodded, the firelight glancing off his dark, angular features. Lifting a finger away from the glass in his hand, he pointed to the man in question. "I've seen you at the tables too many times to gamble with you, as well."

Renowned for his charm, Lucan Montwood ignored their comments and tossed the cork from another bottle into the fire. Lying on the floor in front of the hearth, the lanky gray dog that had made his home here in recent weeks didn't even flinch.

Arching black brows over amber eyes, Montwood considered the label of a rather costly scotch. A slow, appreciative grin followed.

Gabriel knew firsthand that it was costly. His own father, the estimable Duke of Heathcoat, had railed at him over the price. The tirade had expanded to encompass an entire life of imprudent choices. *"A waywardness that is unbecoming to the heir of a dukedom."*

No stranger to these lessons in castigation, Gabriel shouldn't have been bothered. Yet his convenient deafness during these moments had abandoned him of late. He was actually starting to *hear* his father. *Bugger it all.*

"Then in celebration of the departure of our most recent guest, I offer a toast—"

"Thank the Lord that Brightwell's mother-in-law left today," Danvers interrupted.

Montwood continued without missing a breath. "To Fallow Hall, where the rent is cheap and the friends are wealthy."

"And good riddance to those ankle-biting terrors she kept with her." Danvers bumped the rim of his glass against the bottle for another finger or two. In truth, the three of them had stopped counting the amount of fine spirits they'd consumed. It was more a measure of how close to filling without spilling that mattered now.

Filling without spilling? Gabriel rolled his eyes to the cornices outlining the domed ceiling overhead. This wasn't a good sign. He always started to rhyme when he'd had a too muc to drink. Although, he distinctly recalled several instances the past when he'd imbibed in a greater quantity and it hadn't taken hold so soon.

He blamed the Dowager Duchess of Heathcoat. Being under the constant scrutiny of the *ton*'s most formidable dragon had turned him into a one-bottle man. A sad day, indeed.

But there was nothing he could have done differently. At the time, she'd threatened to have his father cut him off. *Completely and without a shilling!* Well, except for the six thousand pounds he lived on each year. *Still…* What a fine threat, and from his own grandmother too.

Now, safely tucked away in the wilds of Lincolnshire, he could once again be himself. He'd had his fill of reforming. Especially when it had served no purpose, other than to make his father expect more from him. Until *more* had become too much.

Gabriel lifted his glass as soon as Montwood filled it to the brim. "To Fallow Hall—where neither brides nor babes may ever roam!"

The two other bachelors cheered *"Huzzah!"* and tossed back another swallow.

Danvers tipped the glass a bit too far and wavered on his feet. Swaying, he dropped into an upholstered armchair at his back. Yet with an outstretched arm, he managed to save the liquor with nary a splash and gave a low whistle.

Gabriel saluted his fellow one-bottle man.

Montwood made the rounds, topping them off, his pouring hand suspiciously steady. "Alas, there is a bride in residence already."

"Not mine. *Never* mine." The gratitude in Gabriel's voice echoed down from the ceiling. "Brightwell"—absent from their party, the poor bugger—"is stuck with that baggage. I was merely being charitable to allow an old friend and his wife a bit of respite."

"The carriage accident was a month ago," Danvers pointed out needlessly.

Gabriel was all too aware of how long ago the accident had been *and* how long their guests had been in residence in the east wing. Far too close to his own suite of rooms. For that reason, he spent most of his time here, in the north tower.

The map room had been his haven in recent weeks. Framed atlas prints adorned the walls, each one hosting places he'd been or new ones he'd yet to explore. At the back of the room, a spiral staircase curved up toward an open loft filled with books and journals of fellow travelers, in addition to enormous volumes of charts he was eager to inspect.

He was itching at the prospect of another expedition. The need to be aboard a ship, with the wind in his face and England at his back, filled his thoughts. That was something he was good at—running away. Staying one step ahead of guilt and responsibility.

"Not to add bumble broth to our merriment," Montwood interrupted, his tone ominous, "but the physician suggested continued bed rest until Lady Pamela's"—he coughed—"mental faculties return."

Gabriel didn't appreciate the reminder, but laughed nonetheless. "Though I have not been acquainted with Lady Brightwell overly long, she's been rather bird-witted the entire time. If bed rest will aid her, then surely another glass of scotch will *prevent* me from becoming foxed."

"Aye!" Danvers nodded and squinted in agreement as if Socrates had just spoken.

Montwood held his empty glass to his eye as if it were an enormous monocle. "Ah. A mystery solved at last! The reason Everhart hasn't married is that he would prefer a bluestocking for a bride."

Gabriel frowned. This conversation rang with too many familiar notes, bringing to mind the demands of his father. *"This tomfoolery has gone on long enough. It is time for you to take your rightful place in society. No more gadding about, wasting your life on games, expeditions, and light-skirts. Find a sensible girl, settle down, and become a responsible adult."*

But at what cost? Turning into the same shell of a man that his father had become?

"I will never marry," he said, and likely with more vehemence than his friends deserved. Neither seemed to notice, however, because they were too busy laughing.

"Ha!" Montwood challenged. "You are your father's heir. You must marry."

Unruffled due to years of weaving away from that type of bare-knuckled blow, Gabriel shrugged. "Let my younger brother be the responsible one." Clive was nearly thirteen. Plenty of time left for their father to groom him into the perfect ducal candidate.

With the thought settled in his mind, Gabriel pointed with his drink, amber liquid sloshing. "Danvers is the only one of us who *must* marry. He is his father's only son."

Danvers's grin faded. "Not I. My father holds no title to hand down to me, nor a name that garners much respect among the *ton*. Unlike yours. Besides, with my sister married to your cousin"—he pointed back to Gabriel as if the fault for the marriage lay with his side of the family—"my parents will have scores of infants to coddle, with the first arriving shortly."

At the mention of the anticipated arrival, another enthusiastic—and somewhat slurred—toast made the rounds. "To Rathburn, his bride, and his babe!"

Before Gabriel knew it, he was looking at the bottom of another empty glass. Montwood was quick to remedy that situation. Making himself more comfortable in the corner of the sofa, Gabriel was careful to keep his leg propped on a pillow. He thought of Hawthorne Manor and how downright blissful his cousin had been during their last visit.

Absently, Gabriel scratched his leg through the slats. "The marriage noose fits Rathburn's neck quite well."

"And so it shall remain," Danvers added with a fierceness that suggested he still thought of his sister in leading strings. His friend was a veritable beast when it came to protecting his family. Those who knew him best understood that his claws were reserved for enemies, but for everyone else, he was full of stuff and fluff.

Stuff and fluff? Gabriel stared down at his drink. Perhaps he should make this one his last.

"I seem to recall a time when Danvers welcomed the knot." Montwood sat forward, extending the bottle to add another splash to each glass. It seemed he was baiting both of them now. "But your betrothed decided to tie her rope around a rich American."

"Precisely why I will never marry," Danvers declared with only the slightest slur. He rose a bit unsteadily to his feet, made his way toward the hearth, and crouched down to pet the dog. "Fortune hunters, the lot of them."

The dog thumped his tail in agreement.

Gabriel remembered the day that Rafe Danvers had been left standing alone at the altar. His betrothed had set her cap on a fur trader from the former colonies and then set sail across the pond. Montwood shouldn't have reopened the wound.

"Quite right." Montwood topped off his own glass. "I say we pledge our troths to bachelorhood."

"Hear! Hear!" Danvers held onto the mantel as he stood.

Seemingly encouraged, Montwood held his drink aloft. "Let nary a woman break our bonds."

They all drank to that.

"Let them pine for our—or rather *your*," the amber-eyed snake-charmer corrected, pointing first at Danvers and then at Gabriel, "fortunes, and waste away on the doorstep of this grand edifice."

"To Fallow Hall!"

A friend of theirs, Lord Knightswold, had won this property, and countless others, in wagers throughout the years. After his recent marriage and subsequent desire for a family, he wasn't interested in keeping a property that not only was named for the deer that grazed the lands but also hinted at infertility. Therefore, he'd offered to let the property for a small sum and even encouraged Everhart, Danvers, and Montwood to purchase it from him. For now, however, Gabriel's fellow bachelors were content with impermanence.

"And for a little fun, we'll make a wager." Montwood was uncharacteristically verbose this evening. Among the three of them, he was usually the most reserved when not required to perform for a crowd. "The first of us to marry must pay a grand forfeit."

"To forfeits!" Danvers drained the last of another glass.

"How grand?" Gabriel was sure he'd asked the question, but the skeptical, almost *austere* tone of his voice made him look over his shoulder, expecting to see his father standing there. He shook his head to clear away the echo. Nonetheless, the way his friend seemingly steered the conversation back to this avenue of wagers pricked his suspicions.

Montwood grinned like a cardsharp. "Enough to make it memorable. Enough to make it...*irresistible*. After all, it wouldn't be much of a wager if we weren't plotting against one another."

At that, Danvers stepped back into their circle, sudden clarity alive in his dark gaze. "For us to plot against each other, it would have to be an extravagant sum." And yet, apparently, he wasn't opposed to the idea. They all knew he'd give his right leg to buy a certain estate he'd had his eye on for years.

"Enough for you to buy Greyson Park, my friend," Montwood said with the persuasive charm that had kept him in the good graces of the *ton*, even though his own family had cut him off without a shilling. "Enough for Everhart to buy... well, whatever his latest whim might be."

Gabriel winced at the unexpected sting. Though why it stung—when he'd done nothing to dispel the mark of the *aimless wanderer* he carried with him—he had no idea. Still, he felt compelled to fire back a shot across Montwood's bow. "And enough for you to pay off the mysterious debt of which you never speak?"

Montwood flashed a grin that was more teeth and less charm. "Precisely."

Gabriel tested the depths of the water in which they were suddenly wading. "One thousand pounds, then?"

"A trifling sum!" Montwood scoffed. "Knowing the vulgar riches you both possess, I wouldn't wager for five times that amount."

"Not for five thousand pounds? That is my yearly income." Danvers laughed as if in disbelief and then sketched a courtly bow. "Would you wager as Prinny does for a mere *ten*, Your Highness?"

"I believe you have the right of it. Ten thousand is quite a savory number." A calculating gleam stole across Montwood's gaze. "Besides, it isn't as if you need to worry. We've all declared never to marry."

Never. Until this moment, Gabriel hadn't fully appreciated the utter finality of that particular word. He cleared his throat. "Perhaps a set period of time would make the wager more interesting. Say…a single year?"

"Better and better." Montwood rested his glass on a low table, stood, and extended his hand. "Then our wager is set."

"Perhaps clarification is in order. This is a grand sum, after all." Danvers appeared more sober by the minute as he raked a hand through his unruly dark mane. "To be clear—for the following twelve months we will each be pitted against the other in the hopes of being the last bachelor standing."

"Simple enough," Montwood said with an encouraging nod, his ready handshake tucked away for the moment.

If Gabriel had learned anything during his years of friendship with Montwood, it was to be well versed in *all* the rules beforehand. "In theory, the last bachelor earns ten thousand pounds, when the two of you pay me five thousand pounds apiece. Correct?"

"Interesting *theory.*" Montwood's grin said that he accepted the challenge. "The figures, however, are spot on."

Danvers frowned. "If our wager is set to declare *one* bachelor the winner, it hardly seems fair if there are *two* of us left who gain nothing."

"Very true," Montwood said, stroking his chin. "After our year has ended, the winnings should be split amongst the winners. Therefore, a solitary loser would have to pay ten thousand pounds. Such a loss makes the stakes higher, doesn't it?"

It did, indeed.

"Of course, it goes without saying," Montwood continued, "that there can be no betrothals or binding declarations during this time. Also, no elicit affairs with women whose reputation would be ruined; ergo, no debutantes, spinsters, cloistered nuns, et cetera." The last bit earned a chuckle.

"What about a betrothal that happened prior to this wager?" Even though Gabriel purposely kept his gaze on Danvers when he spoke, the anticipated answer was more for himself. Little did his friends know that he was once a very foolish young man. Five years ago, he'd fallen in love at first sight. Or rather, *imagined* he had.

Fallen? No, the act had been much harder than a simple fall. He'd plummeted. The earth had disappeared from beneath his feet and kept him falling endlessly. Then one night, drunk on the very thought of her, he'd proposed marriage in a letter.

If that letter was still in her possession—and if it should ever see the light of day—then he stood to lose more than a fortune. Life as he knew it would end.

His father refused to fund any more expeditions or endure any more scandals. His grandmother, whom Gabriel loved dearly, held propriety in high esteem. Maybe it was the guilt of his more recent actions niggling at his brain, but he couldn't let her down again.

A debt of ten thousand pounds? *Well, that would certainly brew a scandal and scream a lack of propriety.*

But if he won? With ten thousand pounds, he could fund his own expedition.

"Since Danvers's bride married another, his prior betrothal no longer counts. It would be different if she were yet unmarried," Montwood answered offhandedly. Then his gaze sharpened on Gabriel. "Unless…you're asking on your own behalf? Could it be that there *is* a bluestocking in London who's shaken the insouciant foundation you've so carefully crafted?"

If Gabriel ever were to come clean about the proposal he'd made and explain the details, now was the time.

Yet knowing his friends as he did and weighing the odds of a likely encounter with Miss Calliope Croft—in addition to her discovering that it was he who wrote the letter—Gabriel felt little need for concern.

Certainly nothing that would induce him to enlighten his all-too-curious friends. "Of course not."

"Then it appears, gentlemen," Montwood said with a grin, "we are all agreed."

Gabriel was the first to extend his hand, confident that nothing would go wrong.

Chapter Two

The carriage jolted, startling Calliope from the pages of her book. Outside the window, the scenery dipped sharply but quickly righted again. Apparently, they'd hit a cavernous rut on the road to Fallow Hall. Thankfully, the carriage continued to roll on without event.

Across from her, her brother tapped the carriage's folding head with his walking stick and spoke with the driver, while her sister-in-law roused from another nap.

"I cannot believe that I fell asleep again," Delaney said on a yawn, her auburn hair in wild disarray. "I am positively the dullest traveling companion. Calliope, you must forgive me. I promised you a grander adventure than your sisters and mine would have in Bath, and so far I've given you nothing letter-worthy."

"This is already a grand adventure, for I have never been to Scotland or on the road that would take me there." Calliope shook her head by way of reassurance. "I'll have plenty of new sights to remark upon when I do write to them."

Even if their entire party had slept through the journey, Calliope would have preferred it to returning to Bath.

Especially since Bath only reminded her of refusing Brightwell's proposal. *A clear reminder that some endings do not bring about wonderful new beginnings.*

"Besides," she continued. "I can also inform my sisters that Griffin is a frightful snorer. The endless years of teasing and torment we will bring unto him are worth their weight in gold."

"A *bear* snorer, to be sure." Delaney laughed, her violet eyes bright with mischief as she finger-combed wayward curls away from her glowing cheeks. "But I find the rhythmic cadence pleasing. If I were to walk past his cave on a winter's day like this, I would be reassured by that sound, knowing I would come to no harm."

Closing the flap in the roof, Griffin scoffed, pretending a great offense had befallen him. "Wound this hibernating bear and suffer the consequences." He reached out as if he meant to tickle his bride but then stilled as his gaze drifted to her middle. A resplendent smile transformed his face into an expression Calliope had never before witnessed on him. Instead of tormenting his wife, he took her hand in his and brought it to his lips for a kiss. "But not quite yet. Perhaps there is a reason you've been sleeping so much of late."

Delaney brightened like a flame and settled her free hand over her stomach before she beamed at Calliope. Immediate understanding dawned.

A baby?

"We aren't certain," Delaney said as if she'd heard the unspoken question. "I know how much the news would please your mother and father. For now, however, it should be our secret."

"Of course." Calliope found herself nodding and grinning and then nodding some more. *The perfect beginning.* "Although I must mention that Mother's happiness would exceed any that mankind has ever known if she were to have a grandchild *before* her younger sister, Augusta."

Knowing it was the truth, they all laughed.

Then, in Calliope's ever-wandering mind, a vision of herself sitting for hours upon hours, cuddling and reading to a little bundle, filled her with such joy that she began compiling a mental library.

If truth be told, she'd had the list tucked away for years now—a list that hadn't always been intended for a niece or nephew...

"*Calliope,*" Griffin said, drawing her gaze away from the fogged window to see that he was now standing outside the carriage, extending his arm to assist her.

She blinked and rubbed a hand over her eyes. "Have we arrived at Fallow Hall already?" Only a moment ago, they'd been having a conversation about a new baby. How could they have arrived so quickly?

"You've drifted off on another of your journeys." His brow furrowed. Mother had called them *spells* at one time, before a physician informed her that Calliope was nothing more than a daydreamer.

Calliope shook her head. "It's merely the effects of a long day's ride and the chill in the air."

Stepping out of the carriage, she stopped short. There, on the stone landing, was none other than Lord Brightwell. His pale features and attire stood out in sharp contrast to the dark door behind him. The last time they'd all been standing together like this had been at Pamela's wedding breakfast.

"Brightwell," Griffin said in greeting. "It's good to see you again. I hope our spontaneous visit will not cause trouble."

Brushing an errant forelock from his brow, he nodded to both Griffin and Delaney. "I'm certain our hosts would agree that your timing couldn't be better."

Their hosts were the three gentlemen who rented Fallow Hall. Calliope knew little of Rafe Danvers or Lord Lucan Montwood. As for Lord Everhart...

Once upon a time, she'd been in the same circle of friends with him, but that had ended abruptly. In fact, Everhart had ceased their acquaintance on the same night she'd refused Brightwell's proposal.

"I heard Danvers mention the damage." Brightwell gestured to Rafe Danvers, who was a short distance away, speaking to the driver while examining the wheel of their carriage. "For your sakes, I hope it is an easy repair. For my wife's sake, however, I hope for an extended visit."

Then his gaze shifted to Calliope. In that moment, her refusal seemed like a living, breathing entity between them. Adjusting her grip on her satchel, she felt the tension in her muscles climb up her arms and settle at the base of her neck.

"Miss Croft," Brightwell said with a familiar smile. "How serendipitous that you should be among the traveling party. Your cousin will be most pleased by the news."

"Thank you, Brightwell"—she paused, correcting the too-familiar address—"*Lord* Brightwell." Years ago, he'd just been *Brightwell*. He'd been her friend, and in their close circle no one bothered with formality. Now, it was impossible to refer to him as such. Adding the title helped to remind her of the choice she'd made.

She'd chosen a letter over him—and thus, a broken heart.

Sweat dripped from Gabriel's brow as he neared the top of the circular staircase. If he'd have known that hopping on one foot up stairs took such skill, he would have added it to his regimen ages ago. Apparently, neither broadswords nor boxing had anything on hopping. He suddenly had a new respect for his younger half-sister, Raena, and her tendency to hop and skip from one room to the next—as long as she wasn't caught by her mother.

"Only months away from town and you've already gone soft, I see," a familiar voice called up from the open doorway of the map room. But it wasn't Montwood or Danvers.

In bewildered disbelief, Gabriel ducked his head to peer down behind him. "Croft?"

"The one and the same," Griffin Croft answered. "When we were last at Gentleman Jackson's saloon, you knocked me on my arse. I thought I'd return the favor with an unexpected visit."

"You have succeeded." Gabriel turned to make his way back down, one step at a time. Croft and he were more sparring partners than friends. In fact, this was their first social call of any sort. One did not typically make friends with the man who'd blackmailed you and threatened to end your life, after all.

Normally, Gabriel wasn't of a superstitious nature. Yet after the drunken wager he'd made last night—along with his thoughts concerning Croft's sister—he was beginning to wonder if he ought to be.

Then again, there *was* a perfectly obvious reason for the visit. "I imagine you've come to see how your cousin fares."

Croft offered an absent gesture as he stepped into the room. "Since we are journeying to Scotland regardless, I would have been remiss not to at least entertain the idea... although, knowing my cousin, I feel I should ask how Fallow Hall fares instead."

We. That was all Gabriel heard. The perspiration on his skin cooled considerably. Was the "we" simply Croft's referring to his wife? Or was he traveling with one or more of his sisters as well?

Croft's amusement abruptly transformed into frown. "Say, how bad is that break? You've gone pale." He stepped forward as if to offer assistance, but Gabriel waved him back.

"It's nothing. In fact, I should be able to remove the splint within a fortnight." To prove that he was fine, he descended the length of the penultimate curve, the sole of his boot clanking against each iron tread. "So, you've come here with your bride, then?"

Before Croft could answer, Danvers strolled into the room. "I went to tell Montwood that we have guests, but he has disappeared again."

"He has a knack for doing that whenever I am around," Croft said. "And in my opinion, he should keep to that habit."

Danvers laughed. "Strangely, you are not the first to have said that. Apparently, Montwood collects ill favor as one collects snuff boxes." He walked over to the mahogany sideboard and poured a dram of Irish whiskey into each of three glasses. "But all in all, he isn't a bad fellow."

Croft accepted a glass with a salute. "Perhaps you would think differently if he'd threatened to elope with your wife."

"Then I need never worry." Danvers tossed a nod in Gabriel's direction as he set the third glass on the oval table in front of the sofa. "Nor Everhart, I imagine."

"True," Gabriel agreed, but the word came out dry, parched. He sensed a need for the fortifying drink but didn't trust his good leg to hop down the final two steps and across the room to get it. Unfortunately, that was also where he'd left his cane.

Croft tossed back his drink. "Gentlemen, my curiosity is piqued by your certainty."

"Some may call it an oath. While others..." Danvers added as he returned to the sideboard, "might call it a wager."

"Do not tell me you've tossed your coin into the same pot against Montwood." Croft shot to the heart of the matter quickly. When he looked from one man to the other, he shook his head and laughed. "For your sakes, I pray it was a small sum."

Danvers shrugged. "This is no card trick; therefore, no risk involved. It comes down to a choice of *will* or *won't*."

The words were stated with such simplicity that it was impossible not to believe them.

Croft shook his head again. "The same way you choose to take each breath, I suppose? *I will breathe—I won't...*"

Gabriel swallowed. Hard.

He knew precisely what Croft was saying. Gabriel had once felt so consumed by love that he'd had no choice in the matter. Or at least, that's what he'd *imagined* at the time. Thankfully, he need not worry about being so foolish again. Croft's interference had *helped* Gabriel come to that realization five years ago.

They'd been at Vauxhall Gardens. Croft had accompanied his sister on an evening tour. Gabriel, Brightwell, and their small circle of friends were also among the party. When the fireworks distracted the group, Croft had pulled Gabriel aside, shielding them from the others. "*You have wounded my sister, Everhart, and for that I could easily kill you,*" he'd said in a lethal hiss. "*If anyone harms my family, I repay them tenfold.*"

Gabriel remembered taking an involuntary step back. "I don't know what you mean, sir."

"*I am speaking of the letter. Yes, that letter.*" And that was when Croft had taken him by the throat. "*If you thought that omitting your signature would keep me from discovering your identity, you were mistaken. You encouraged her affections only to toy with them, the same way you've done to those other young women to whom you wrote. With what I know, I could have you arrested under charges of Unlawful Intent and Licentious Seduction of an Innocent. Upon conviction, they would burn a brand into your flesh that you would wear for the rest of your days. Do you want to bring utter humiliation to your father and grandmother? Is that what you choose?*"

"To make amends…I could marry her," Gabriel had rasped, unable to swallow. Delirious, he clearly hadn't known what he was saying. Essentially, he'd offered to exchange one form of death for another.

"*And have my sister married to a man who would so easily dally with her emotions? Never.*" Croft had tightened his grip.

"*There will be no more letters. And you will not see my sister again.*"

Now, years later, Gabriel still felt the chill of the memory. Absently, he slipped a finger beneath his cravat. He tried to shake it off, but it was difficult when the man who knew his secret was standing here in the same room. "Speaking of marriage—*yours*, of course—you and your wife are welcome to break your journey here."

"If you will have us, I thank you," Croft answered graciously. "The wheel of the carriage is in need of repair and may take a few hours."

Gabriel relaxed marginally. He need not worry that Calliope Croft had journeyed with them. In fact, the last he'd heard mentioned from Lady Brightwell's mother was that the Crofts were traveling to Bath. Likely, all the Crofts but the one before him now were far, *far* away from Fallow Hall. And all the better for Gabriel.

Feeling restored, he began to hop down the remaining stairs—

"Though my sister is here as well," Croft added offhandedly, placing his empty glass on a nearby table.

Gabriel slipped. The heel of his boot missed the bottom tread and sent him reeling backward. Fortunately, with the stairs so steep, his fall was brief. Still, he hit the rigid iron treads soundly, knocking a grunt of pain from his lungs.

Danvers stared at him in open-mouthed shock. Gabriel wasn't usually clumsy, but one had to account for the broken leg. In the very least, Danvers could have offered assistance.

In the end, it was Croft who came forth to lend a hand in a timely fashion. "Here. Allow me to assist you to the sofa."

He took Gabriel's arm and placed it over his shoulder. Since they were primarily sparring partners—and with a sordid history—this degree of familiarity felt somewhat...awkward.

Gabriel had known for some time that it was odd for him to spar with Croft, of all men. Yet in his own mind, he saw those weekly sessions—of letting Croft pummel him—as a penance of sorts.

"Your stamina must be waning." Croft issued one of his typical provoking remarks, reminding Gabriel where they stood. "Then again, you never could best me."

Gabriel wanted to taunt him in return but found himself shaken by the previous announcement. "Your sister, you say?" He cringed as the words came forth. This degree of obviousness was even worse than rhyming when he was drunk. He might as well have asked "Which one?" and listed them all by name.

Still, there was a possibility that it wasn't *Calliope*...

Once they crossed the room, Croft released his arm and stepped away. "Yes. I believe you've met," he said, as if for Danvers's sake, "but it would have been years ago."

Croft was keen on torture, Gabriel realized. He resisted the urge to shout, *DAMN IT ALL, JUST SAY HER NAME!* Instead, he reached down for the glass on the table. "Ah, years ago? Then it would have been..."

"The eldest of my sisters, Calliope." Croft slid a cold stare his way. A clear warning. "And speaking of her, I suppose it's time to offer her a reprieve from our cousin's illness. I'll see you at dinner, gentlemen." He moved to the door and then added one parting remark. "Although with Fallow Hall being such a grand estate, I imagine that it would be difficult for someone in your condition, Everhart, to wait upon his guests. Please do not trouble yourself. We would not be able to *live* with ourselves if you were left with a *permanent mark* or injury because of us."

Croft left, but his threat remained. Gabriel's hand shook. Amber ripples disturbed the surface of the whiskey. Calliope was here at Fallow Hall? And not even twenty-four hours from the time of the wager. Clearly, the Fates were laughing at him.

"I've never seen you flustered or known your wit to be absent," Danvers said, watching him closely. Too closely. "Croft's insult was an easy jab to counter, yet you said nothing. You seemed tongue-tied. And when you unknotted it, you were more concerned about…" He paused, studying him. Gradually, one corner of his mouth lifted. "About the identity of his traveling companions. Hmm… You've gone pale, my friend, like a man haunted."

Gabriel knew that look, the *I know you're holding the trump's ace* look. He needed to put Danvers straight and erase the calculating gleam in his eyes. "Or like a man who'd imbibed too much the previous evening."

"Or perhaps"—his friend grinned—"like a man who is about to lose a great deal of money."

"You're acting like Montwood. Greed is causing you to see things that are not true." That austere tone had returned to his voice, nearly making him wince. "I never thought *you* would plot against me."

"I never thought you would make it so easy." Danvers's ribald laughter echoed off the walls as he moved to the door and quit the room.

Gabriel blew out a breath. The arrival of their guests had taken him unawares. If he'd been prepared, he never would have revealed his cards to Danvers. Now, the only option left was to prove that he was completely unruffled. Since it was the same mask he wore each day, it would be easy to secure for a single evening.

Then, by tomorrow, the Crofts would be gone and Gabriel's ten thousand pounds—along with his life—would be safe once again.

CHAPTER THREE

"A bite of bread, please, cousin," Pamela said, her voice weak and frail. "I prefer it without the crust. Just a small piece, barely large enough to fit on my tongue. And if you could butter both sides, I'm certain I would be content."

Calliope reminded herself that she'd *volunteered* to keep her cousin company while the others were dining. She'd had no desire to sit across from Brightwell.

So far, all she'd managed to accomplish in the past hour was to serve broth that was "a trifle too hot" at first, and when she blew on it, became "a trifle too cold." The bread pieces near the center of the loaf were too moist and the outer part too dry. The wine was too sweet. The cheese too salty. The tart too crumbly.

"Of course." Calliope clenched her teeth in a smile. "For what is bread without butter?"

Queen Pamela sat propped up against a mound of pillows draped in rose silk, the same color of ribbon woven through her pale tresses. All around her was designed for her comfort—a wine-colored velvet coverlet, matching brocade bed curtains tied to each corner post, sumptuous furs draped over her feet, mulled wine in a pewter goblet on a Pembroke table, a softly crackling fire in the hearth, and a portrait of fluffy white lambs frolicking on a hillside above the mantel.

Still, Pamela was not content. Her next sigh proved as much. "It is unfortunate that the servant girl had to assist with dinner. I should like to hear more harp music. It relaxes me."

Calliope stiffened. A golden harp sat in the corner, and likely with tiny droplets of blood on the strings because of how long poor Nell had been asked to play. "As you know, I never learned. So in this one thing I cannot ease your burden," Calliope said, producing a small laugh in order to keep censure from her tone. "Besides, the girl needs to rest at some point."

Her cousin sniffed. "I don't see why. If I prefer her to remain here, the household staff should make allowances."

Incredulous, Calliope's mouth fell open. She nearly dropped the tiny piece of bread before she had the chance to lay it on the spoon. "I'm certain not even the greatest houses keep harpists on hand."

"Then the world we live in is cruel, indeed," Pamela whined. Then, blinking up at Calliope, she shook her head. "I am too distressed to eat another bite."

Calliope looked from her cousin to the miniature square of perfectly buttered bread. Irritation made her fingers tighten around the spoon handle. Turning, she placed the spoon on the tray—minus the deliciously buttered bread. There was no point in letting it go to waste, not when servitude made her so hungry. "Then we shall have a nice visit instead. I could share with you news of our travels thus far."

"I should rest," Pamela whispered, letting her eyelids droop. Any topic of conversation that did not revolve around her was usually too tiresome. "If I shan't have a harpist, then nothing but dreams can comfort me now. Tomorrow, I shall tell you about my letter."

Calliope wasn't interested in any letter that her cousin received. In fact, she was already looking forward to leaving at first light. "If only you could. Likely, we will be gone before you awaken."

"I'm certain it was one of *those* letters," her cousin continued as if Calliope hadn't spoken. "You remember, don't you? They'd caused quite the scandal years ago, but I can't think of the name. Cupid's letters? No, that wasn't it…"

Calliope's heart stuttered to a halt.

There was, perhaps, *one* letter that she was interested in reading. Could it be that her cousin had received a letter such as that?

No. Surely, not. There hadn't been any reported for years now. In fact, Calliope had thought the author had either died or married one of the other letter recipients. Secretly, she'd mourned for him for months, wearing only gray and lavender frocks.

"The Casanova letters," Calliope whispered, a tremor coursing through her.

"Oh, yes. That's what they were called." Pamela lifted her arms, expecting Calliope to tuck the coverlet around her. "It is a pity that you are leaving so soon. The letter came as such a surprise too. I'm certain no other married woman has ever received one from him."

This was the first instance Calliope had heard of as well. Curious, more than she cared to admit, she was even willing to endure servitude in order to hear more.

Leaning down, she situated the blankets over her cousin. "We could talk about the letter now. Or if you are too tired, perhaps you could direct me to it and I could…read the letter to you while you rest."

"What a lovely thought. You would make a very good companion for me, cousin," Pamela said, offering a regal smile.

Calliope bit back a rise of annoyance. "You are too kind. Though now that I think on it, I would enjoy reading to you."

"I'm afraid Mother moved the letter." Pamela smoothed her hands over the velvet. "She worried that distraction was hindering my recovery."

"I'd be more than happy to retrieve it for you, if you would but direct me."

"Perhaps one of the servants knows where it is." Her cousin flitted her fingers toward the opposite end of the room and closed her eyes. "Oh, I have done too much. The weariness is overtaking me. I must rest. Please consider staying, cousin."

Consider staying? Here, to act as companion to her cousin? Absolutely not.

Not to mention, staying would nearly demand that she engage in conversation with Brightwell eventually.

She couldn't possibly stay. And yet—at the risk of sounding very much like a character in one of her novels—she wanted to see that letter more than life itself.

Out in the hall, Calliope released her pent-up frustration in a growl. In the next instant, she heard an answering chuckle. Rafe Danvers stood down the corridor, angling his head to light a cheroot from one of the wall sconces.

"Pleasant visit with your cousin, Miss Croft?" He paused from smiling only long enough to draw on his cheroot, making the end glow bright orange.

Embarrassed at being caught with her guard down, she lifted a hand to her neck. "Very, but I find that my throat is quite dry from all the…conversation." She cleared it in an imitation of the growl, on the off chance that he'd believe her.

His smile told her he didn't. Much to his credit, however, he didn't challenge her either. "I know of a perfect remedy. If you will allow me to show you the way." He gestured with his cheroot toward a turn off the main hallway.

"Time seems to have gotten the better of me," Calliope said. "I imagine the supper hour has long since ended. Are my brother and sister-in-law in the parlor now?"

"They retired to their rooms not long ago. I'm afraid we spoke exhaustively on the topics of town, pugilism, and the apparent felicity of marriage." He said the last in wry humor, his mouth puffing out a ring of smoke.

Calliope was little acquainted with Rafe Danvers but knew enough that he was a confirmed bachelor. While the tragic circumstance of his wedding—or lack thereof—had happened a year prior to her debut, it had still been the foremost gossip on everyone's lips. Yet because he remained apart from most of genteel society, she'd had little chance to know him. Certainly not enough to add his character classification to her once-thorough list.

*Hmm...*Rafe Danvers did *not* have a completed page in her book. With his wavy dark hair and the short side-whiskers trimmed at an angle, defining the line of his cheeks and jaw, he certainly possessed the *appearance* of a romantic hero. Considering his dreadful history, however, she doubted he was the scribe of those infamous letters. Still, she couldn't pass up an opportunity to inquire.

"Earlier, my cousin was speaking of a letter she'd received." Calliope studied him askance, watching for any sign of artifice that would suggest he was guarding a secret. So far, nothing in his countenance betrayed him. "I'm certain she would enjoy reading it again, but I was unable to find it."

"Tell me, Miss Croft..." He stopped at the threshold of a pair of open French doors and squinted at her as if she'd presented him with an unsolvable puzzle. "Women tend to read letters over and over—some gentlemen too, I suspect— but the content therein never changes. I see no purpose in it, unless one is of a mind to find flaws or twist the meaning of each phrase into something that was never intended."

Calliope laughed. "I see your point. I have found myself in an argument with ink and paper at times. Yet you are forgetting one immeasurably important fact. The power of a well-written letter can be as transformative as a chrysalis. Emerge from it, and the world is new and vibrant in a way you never imagined."

Rafe Danvers shook his head. "There is more power in speaking face-to-face," he said firmly—conviction enough for her to completely cross him off the list.

1. He did not possess a poet's soul.
2. There was no undisguised yearning in his gaze.
3. Not even a hint of an inclination to marry.
4. His vehemence on their topic suggested a passionate nature. That passion, however, was not directed toward her.

She didn't even bother to check for ink stains on his fingertips.

Now, back to the matter at hand. "You are quite right, I am sure," she offered. "But there are those of us—my cousin included—who reread letters to ensure our connection with others is never severed. It's an ongoing conversation, even though we may be miles apart. So you see, it is imperative that I find that letter."

Inside the room, something crashed to the floor with a loud clanging sound. "*Bugger it all,*" quickly followed.

Rafe Danvers chuckled as he glanced into the room. "That would be Everhart. He's recently become quite clumsy."

Surprise jolted through Calliope at the mention of Everhart's name. Though why she should feel alarm when she was already aware of the inhabitants of the manor, she didn't know. Well, perhaps she did. The truth was, the last time she'd seen him, he'd made it quite clear that he disapproved of her treatment of Brightwell. More to the point, he did *not* like her at all.

"Have the two of you been introduced?" Danvers asked with a decidedly devilish grin as he gestured for her to precede him into the room. "Of course you have. How silly of me."

While Calliope didn't know her escort all that well, from experiences with her own family she knew what mischief looked like. The only thing was, she didn't understand the reason behind his.

"Yes. We've been introduced," she said with trepidation. Crossing the threshold, she didn't know if Everhart's resentment toward her had lessened since their last encounter, nearly five years ago at Bath.

The man in question was now bent at the waist and playing tug-of-war with a monstrously large dog over a baguette. The lean, gray beast gave a low growl, but the ferocity of it was undermined by his wildly thumping tail.

On the opposite end of the loaf, Everhart's scowl was genuine. Beneath a crown of short-cropped flaxen hair, his tawny brows drew together. The sharp angles of his nose, cheekbone, and jaw appeared hard as granite, and faint crescent-moon lines tightened the flesh at the corners of his well-defined mouth. Even in anger, it was impossible to dispute the fact that he was the most handsome man in all of England. Perhaps even the world.

Then again, she'd always had a foolishly romantic view of the world.

The exchange between man and beast only lasted a minute, each straining for a baguette that surprisingly did not give way. Everhart's dark blue evening coat did nothing to disguise the lean musculature of his shoulders, arms, back, and even farther down to the outline of his thighs straining against the dove gray breeches and to his calves—

Seeing the thick splint encasing his lower leg, she started.

"You're injured," she said, her voice louder than she expected. Loud enough to draw Everhart's attention and cause him to lose the battle.

The dog scrambled back and then gave the loaf a vigorous shake, the ends of his short floppy ears swaying. On the floor between them was an empty silver platter, a knife, and a hunk of blue-veined cheese.

"Everhart's a veritable invalid," Rafe Danvers said with a laugh. "So much for our evening snack, though."

Calliope couldn't look away from the man across the room. She felt...arrested more than alarmed, as if every one of her organs had ceased functioning. Her breathing halted. Her heart sputtered. Her eyes could no longer blink. She simply stood there, staring at the splint and then up to those blue-green eyes. Eyes that had once shown her so much censure for refusing his friend's proposal. Those eyes did not hold censure now but something equally as intense, though she could not name it.

"Miss Croft," Everhart said by way of greeting, his voice low and clipped. His gaze snapped to Danvers with what looked to be annoyance, and then back to her. "I trust you've found your cousin well?"

She nodded, and with that simple motion, her heart started to beat again and her lungs expanded. "I have, thank you. It was very kind of you to allow her and her husband sanctuary here for her recuperation. Especially when it is apparent that you require rest as well."

"It is nothing—more nuisance than injury." He waved in a gesture of dismissal. "I apologize for the state of the room and for the loss of the 'evening snack,' as Danvers said. We have made it somewhat a habit to have our bread and cheese here in the evening. While the bread is usually inedible, the cheese is quite—"

The instant he said the word, the dog loped over, snatched the large hunk with his teeth, and gobbled it up in no more than two bites. Then, as if in thanks, the gray beast nudged Everhart's hand with his nose, earning an absent scratch behind the ears.

"He rather likes cheese." Everhart shrugged, his tone no longer clipped but instead laced with the easy fluidity that one adopted with friends. She liked this far more than his censure.

Her lips drew up into a smile. "Apparently. What is his name?"

"So far, he has four: Boris, Reginald, James, and Brutus. The last was given to him by your aunt when she'd caught him in the vicinity of her small dogs and summarily declared him a brute."

Calliope could easily imagine the shrieking that must have accompanied such a name. Her aunt tended to coddle those she loved to the point of giving way to snobbery. The same could not be said of Boris Reginald James Brutus, who thumped his tail soundly on the floor in blissful surrender to the scratching behind his ears, his tongue lolling to one side. "Which of the names did you assign him?"

"None," Everhart supplied. "I simply call him *Dog*, unless I am cross with him and then I call him *Duke*." A telling remark from the son of the Duke of Heathcoat, but she knew better than to comment. All the same, a look in Everhart's gaze and the quirk of his lips seemed to possess insight into her thoughts.

"You must admit, Miss Croft," Rafe Danvers said beside her, startling her with his presence, for she had nearly forgotten he was there, "that he rather looks like a Boris."

She made an effort to pull her gaze away from Everhart to answer. "Perhaps it would be better to ask the dog to see which name he prefers."

"That's the thing," Danvers said with a shake of his head. "He doesn't yield to any of those names. We have spent too much time trying to persuade him, I suppose, and now he believes we are all idiots for not knowing what to call him."

Calliope laughed. "Then perhaps *Duke* is the perfect name for him."

"He won't respond to that either." Everhart's smirk turned into a lazy grin as he continued to watch her. His blue-green gaze seemed to shimmer in the same way a ray of light glanced across jewels, disorienting her for an instant.

She'd forgotten the seductive power he held in a single look. That same look had inspired her to write four full-page lists in her journal on him. For a time, she'd actually had him at the top of her list for possible Casanova candidates. But in the end, when he'd scolded her so harshly for refusing Brightwell, she'd realized her mistake. He'd only tolerated her company out of deference to his friend.

Remembering that event now helped her break the spell she was under. She blinked and took a step back for good measure.

"Then perhaps I will come up with a name to give him before I leave in the morning. For now, I must bid each of you a good night." She inclined her head to Danvers and offered something of a curtsy to Everhart, but without meeting his gaze again, and summarily left the room.

Halfway to her own chamber, she realized that she'd forgotten to ask Everhart about Pamela's letter.

Tearing his gaze away from Calliope Croft's retreating figure, Gabriel held himself in check. When he'd heard her say *"It is imperative that I find that letter"* to Danvers in the hall, he hadn't been sure he would be able to.

Gabriel wanted to forget about Calliope's letter. Forget about all letters—especially the one he'd written to Pamela. *What a horrendous debacle that was.* Right now, he needed to move on with the simple, unfettered life to which he'd grown accustomed.

Knowing that Danvers was scrutinizing his every gesture and expression at that very moment, he refused to reveal the relief he felt at having survived this encounter. Both Montwood and Danvers had once taunted him by claiming they knew his *tell* when he gambled, but neither had told him what it was. Therefore, in order to keep himself from giving anything away, he turned to pet the dog with more affection than the beast deserved.

"You have spoiled my supper, Dog," he said with one final pat to the side of his neck. The bread wasn't a great loss, but the cheese had come from their remarkably efficient head butler—private pantry and would have been marvelous with a glass of port.

Summarily dismissed, the dog loped over to the hearth, turned around three times, and plopped down onto the floor, wholly unconcerned over the reprimand.

Danvers leaned a hip against the side of a wing-backed chair opposite the sofa. "I must admit, that encounter left me with a modicum of doubt. Earlier with Croft, you were decidedly unsettled, but just now, you seemed moderately at ease."

"When you expected disaster?" Relief swept through Gabriel, though outwardly he remained the same. "As I mentioned, you had no reason to make such grand assumptions regarding our wager. If I displayed a measure of unease before, it was because I'd been rather unkind to Miss Croft when last we met. She'd abused my friend's affections, and I might have been too harsh. In learning she was here, I merely wanted to avoid any need to discuss prior events again. You know how I detest apologizing for my actions."

"True." Danvers seemed to take this explanation as fact. "You are fortunate in the fact that Miss Croft appeared not to have been scarred by the previous encounter. In fact, I wonder if she remembered you at all."

Oh, she remembered him. Gabriel had seen it quite clearly in her slow perusal of his form and the utterly beguiling way she'd held his gaze. "I always took you for a hunter, Danvers. Instead you are dangling bait before me like a fisherman," he said with a chuckle. "I suggest you focus your plotting elsewhere."

"Yes. Perhaps, you are right. I wonder if Montwood would be taken in by her. I should arrange for a meeting to determine if—" Danvers stopped. A wide grin broke over his face.

Damn. Gabriel felt a muscle twitching in his jaw before he'd had the chance to control it. Was that his *tell*, he wondered? He could hardly think straight. At the moment, all he could see was the all-too-charming Montwood alone with Calliope.

That would never happen. Ever. Not if he could help it.

"A fisherman, indeed." Danvers sketched a courtly bow.

"Be careful that someone does not put a hole in your boat or net," Gabriel warned. "Our wager is for friendly purposes and not designed to ruin the reputations of our guests. Or had you forgotten?"

Danvers's only response was a hearty laugh as he left the room.

Chapter Four

"I'm so very sorry, Brightwell. I cannot marry you."

Calliope watched Brightwell's pale, unremarkable features turn hard. She'd expected nothing less after refusing his proposal. But instead of questioning her further, he took her answer and simply left her on the terrace, disappearing into the cold darkness of the Randalls' garden. Perhaps he'd noticed how distracted she'd been of late—ever since she'd received that letter.

Before stepping back inside the ballroom, she lifted her gloved hands to her cheeks to check for any sign of wetness. There was none. Surely, she should be crumbling into tears. Brightwell deserved proof that he meant something to her, didn't he? And yet, while she felt sadness at knowing she was losing a dear friend and hurting him as well, most of all she felt relieved because he hadn't demanded to know why she had refused him.

After all, she couldn't have told him that she'd fallen in love with a letter, could she?

Preoccupied by her thoughts, she walked through the veil of diaphanous curtains hanging from the top of the archway. A sweeping melody rose above the crowd of dancers. The strains of violin and cello mingled with the sway and swish of pastel silk skirts, and somehow the combination caused a terrible yearning in her heart. It ached from being empty. She longed for the man she loved to fill the void.

Everhart suddenly appeared in front of her. Without asking permission, he seized her hand and pulled her into the waltz.

In no mood for dancing, she prepared a set-down, willing to leave him stranded on the floor this very instant. Yet the intensity in his gaze kept her silent. The power of it coursed through her as if the ground were quaking at her feet, preparing to swallow her into the depths of the earth. She was unable to look away.

They were friends, or at least they were among a small circle of friends. He smiled and laughed easily with the others. But not with her. He always looked at her as if he disapproved of her. Perhaps he'd guessed that her heart was not set on his friend.

Gazes locked, they swept turn by turn throughout the ballroom, as if all the other dancers had disappeared. When it ended, she'd stood in his arms for a moment too long. Her breath rushed over her parted lips. For all the world, it looked like he was going to kiss her. Right there and then—

Calliope awoke with a start.

Breathing heavily, she sat up and looked around the room. The golden brocade bed curtains and satin coverlet were unfamiliar. She wasn't sure where she was. But wait. *Oh.* Then it came to her: Fallow Hall, Pamela, Brightwell, Everhart, and quite possibly…a Casanova letter.

That explained why she'd had the dream again. Although in truth, it was more a memory than a dream. The only difference was how it had really ended.

When she'd refused Brightwell in Bath, Everhart *had* seized her for a waltz. After their dance, however, the intensity in his gaze had felt more like he was scolding her than any likelihood that he might have kissed her. His words, the only thing he'd said to her that evening, confirmed it. "You shed no tears over Brightwell."

At the time, she'd taken the full force of his censure and felt the first sting of tears that should have been for Brightwell instead of herself.

Everhart had always been so affable with everyone else, but not with her. Perhaps it was because he'd felt his friend deserved someone better. It had been the truth, hadn't it? Brightwell deserved someone who loved him. Someone who hadn't been pining over a letter. Because of that, she'd borne Everhart's reprimand, left the Randall ball, and promptly crumbled into tears.

The memory of her foolishness still festered.

Parting the bed curtains, she noted the warm glow of the embers in the hearth and surmised it was still hours until dawn. The sight awakened an irrepressible desire for toasted bread and warm tea. Her stomach rumbled. Pressing a hand to her middle, she knew it was no use. Sleep would evade her if she tried to reclaim it. She was still hungry from missing dinner. Perhaps if she slipped down to the kitchen…Then afterward, she would attempt sleep once more.

Donning a wrapper over her soft flannel night rail, along with a pair of thick wool stockings, she left her chamber. In the hall, the sconces had all been doused, likely by Valentine. If not for the taper in her hand, she would have tripped over the large gray dog she'd met earlier in the map room. Sprawled out on the Persian runner outside her door, he merely lifted his head at the sound of her gasp, as if he was used to startling women in the dead of night.

"Hullo, Boris Reginald James Brutus," she said in the hopes of sounding more friendly than alarmed. Was it true that the scent of fear excited the appetites of large, beastly animals? If she were the lead character in her own novel, then she might very well need a dashing hero to stride down the hall and save her from harm.

But the beast in question merely lowered his head to his paws, apparently bored by their brief exchange. One had to wonder how many women the rakes of Fallow Hall entertained to inspire such a bland response. Perhaps she didn't need a hero after all, but someone who could figure out the dog's name.

Looking down at him, she recalled the name Everhart had used and decided he looked very much like an indifferent duke. "Hullo, Duke."

Since she didn't expect a response, the quirk of his ears and thump of his tail caught her off guard. It wasn't a complete victory in the name category, but he seemed to like it.

Bending down, she gave him a scratch behind the ears, earning faster tail-thumps as her reward. "I don't suppose you'd know the way to the kitchen."

Duke Boris Reginald James Brutus licked her hand and gradually assembled his large frame into a standing position atop his four saucer-sized paws. He took a few steps down the hall and then looked back at her, snuffing through his nostrils as if asking whether she planned to follow or stand there like a ninny.

Beset by another rumble of her stomach and imagining a dog that size would know the precise location of the kitchen, Calliope followed.

He headed down the curving main stairs, through the great hall, down a corridor, past the drawing room, and around a series of corners until he suddenly stopped in front of a familiar set of French doors. *The map room.*

"This isn't the kitchen," she scolded quietly.

Unconcerned, Duke sank down onto the floor, forming a rather large, dog-shaped, lumpy gray puddle. She had a mind to come up with her own name for him. Something far less noble to serve as a punishment for elevating her hopes.

Pressing one hand to her stomach and contemplating which direction the kitchen would likely be, she let out a sigh—and promptly blew out her own candle. Then, she let out a second sigh because of her own stupidity.

Now, she was completely immersed in darkness. Even down on the main floor, the wall sconces had been extinguished. Not to mention, the odds of finding flint and steel in an unfamiliar house without tripping over something first was remote at best.

"Perhaps I should name you Prometheus and see if you can light this taper for me." She glared down to the floor where she'd last seen the dog. That was when she noticed a faint glow, radiating through the gap beneath the bottom of the doors to the map room. If there was light, she thought, then there was a hearth fire enough for her wick.

But just as she gripped the knob, it went stiff in her grasp.

Suddenly the door swung inward, pulling her along with it. Too startled to make a sound, she tumbled forward—*or nearly did.* An instant before she fell to her knees, a pair of strong, warm hands caught her by the shoulders.

"Thank you. I—*Everhart!*"

His stunned expression matched the abrupt stillness that moved through her.

Like that moment at the Randall ball, her heart and lungs seized when her gaze collided with his. She was trapped, mouth agape, unblinking. And standing *far* too close for propriety's sake.

Of course, it went beyond mentioning that unmarried women wearing nightclothes, thickly made or not, should never visit a gentleman in a secluded part of a dark house. Especially not a reputed seducer. One who'd abandoned his coat and cravat, no less. The dusting of fine golden hair emerging from the open neck of his shirt served as a potent reminder of this fact.

She swallowed. "At this hour, I never imagined that you... In fact, I thought the house was... You see, I was hungry... But the dog... And then the candle... So I came in here to light it," she explained in one breath, exhaling the last of her air. It was quite possible she would faint next.

Calliope had never fainted before. Doing so would be a novel experience. Everhart was already holding her; therefore, she wouldn't crash to the floor. In addition, if she fainted now, then she wouldn't have to endure any reproach for disturbing him, or for being out of bed in the dark, or for any number of reasons.

Unfortunately, it appeared as though she wasn't going to faint. She distinctly felt her heart start beating again, albeit wildly. Her lungs filled, emptied, and filled again.

Yet, Everhart still held her. Although his large hands *had* slid an inch or two lower. The tips of his fingers curled around to the underside of her arms, where she was certain no man had ever touched her before. That sensitive, undisturbed part of her tingled with awareness, just shy of tickling. His thumbs grazed her in tiny circles, as if he were worrying a coin-sized mark through the soft cotton.

"That still does not explain why you are here in Fallow Hall, bewitching both man and beast in the wee hours of the morning," Everhart said with the hoarse gruffness she'd come to expect from him. What she did not expect was the way his gaze shifted to her mouth.

She blinked. He was impossibly close. His breath was sweetly scented with cloves and cinnamon as if he'd been drinking mulled wine. The firelight caught the growth of golden whiskers along his jaw, his chin, and lining the edge of his upper lip. A wild impulse to brush her fingertips over those short hairs rushed through her.

She managed to tamp it down when she saw his lips compress in a line. Lifting her gaze to his, she noted the blue-green intensity had returned. He was either going to shake her or scold her. She wanted neither.

Bewitching? Hardly. "I had no intention of doing so."

Everhart scrutinized her face quite thoroughly, as if searching for evidence to support his statement. "Your hair is down."

Unsteady from the oddness of this exchange, Calliope tilted her head, hoping to find understanding at this new viewpoint. She didn't. However, she did note that his lashes were quite long, and darker too, like his brows. "The strands are rather fine and tend to escape their confines."

"Like attracts like, or so they say."

She frowned, absorbing the meaning. "Are you suggesting that *I've* escaped my confines as well? I was not under the impression I was a captive here."

"Perhaps you should be," he said, his voice softer, lower but no less accusatory. "You certainly shouldn't be wandering the halls, disturbing those who would rather be sleeping."

She harrumphed. "I would happily leave you to your slumber, if you would unhand me."

"That I cannot do." Unexpectedly, his lips spread into a slow, swoon-worthy grin—*if* one were inclined to swoon. She, however, was not. "You are holding me up."

"Oh." She'd forgotten about his injury. Looking down, she saw that he was balanced on one leg, the other bent at the knee. Even standing like a wounded pirate captain at the helm of his ship did not detract from his virility.

There I stood, transfixed by a foreign sensation. In that moment, I was a voyager witnessing land after a lifetime at sea, and blind to the rocks jutting up between us…

The words from the letter suddenly thrummed through her heart. *No,* she said to herself. *Absolutely not.* She was not going to slip into another one of her daydreams while standing in front of Everhart. She could only bear so much humiliation.

In a hurry to end their encounter, she turned to stand beside him and settled her arm around his lean waist. Ignoring the staggered look he cast down at her, she took a step, urging him forward. "Do not be alarmed, Everhart. I'm merely offering assistance, as I've learned to do for my father when he suffers a bout of weakness."

Yet even she knew that this was not the same. A quaking sensation trampled through her limbs. Which was not entirely unpleasant. Far from it. At the moment, she didn't want to think about how overly familiar or inappropriate the gesture was, or how warm and solid Everhart felt pressed to her side. She only wanted to help him to the sofa and leave as quickly as possible.

His acquiescence came by way of his arm draped over her shoulders. "Offering assistance? No, what you are doing is ensuring that I will not sleep at all this night."

Not even a word of gratitude. "Perhaps you are the one disturbing me and deserve the full blame." She produced a believable huff of exasperation to let him understand that she was acting against her will. Mostly.

"I think not." He ground out the words.

"You needn't have opened the door with such force. In addition, I would not have stood there at all, had you not employed nefarious tactics." The gall of him, standing in front of her with so much of his flesh exposed for her to admire. No matter how many novels she'd read, nothing could have prepared her for that.

He chuckled, the sound rumbling from his body and through hers, eliciting all sorts of unwanted but enthralling sensations. "And what might those be?"

"You know very well what they are." She did not appreciate being the cause of his amusement when she was sacrificing her humility for his sake. They had been among the same circle of friends at one time, but apparently he'd forgotten. "Every nuance of your character heightens your reputation as a rake and seducer. I was merely startled at being a first-time recipient. Normally, I am singled out for your reproach, though you did manage to add enough of that as well." Calliope nearly gasped at the boldness of her speech. Perhaps being on the shelf for so long had made her more brazen and less willing to leave matters unsaid.

Everhart made no comment.

The heat of a blush rose to her cheeks. "Never fear, Everhart, your resolve to detest me is still very much intact."

Gabriel held his breath. This torment went beyond the pale.

Surely, this must be a dream that brought Calliope Croft to him. Any moment he would awaken to see the vast empty map room. The softness of her body pressed against his side, the subtle shifting of her supple breast with every step must be a fantasy created by his cruel mind. "*Yes.*"

"Is that your only response?" She lifted her face, annoyance evident in the way her slender brows drew together. Her brown eyes glittered like moonlight across wet sand or, given her mood, more like lightning striking the shore. Dark golden waves of hair cascaded down from a center part in her hair and swayed like a curtain against her cheek. He was so tempted to lift those strands to his lips, to feel the softness and draw in her unique rosewater-and-mint fragrance, that his hand twitched. Fighting the impulse, he curled his hand into a fist and then nearly laughed aloud at the absurdity of his action.

It had been five long years since he'd stood near her, let alone touched her. Did he actually think that the simple act of keeping his hand fisted would be enough to rein in his desire?

He shook his head. "I do not detest you."

"It is fine with me, you know. I am a complete person with or without your approval." She stopped as they neared the sofa and lowered her arm from around his waist.

He'd always like that about her—the aura of *completeness* that surrounded her. She knew her own mind, her likes and dislikes, and hadn't cowed to the influence of those around her. Part of him wished she'd married Brightwell—so that she was beyond his reach in a manner that would have put a stop to the incomprehensible yearning he'd once felt. And perhaps still did.

"I did not plan to hurt your friend all those years ago," she added suddenly, as if her thoughts were in alignment with his. What cruel joke would it be if they were always in line with his, even after all this time?

Or perhaps that was fanciful thinking and the reason was because Brightwell—both in her refusal and Gabriel's involvement—was *always* between them.

"Surely even you can see that it has worked out the better for him in the end," she continued. "I would not have made Brightwell happy."

The notion was preposterous. "And why wouldn't you have made him happy?"

"Because I did not love him."

The forthright simplicity of her statement irritated him, but he did not take any time to question the reason. "Perhaps you do not know what love is." *Love is agony, sacrifice, and seeing what you want but knowing you can't have it. Knowing that there would be nothing left if you surrendered to it.*

"I have a deeper understanding of that emotion than you could ever comprehend," she spat, her nostrils flaring. "And I've had quite enough of your censure for one evening."

Without thinking, he reached out to stop her from leaving. Once again, his hands encircled her upper arms, his fingertips nestled into her warmth. He couldn't resist the barest caress. Odd, but even after five years it seemed impossible to be this close and not touch her.

"First you accuse me of seduction, and now censure. Pray, which one is it, Miss Croft? For one cannot do both simultaneously."

"Are you sure of that?" she challenged, her chin jutting forward. "You've made no effort to conceal your state of undress since my arrival. I'm quite certain you are aware that my eyes are at the level of your exposed flesh. Therefore, I would be unable to avoid noting your obvious display of...*masculinity*." She swallowed. "And—do correct me if I am mistaken—but are you not, even now, caressing my arms as you hold me close?"

He was, *bugger it all!* And he wanted to do so much more. A keen, throbbing ache filled his entire body as he pulled her closer. He couldn't seem to help himself.

"A moment ago, I was assisting you to the sofa," she continued, her voice no more than a breath against the open V of his shirt. "And now you've maneuvered me into your embrace again, all the while leveling me with the intensity in your gaze and the harshness of your tone. If anyone could manage both seduction and censure, then it is you."

He stared down at her, fighting the urge to kiss her with every ounce of his being. It was like trying to hoist the mast of a ship with a single finger. He strained to keep himself still and not lower his head even a fraction.

If he kissed her now, he would never be free of her. His life would change forever.

If he kissed her *right* now, he wouldn't be able to stop. Ever. That knowledge hit him like a blast of arctic water off the bow of a ship.

"Miss Croft," he began with surprising calm, while a sea of thwarted desire raged inside him. "Has anyone ever accused you of having an overactive imagination?"

She blanched as if he'd thrown the words at her. Beneath his hands, he felt her tense. "Another perfect example of seduction and censure. Very good. You've managed to wound me while drawing me closer still."

His level of restraint grew weaker by the moment. "Perhaps there is no censure at all, but your own bad opinion of me that overshadows this encounter."

"It is not my opinion that needs alteration," she said on a breath, her ripe bosom rising and falling, drawing unnecessary attention to her own state of undress and forcing him to imagine how easy it would be to remove so few clothes. "It matters not what we think of each other. I will be gone in mere hours. We can both keep what is ours—opinions, censure, and overactive imaginations—in separate houses."

"Do not forget to mention nefarious tactics of seduction." To prove a point, and because he couldn't resist the urge, he loosened his grasp of one arm without freeing her. In a slow caress, he trailed his fingertips along her shoulder toward her throat, lightly grazing the silken flesh exposed above the prim ruffled edge of her night rail. "Be warned. Should you enter my house again, I cannot be held responsible for my actions."

Lifting her hands between their bodies, she settled them atop his chest. Cool on contact, he felt a wayward need to warm them, to chafe them between his own hands.

"Nor I," she said with a shove as she stepped out of his embrace before turning on her heel.

Taken off guard, he lost his footing and fell backward onto the edge of the sofa. His splinted leg shot out and nicked the edge of the low table. Pain knifed through him as he hissed through his teeth. Wincing, he looked up to see if she would look back with concern.

She didn't. Instead, she absconded with a brace of candles and left him alone in his misery.

CHAPTER FIVE

"You are heavy-footed this morning, cousin," Pamela remarked from her perch on the vanity stool, while her maid brushed her pale hair.

Calliope suppressed a yawn as she moved about the room, surreptitiously searching for the letter under the guise of positioning trinkets for her cousin's admiration. Drowsy, she couldn't stop shuffling her feet. Her slippers felt weighted, as if the ground beneath Fallow Hall were trying to root her in place.

"A long journey can make one overly tired, I suppose." There was no need to mention her predawn jaunt through the manor or her encounter with Everhart. Nonetheless, she hadn't slept a wink after she'd returned to her chamber. Why that man set out to provoke her, when he was always so agreeable to everyone else, was beyond her understanding.

More than that, she hated that it bothered her.

"Ah, yes. As does a long illness." Pamela gestured for Bess to stop brushing and then lifted a bent wrist, as if in a silent command for assistance in making her way back to bed. "I tire so easily."

Poor Nell, already tucked away in the corner, strummed the harp strings. Noting the tiny strips of linen tied around the girl's fingertips, Calliope felt even sorrier for her. "Then perhaps we could let the servants adjourn for a few minutes while we have a *visit*"—though what she really intended was a more serious interrogation about the letter—"before you are *too* tired and before I must leave. As we speak, Griffin is ensuring our carriage is in order."

"Even when mother was here, I had a difficult time enduring long conversations. They are so taxing." Her cousin sighed and sank down onto the mattress. Bess fluffed the pillows behind her. "Nevertheless, I believe a lengthy visit is required. Since you are still *unmarried*, it can be of no consequence to remain as my companion here."

Calliope clenched her teeth.

A dark cauldron of emotions roiled within her—hot prickles of irritation, a simmering tension at the pit of her stomach, and the sour taste of jealousy at the back of her throat.

If the letter was truly from *him*, then this Casanova was playing with her cousin's affections. The same way he had with hers, when he'd so easily dismissed his ardor for her and gone on to someone else. *Several someone elses.* The fact that Brightwell had moved on hadn't bothered her quite so much before...

Until now, when it appeared that both men wanted her cousin. And no one wanted Calliope. Which was a silly thought—one that made her annoyed with herself—considering how *she* was the one who'd refused Brightwell in the first place.

Casting those thoughts aside, she focused on her task. All she needed to do was find the letter and read it for any clues to the anonymous author's identity. In addition to his distinctive handwriting, the other letters had been postmarked from London with a WMO for the Westminster office. Of course, confirming the postmark and date might not identify him, but it would be another step to narrowing down the candidates to one area.

"Alas, I am out of time," Calliope said, hoping that her cousin might feel a sense of urgency as well.

Pamela pouted. "You cannot leave. I haven't discussed the letter with you. I believe I mentioned how I am the *only* married woman to have received one."

This Casanova's heart was fickle indeed. Part of Calliope hoped this letter was merely a product of her cousin's desire to be the center of attention. "But how are you even certain it was one of those?"

"It started off with *My dearest Pamela*…the same as all the others." Her brow furrowed in confusion and her gaze glazed over. "Although their names weren't Pamela. So I suppose it wasn't exactly the same."

It was common enough to begin any letter with such a salutation. Yet none of the other letters had started with *My love*, as Calliope's had. *My dearest Marianne* had been the second. *My dearest Petunia*, the third. *My dearest Beatrice*, the fourth. *My dearest Johanna*, the fifth. *My dearest Gertrude*, the sixth. *My dearest Honoria*, the seventh. And now, potentially, *My dearest Pamela*. Most of the recipients had since married.

Had one of *them* found Casanova and married him posthaste?

"Was it signed?" If the signature were missing or torn away, that would be another clue.

"Of course not, silly. *He* never signs them." Pamela laughed and then pursed her lips in a very queen-like manner. "But I don't suppose you'd recall something like that since you've never received one yourself."

Not signed. Was it true? Had Pamela received a Casanova letter?

The only person Calliope had shared her letter with was Griffin. She'd wanted her brother's help in finding the author who'd stolen her heart with his words. Griffin, however, had advised her to have caution. "*Only a coward would omit a signature,*" he'd said, while reminding her that she'd already secured Brightwell's affections.

"I suppose not," Calliope murmured. Anxious, her gaze darted around the room once more, as if the letter would suddenly appear in plain sight, even after repeated searches had produced nothing. She didn't like not knowing where it was, or *if* it was even here. The love-letter Casanova had already taken her unawares once. She didn't want it to happen again. "Although, there is one way for me to have a full understanding…and that is by reading the letter myself."

"But Mother had it removed," Pamela whined. "I believe she feared I was falling madly in love with him."

Calliope forced a laugh. "Ridiculous. You are newly married and madly in love with your own husband."

Pamela's gaze drifted off. "I should still very much like to see the letter again. Mother packed it inside an ivory-handled patch box, along with a bit of needlework, a few ribbons, earbobs, and a silk fan. She wanted me to concentrate completely on my recovery."

"An ivory-handled patch box," Calliope remarked, thinking about the carriage outside and the day's journey ahead to Scotland. She had a choice to make. A difficult one.

"Yes, trimmed in gold and with a mirror on the inside. It was a wedding gift from Milton." Pamela didn't even bat an eye. Apparently, she was blind to the hypocrisy of having a letter from her ink-and-paper lover tucked away inside a wedding gift from her husband. "It shouldn't be too difficult to find."

Look for me, dear siren...Calliope had done that to the best of her ability. Still, her efforts hadn't been enough. Now, she was presented with another opportunity to find him. Another opportunity to unmask this scoundrel and expose his identity.

The only question that remained—was she was willing to sacrifice more of her life for this pursuit?

Anxious for his guests' departure, Gabriel grabbed his cane and headed toward the foyer. It was still early, but he hoped their carriage was packed and ready.

He'd slept fitfully, waking from a nightmare in which Calliope Croft stood before him, dressed in her night rail, and handed him a small, green seedling. The moment he took the gift, the plant sprouted to life. It transformed into vines that grew as thick as saplings and twisted viciously around his arms, his legs, and his throat, shackling him to the edifice of Briar Heath, his childhood home.

Even now, Gabriel shuddered. He did not want to return there. Ever. He did not want to think about what life had once been like, or the fear that had dogged his heels since the moment he'd met Calliope Croft.

More than anything, he needed to win this wager. Or in the very least, not lose.

At the sight of Griffin and Delaney Croft conversing with Danvers and Brightwell near the door, relief washed through him. Fortunately, the only people who stood in his way would soon be gone, and he needn't worry about the letter he'd written all those years ago. Everything would return to normal soon.

"It disheartens me to see you go, Croft," Gabriel said as he approached, relying on his cane to minimize the weight to his broken bone. "I was interested in proving that I can best you while standing on one leg."

Croft grinned. "I *almost* feel guilty for pummeling you when all your limbs are in order. But the truth of the matter is, you couldn't best me if you had a dozen legs to stand on, Everhart."

This familiar sparring assured Gabriel that all was right with his world once again. "I look forward to proving you wrong when we are next in town." He transferred his cane to the other side so he could grip Croft's hand. Strangely enough, over these past few years of boxing with him, he'd actually started to like the chap, despite the threat he'd issued. Croft lived by a code of honor where he put his family first and stayed true to his character. Gabriel respected that, even now, when Croft wasn't holding back from a good, solid handshake. "You're going soft already. I guess it's true what they say about married men."

"That only the best of men are designed for it? Yes, that's entirely true." Croft chuckled and gave one final bone-crunching squeeze before he released his grip.

"Hear, hear," Brightwell cheered with a resounding clap that caused one of his pale forelocks to droop. Years ago, their friendship had merely been a convenience for Gabriel. He'd wanted an excuse to spend more time with Calliope. Then, after the letter and her refusal of Brightwell, he'd experienced guilt over having misled them both. To make amends, he'd decided to become Brightwell's friend in truth and suggested an expedition that would, essentially, help both of them heal their wounds.

Gabriel hoped the plan would finally work for him on his next expedition.

"All right, gentlemen," Delaney Croft said with a laugh of her own. "You've proven yourselves worthy opponents. However, if we do not leave soon, I fear Valentine will fetch some rope and turn the foyer into a boxing ring."

"Capital notion." Danvers hailed Valentine who waited near the door. "Some rope, if you please. I should like to see Everhart pummeled."

"You forget, *my friend*," Gabriel said, "that you will not collect on our wager if I die."

"Never mind, Valentine," Danvers said with a tsk. The butler, however, never once moved from his spot, having become an expert at ignoring their nonsense in the short time they'd resided at Fallow Hall.

"My husband told me about the wager," Delaney said. "I cannot believe you bet against Montwood."

Gabriel shrugged, daring not to reveal how the statement made him want to look over his shoulder with dread.

Knowing what he stood to lose, he never should have been so foolish. "Where is the cheat, by the way?"

"I imagine he's a safe distance from the reach of Croft's fists." Brightwell smirked, apparently amused at being excluded from those who were targets, either of Croft's fists or Montwood's wager. Not to mention, since Brightwell had come to stay here with his wife for her recuperation, he'd done nothing but try to convince Gabriel to find himself a bride. Of course, the accident had much to do with that.

The uncomfortable weight of culpability settled in his stomach.

Delaney sighed in exasperation. "Montwood needn't worry about that any longer. My husband has quite a forgiving nature."

Forgiving nature? Gabriel bit back a laugh.

Croft issued a low grunt. His stern countenance suggested that he did not seem to share his wife's certainty on the matter. Then, when his gaze shifted to Gabriel's, the warning was clear. Sparring partner or not, Croft had not forgiven him for wounding Calliope.

Gabriel couldn't blame him. He hadn't forgiven himself either. As far as he was concerned, the sooner the Crofts left Fallow Hall, the better. "And speaking of those absent from our farewell party," he added with an unnecessary glance around the room, "your sister appears to be missing."

"Here I am," said the woman in question from the top of the stairs. Hand atop the wide rail, Calliope raced down quickly but lost her muff along the way. Then, retracing her steps, she snatched it before turning back around and finally descending to the foyer.

Out of breath, she stood there in a blue redingote trimmed in white fur, her honeyed tresses already slipping free of their confines to brush against her collar. Her cheeks were rosy, her eyes bright, her lips parted and inviting…just as they'd been last night for a single moment. Until he'd come to his senses and realized how dangerous it was to be alone with her.

He'd forgotten how easy it was to *forget* himself around her. Even now, he found himself taking a half step nearer. It was only a half step because he realized what he was doing just in time. Thankfully, he would not have to be on his guard for too much longer.

He tore his gaze away but not before spotting a smirk from Danvers. Gabriel glared back with a "bugger off" look. His friend snickered.

"And how does our cousin fare?" Croft asked. "I did not have the time to see her before her maid informed me that she was resting."

Calliope tensed. It was nothing more than a subtle shift in her posture, a slight adjustment of her shoulders, but Gabriel noticed. "She *is* resting but doubtless hoping that I will still be here when she wakes. Pamela has requested that I stay behind to keep her company."

Brightwell cleared his throat. "She mentioned the same to me earlier."

Until now, Brightwell had said few words and lingered more along the outer rim of the foyer. Now, he took a step forward and drew everyone's attention. Of course, Gabriel paid more attention to how Calliope reacted.

How often, years ago, had he watched her gaze alight on Brightwell? Dozens of times, at least. Back then, Gabriel had always felt a rise of annoyance. Strangely, he still felt it now.

"I imagine you found that an odd request, considering…" Calliope's words drifted off, likely because everyone in the room was thinking the same thing. Why would Pamela want her husband near the woman to whom he'd once proposed?

"Not at all." Brightwell's gaze softened with a familiarity that made Gabriel tighten his grip on the head of his cane. "My wife knows that there is no animosity on my part. What is in the past remains there, Miss Croft. Please do not allow your concern for what you believe to be my discomfort sway your opinion. Your cousin's health is all that matters now."

Calliope drew in a breath and nodded. "Yes. You are quite right, Lord Brightwell."

"No. It is not right," Gabriel heard himself say. The vehemence in his tone must have shown on his face because there were startled glances his way. He didn't care. He didn't want Calliope to talk to Brightwell any longer. He didn't want her to stay for her cousin's health. He didn't want her near enough to tempt him to insanity. *She must leave immediately.* "Croft, you could not possibly consider leaving your sister here with the likes of us." *With me.*

"Be careful, Everhart," Croft warned, his tone tinged with a reminder of the threat in Vauxhall Gardens. "Do not forget that you have your own family to worry about."

Ah, yes. A perfect example of his forgiving nature. Croft could still ruin him. Gabriel had hoped that after five years of penance, he would be free. Yet having the Crofts here only made it clear that the letter he'd written had not faded from their memories, just as it had not faded from his.

"By all accounts," Delaney offered, "Calliope would be here with her maid, her cousin, her cousin's happily married husband—and three gentlemen who have declared never to marry."

"If I may…" Danvers interjected, holding up one finger. "It behooves me to mention that part of the wager included steering clear of unmarried women. Miss Croft is quite safe."

"It *behooves* you, does it?" Gabriel knocked Danvers in the shin with his cane before turning to Calliope's brother. "Croft, if Raena were in her place, I would never allow—"

"Lord Everhart," Calliope Croft interrupted, pointing at him with her muff. "When your sister turns four and twenty, I do not believe you will *have* a say on what she can or cannot not do. While I will respect my brother's decision, I have a mind of my own. In addition, being a spinster *allows* me certain freedoms, I'm sure."

The word *spinster* seemed to echo like the toll of a bell. A specter of guilt crept up behind Gabriel. Her unwed state was partly his own fault—or *entirely*. If he hadn't written that letter, she would have married Brightwell. Gabriel swallowed and noted how Croft narrowed his eyes at him.

"Your sister has a good head on her shoulders. Quite like her brother, I think." Delaney patted the place above her husband's heart. By all appearances, the gesture worked some sort of magic. Instantly, Croft's gaze softened as he looked at his wife.

No.

Calliope seemed to notice too. A smile bloomed, bathing her features in a warm glow. "Then you are leaving the decision up to me?"

No. Croft would not permit such a thing, Gabriel assured himself.

Then, Croft gave a nod of consent.

Gabriel felt betrayed. He'd counted on Croft's overbearing nature.

"But of course it would be wrong of me to extend my stay at Fallow Hall without an invitation." Calliope cast a sly glance to Danvers.

Danvers—*the traitor*—posed a ready reply. "It goes without saying. You are welcome to stay as long as you wish. Let Fallow Hall be your second home."

"Thank you, Mr. Danvers," she said graciously and then looked askance at Gabriel to produce a rather smug sniff. "It will only be for a few days, I imagine."

"Then we will all be the merrier for that time, right, Everhart?" Danvers reached over and chucked him on the shoulder.

Gabriel didn't dare answer. This couldn't be happening. Croft wasn't leaving his sister here! The man who'd easily threatened to have him arrested and branded certainly wasn't now relying on Gabriel's sense of honor to ensure Calliope's welfare.

For five years he'd kept to their bargain. He'd kept his distance from Calliope. *Mostly, aside from following her to Bath.* And now he was being repaid with Croft's cruelty?

Gabriel glared at his nemesis and relished the day they would both return to Gentleman Jackson's boxing saloon. Next time, he wouldn't hold back out of a sense of misguided loyalty.

"Of course." Gabriel gritted his teeth and inclined his head curtly. "Any relative of Croft's is welcome."

"Good to know," Croft said, his expression inscrutable. "I'll send a missive to the twins and see if they would like to join their sister here."

Phoebe and Asteria Croft here as well? After a single Season, they were already renowned for the mischief that they liked to call "matchmaking." Forget cruelty; this was downright torture.

"Griffin, stop teasing. Everhart's gone positively pale." Delaney's violet gaze was alive with more curiosity than concern. "We must leave him before Valentine does indeed retrieve the rope."

Instead, Valentine opened the door as the Crofts turned to leave. Gabriel followed the pair and directed the footmen to assist the driver in retrieving Calliope's trunks. During that time, Delaney stood near the servant's carriage, speaking with both her own maid and Calliope's maid.

Standing beside Croft, Gabriel turned his head and kept his voice low so the others wouldn't overhear. "What do you mean by this, Croft—coming to Fallow Hall in the first place, knowing all the while that I was here?" If this was a game or a new condition to their bargain, he deserved to know forthwith.

Croft kept his gaze on the luggage. "I have come to see about the welfare of my cousin. Surely, you couldn't have qualms over that."

"You are leaving your sister under my charge. *Surely*," Gabriel growled, "you could at least find a reason to stay behind as well."

When Delaney had finished with the maids, she cast a concerned glance over at the two of them. Croft waved to her as if in reassurance, and she disappeared into their own carriage.

"I have obligations to attend to—*something* that you should think about for once in your life," Croft said in a genial tone, as if he hadn't struck a low blow.

"For once?" Gabriel jerked around to face him. He clenched his teeth to keep from shouting. "I have seen to my obligations for the past five years. You are the one neglecting yours."

"Our opinions differ." Croft didn't even blink. "By leaving my sister here, I *am* seeing to my family's welfare. However, if you happen to prove me wrong, then you will taste the fires of hell, and I will be the one to feed them to you."

Gabriel strangled the neck of his cane. "Be warned, Croft. Next time we are at *Jackson's*, I will not hold back for the sake of your…*family*."

Oddly enough, Croft smiled at this threat. "I look forward to it, Everhart. I'd always suspected there was more to you than you let on."

Then, before Croft bothered to explain that remark, he stepped past Gabriel and joined his wife inside the carriage.

Gabriel walked back inside, his mood darkening.

It didn't help matters that the first thing he saw was Brightwell bowing to Calliope. "I will inform your cousin once she wakes. I'm certain she will be delighted."

"Yes," Calliope said, a slight weariness in her tone. "I will see her as soon as I've sorted out my trunks with Meg."

Gabriel watched as she tensed again, as if it gave her little happiness to please her cousin. So then, why *had* she decided to stay?

Without another word, Brightwell departed down the hall for the east wing.

Danvers chafed his hands together as he looked from Calliope to Gabriel. "What a merry party we will make. Wouldn't you say so, Miss Croft?"

"Merry, indeed," she answered with an utter lack of enthusiasm.

"Pardon me, Miss Croft, but did you say *merry* or *marry*?" Danvers mused. "Those two words are so interchangeable that it is difficult to tell the difference. Wouldn't you agree, Everhart?"

Gabriel growled but was denied a rebuttal just then because Miss Croft's maid entered the hall with two trunk-wielding footmen in tow.

"Gentlemen," Calliope began, eyeing Gabriel and Danvers warily, "thank you again for your hospitality." Then, after a hasty curtsy, she mounted the stairs and disappeared from view.

The sounds of the footmen's heavy steps pounded through Gabriel like storm waves crashing against the hull of a ship. His stomach churned.

Left alone with the conspirator, Gabriel glared at Danvers. "Whatever it is that you believe, abandon those thoughts. You will only end up making a mockery of yourself."

"Bravo, Everhart." Danvers laughed. "That was said with convincing austerity. If I weren't standing here, watching your mouth move, I would have sworn it was your father speaking."

Now, it was Gabriel's turn to laugh, albeit hollowly. "You cannot force your opponents into marriage. Or set about to compromise them."

"Of course not," his friend said with a look of reproach. "I have a sister as well, you know."

Gabriel conceded this portion of the argument to him. Danvers was too honorable to sully a young woman's reputation solely to win a bet. Which left only one question—what *was* he up to?

Then, as if he'd read Gabriel's thoughts, Danvers mouth quirked in a diabolical grin. "Ten thousand pounds, my friend." Turning on his heel, he walked away, whistling a jaunty tune and leaving Gabriel to dread the coming days.

CHAPTER SIX

Calliope stood outside of the music room and debated whether to enter or to simply retire for the night. In the past three days of tending to her cousin's whims, Calliope had not been able to keep Pamela on the topic of the letter. Each time it was brought up, her cousin grew unaccountably tired. The entire process—furtive questions and manipulating conversations, while concealing her own adamant curiosity and subsequent frustration—was draining.

In the meantime, Calliope had searched the rest of the house, through bookcases, armoires, cedar chests, secretaries, and closets. She'd discovered seven frighteningly large brown spiders, four tiny mice in a corner of the linen closet, three interesting novels in the library, and two stuffed owls in the garret.

But no ivory-handled patch box.

On the bright side, she had not discovered any slimy, crawling insects, which meant the spiders were doing their jobs. There wasn't an overabundance of dust, and other than the mice in the closet, the entire house was quite tidy. Which meant the servants were doing their jobs too.

The housekeeper, Mrs. Merkel, and the head butler, Valentine, kept everything in fine order. Which was even more impressive because Nell, the resident harpist, had been kept away from her duties. Likely, much juggling had to be done, and yet no one suffered for it…aside from Nell, of course. This was all quite surprising, since there was no lady of the manor to oversee these things. So then, who was?

While the notion that one of the confirmed bachelors—none of whom seemed eager to run his own house—had put aside his own desires to uphold his duty intrigued Calliope, she hadn't had a moment of free time to inquire. She was far too busy trying to find the letter.

Calliope squeezed the back of her neck. She ached all over but especially there.

Not too far away, she heard the muffled sound of steady footfalls along the hall runner. Turning, she lowered her hand and saw Lord Lucan Montwood approach. With his dark features and attire, he seemed part of the shadows from which he emerged. Although he'd been absent when her brother and sister-in-law were here, he'd been the consummate host ever since. In fact, both he and Mr. Danvers had been.

"Miss Croft," Montwood said, gifting her with his infamously charming smile. "Still on the hunt for that letter?"

Her pulse skittered to a halt. "Letter?"

Montwood's amber eyes glittered in the torchlight as a dimple flashed in his cheek. "Your cousin's letter."

As any cardsharp ought to be, this gentleman was entirely too perceptive. Always watchful. She'd never seen him let down his guard, though she had glimpsed something other than charm once or twice. Those occurrences were more like the shadows behind him than anything tangible. Yet they were unsettling all the same.

"Oh, *that.*" Calliope offered an absent wave of her hand. Apparently, she hadn't been as stealthy as she'd imagined— or as nonchalant about her quest when she'd asked Danvers that first night. She hoped Montwood was the only other person who'd discovered her secret. If Brightwell found out... Well, she didn't want to think about the pain it would cause him. "You know, it's nothing, really. In fact, I've quite gone on to another task. I've already collected three books to read aloud to my cousin."

Still grinning, he looked pointedly through the open archway beside them. "From the music room?"

"No, from the library." She blinked, wondering why he would think such a thing until she remembered where they stood. *Oh.* Quickly, she attempted to find a believable excuse that was not letter-related in the least. "I was merely curious about...um...sheet music."

This lifted the shadow of speculation from his countenance. "Do you play?"

"Not play so much as read the notes," she explained. "I'm a capital page turner. Once upon a time, I used to sing. Quite singular for a young woman, I know."

"Ah, then you have earned your namesake."

"Hardly." She laughed. "Though when forced, I have managed to land on *all* the notes, and *without* turning any of the audience into magpies."

He chuckled. "Perhaps we should force you to earn your keep after dinner tomorrow evening."

She made a face. "Then I will surely be moved into the draftiest part of the attic."

"Speaking of drafty places..." he added smoothly and with a smile that seemed more cunning than charming, "have you checked the north tower? I'd say that the map room is your most likely prospect for all sorts of papers, random boxes, and such."

Random boxes, hmm? Her hallway companion was sly indeed. Montwood knew quite a bit. It certainly stood to reason that his suggestion would also be on target. Though in truth, she never imagined her aunt would direct anything to a room that was an unreservedly masculine domain. "The map room? I thought Everhart spent a great deal of time there."

After her previous encounter with Everhart in that very room, the thought of seeing him there again caused her heart to quicken. The increasing beats of that organ were from wariness, she was sure.

In the past three days, she hadn't seen much of him. She'd heard the shuffle-slide of Everhart's steps, accompanied by the syncopated rhythm of his cane hitting the floor, but she'd never come face-to-face with him. Sometimes, out of the corner of her eye, she saw him disappear into a room. Yet he hadn't joined the rest of them for dinner or in the parlor afterward for games of whist and loo either. Miraculously, Pamela had garnered the strength to endure these parties each evening. It was clear, however, that Everhart hadn't been telling the truth when he'd said that he didn't despise her.

"Rarely," Montwood answered. "His chambers are actually in the east wing. He complains often enough that the sounds of my midnight playing travel directly into the map room. Surely, if he is there—*by chance, of course*," he added with a wink, "then by the time I begin, he will retire to his rooms, and you will be left to your own devices."

A frisson of hope filled her. Perhaps she would find her treasure tonight and then be gone from Fallow Hall within the week. "Thank you, Montwood. What a fortuitous meeting."

Yet as soon as she said the words, a wave of disappointment hit her as well. Oddly enough, the reason was because of Everhart. She didn't want to leave Fallow Hall with him still despising her.

"For both of us, I hope." Montwood sketched an elegant bow before disappearing into the music room.

Gabriel wrestled a mammoth atlas from the drawer and lifted it onto the expansive table in the loft within the map room. Taking up the entire surface, the South American continent awaited him. Once he had the ten thousand pounds, he could fund his own expedition. Imagine what sights he could explore, what beaches he could walk upon. That was his favorite part—seeing the different shades of sand. The sight had always reminded him of a certain pair of brown eyes...

He stroked the reedy burgundy cover with the flat of his hand. One year. That was all he needed to wait. Of course, it went without saying that he'd have to trick Montwood and Danvers into marrying, but after encouraging Calliope to stay here, Gabriel would aim his sights on Danvers first.

Relishing the idea, he lifted the cover. Just then, he heard a loud *thump* from the lower portion of the map room. At this late hour, he wondered who it could be.

Hopping over to the loft railing, Gabriel stopped short. *Calliope Croft.*

Unaware of his presence, she crouched down to peer beneath a serpentine commode near the door. From his vantage point, Gabriel noted that her burgundy gown was much the same hue as the atlas behind him but with more luster and a short row of pearl buttons between her shoulders. She'd always had nice shoulders. They were among the first things he'd ever noticed about her. In addition to the way her dark golden locks tended to brush her flesh in something of a kiss.

Gabriel swallowed. He'd done a fine job of avoiding her until now. And he had no intention of allowing her to change that either.

"What are you doing in here?" he asked from the top of the circular stairs. Even to his own ears, his tone was harsh. Years of suppressed longing could do that to a man.

Miss Croft jolted upright, sending a stack of papers tumbling from the commode to the floor at her feet. She peered up at him. The lacy white trim of her neckline pulled taut over her bosom and then puckered with each rapid inhale and exhale. "I didn't think you would be here. It wasn't my intention to disturb anyone."

A low grunt of disbelief sounded in his throat. How could she not disturb him? Her very presence in this manor left him on edge and made him constantly aware of where she was at any given moment.

Making his way down the stairs, he continued his study of her. While she'd been enchanting in the pale hues that debutantes wore, bolder colors gave her complexion a warm glow. In his opinion, however, she dressed too modestly now, like a matron instead of a young vibrant woman.

The cut of her gown, while leaving a lovely expanse of shoulder exposed for his admiration, only revealed the barest curve of her breasts. That supple flesh was far too enticing to keep hidden. Five years ago, the gowns she'd worn had held those creamy swells on display for him. His mouth watered, even now. If memory served, she had the faintest birthmark near the outer rim on the left side. It had been a rosy pink color, small, but in the shape of…in the shape of…*the South American continent.*

He shook his head and nearly laughed at himself. *Well, isn't that a telling revelation?*

"Disturbed," he said more to himself than to her. "That is precisely what I am."

She ignored his comment and bent down to straighten the fan of papers. "Montwood said that all sorts of items were brought here on occasion. I thought I might find a few of my cousin's things that were misplaced when my aunt was here."

Montwood, of course. If it wasn't Danvers, then it would have to be Montwood. Gabriel had wondered when the amber-eyed serpent would make his first move. So far, Danvers had been the only one to openly plot against him. What worried Gabriel was the fact that Montwood usually didn't like to play by the rules.

Then again, for this wager, Gabriel didn't plan on playing by them either. Not this time.

Gripping the iron rail and wishing it were Montwood's throat, he descended one step at a time. When he faced Miss Croft again, he saw that she was now standing, perusing one paper after the other while holding a hand to the nape of her neck.

He stopped halfway down. "Why are you holding your neck like that?"

She turned her head with a slight wince. "I should think it obvious."

He experienced a perverse amount of pleasure in the bite of her tone. Miss Croft was cranky. A rarity, indeed. But not without a certain appeal. Of course, since the reason was due to pain, his amusement sobered. "You've done too much. You should abandon this pursuit of yours."

"*Does everyone know?*" She mumbled the words, likely not realizing how well sound traveled in this room. "My pursuit is none of your concern."

Oh, but it was. In so many ways. Surprisingly, his command was not solely for his own purpose. Certainly, he wanted her to end her pursuit of her cousin's letter. It was better for everyone involved if that letter—not to mention Calliope's letter—never saw the light of day. But even more than that, he didn't want to see her in pain.

"I cannot. I have already been here for days and I am—I mean, *my cousin*—is desperate for her letter." Her voice was as weary and bruised as the faint purplish smudges beneath her eyes. "Besides, I must do something to distract her from harp music. Poor Nell has wondrous talent, but she deserves a reprieve from her task."

Gabriel sat down on a filigreed wrought-iron tread, unable to ignore a telltale sting of guilt. He was partly responsible for Calliope's discomfort. Then again, perhaps a great deal more than *partly*. "There's a pillow on the corner of the sofa. Bring it here."

Lowering her hand from her nape, she straightened those lovely shoulders. "Is this a royal decree, or shall I stand here and wait for common courtesy? You'll find that I am not suited for employment, other than what I give of my own free will."

No other young woman of his acquaintance had ever been so eager to flay him with her tongue. Now, he felt as if he'd been cheated by the absence of it. In the past five years, no one had come close to challenging him the way she did. His affairs had been meaningless and lacking in substance, leaving him unfulfilled and empty. He craved more.

A futile desire, he knew. He didn't dare sate his appetite for Calliope. Yet he couldn't stand to see her in pain either, especially not when he knew a remedy. Surely, he could withstand temptation for a few more moments.

"There's a pillow on the corner of the sofa, Miss Croft. I wonder if you would do me the honor of bringing it to where I am, if you please."

"And yet you still manage to condescend to me." She let out a sigh, not moving from her spot.

"If you would but have a moment's patience, I am about to prove to you otherwise."

She studied him through narrowed eyes, pursing her lips in speculation. "Patience for what, precisely?"

"Impertinent *and* impatient." He laughed with wry humor. "What am I to do with you? Here I am, all civility and cordiality, yet you will not accept my friendship."

She pointed to the square object covered in blue velvet, before steadily moving toward the sofa. "Is that what you are offering by way of this pillow?"

Not at all, but he could hardly confess the war between desire and reason that waged within him. "Yes," he lied, his gaze riveted to the delicately boned hand that hovered over the pillow.

She picked it up by the corner. "Very well then, I accept."

Gabriel's heart rose higher in his chest. Anticipation after so many years caused it to beat madly.

Crossing the room, she kept her gaze on his, a slight smile curving her lips. That smile said to him, *I am a complete person, with or without your approval.*

How many times—and in how many ways—had he imagined such a scene unfolding? He had her undivided attention. Other than the open doors, they were alone. There were only six buttons on the back of her gown. He'd counted. Only two combs in her hair. He would like to see her cross the room to him with those buttons undone, her hair teasing her shoulders, but still wearing that smile.

Now, the wild beating of his pulse ventured decidedly lower.

Calliope stopped at the base of the stairs and held out the pillow in both hands as if presenting him with the Sovereign's Orb. "Your pillow, my lord."

He slipped the embroidered velvet from her grasp and placed it on the step directly below his. He spread his legs farther to allow her more room. "Do sit down, Miss Croft, if you please."

"Sit?" She blinked in astonishment. "Surely, this was not your intention—to have me bring a pillow to you and then sit upon it."

"With your back to me, yes." He reached down and gave the pillow a pat. "Come along now, or you'll have *my* patience wearing thin."

She eyed him warily. "I am suddenly wondering at the price of your friendship."

"You are seeing dragons where there are only dragonflies." He tsked at her. "I know of a remedy for your sore neck; that is all."

She shook her head to decline but then winced again. The pain must have made her think twice because she glanced down and then back up at him. "You believe you have a cure and that it involves my sitting on a pillow with my back to you."

He held out his hand, hoping his eagerness did not show in his eyes, hoping she could not hear the heavy hammering of his pulse. "I am merely extending the hand of friendship, Miss Croft."

With undisguised reluctance, she slipped her hand in his and placed her foot on the first tread. The coolness of her fingers did nothing to soothe the roaring heat inside of him. He drew her up a step, then two, and on the third she turned and sat.

His thighs bracketed her like bookends. The slender curve of her neck and shoulders were bared for him. A hot jolt of arousal tore through him, engorging him. As long as she didn't lean back against the fall of his breeches, she would never know.

He placed his hands on her shoulders, *skin on skin*, and nearly groaned with unfettered pleasure. *Her* response, however, was slightly different. She stiffened. He could hear the argument before she uttered a word.

Gabriel couldn't let her balk now. "Surely you've heard of the Chinese medicinal *massage*," he said, attempting to reassure her. Yet the low hoarseness of his voice likely sounded hungry instead. Slowly, he slid his thumbs along the outer edges of the vertebrae at the base of her neck.

"I don't believe I have," she said, relaxing marginally, her voice thin and wispy like the fine downy hairs above her nape, teasing the top of his thumbs.

"Taoist priests have used this method for centuries." His own voice came out low and insubstantial, as if he were breathing his final breath. As it was, his heart had all but given up trying to lure the blood away from his pulsing erection. *This was a terrible idea.*

He was immensely glad he'd thought of it.

His fingertips skirted the edge of her clavicle. Hands curled over her slender shoulders, he rolled his thumbs over her again.

Calliope emitted the faintest *oh*. It was barely a breath, but the sound deafened him with a rush of tumid desire. As if she sensed the change in him, she tensed again. "Are you trying to seduce me, Everhart?"

"If you have to ask," he said, attempting to add levity with a chuckle, "then the answer is most likely *no*." Yet even he knew differently. The *most likely* was said only as way of not lying to himself. He wanted to seduce her, slowly and for hours on end.

For five years he'd wanted to feel her flesh beneath his hands. For a moment this evening, he'd even thought this one touch would be enough to sate him. He hated being wrong.

Those pearl buttons called to him. He feathered strokes outward along the upper edge of her shoulder blades, earning another breathy sound. Only this time, she did not tense beneath the heat of his hands.

"I've read—*heard* stories," she corrected, "where the young woman is not always certain of seduction until it is too late."

Gabriel caught her quick slip and was not surprised. Her penchant for reading was another aspect of her character that drew him to her. Earlier today, in fact, he'd spotted her disappearing through the library doors.

Unable to control the impulse, he'd found a servant's door off a narrow hall and surreptitiously watched her from behind a screen in the corner. Browsing the shelves, she'd searched through dozens of books. Yet her method fascinated him. She only searched the last pages of each book. When she found one she liked, she clutched it to her breast and released a sigh filled with the type of longing he knew too well. He had little doubt that she sought the certainty of a happy ending. All in all, it had taken her over an hour to find three books that met her standards. Yet instead of being bored, he'd been enthralled by every minute.

And now, here they were...

Under the spell of his massage, her head fell forward as she arched ever so slightly into his hands. Rampant desire coursed through him. Even so, he was in no hurry to end this delicious torment.

"I cannot imagine that a woman would not suspect an attempt of seduction in some manner." He leaned forward to inhale the fragrance of her hair, the barest scents of rosewater and mint rising up to greet him. "Aren't all young ladies brought up with the voice of reason clamoring about in their heads?"

His gaze followed the motions of his fingers, gliding over her silken warmth, pressing against the supple flesh that pinkened beneath his tender ministrations. He'd always wondered…and now he knew she felt as soft, if not softer, than any one of his dreams.

"Curiosity has a voice as well," she said, her voice faint with pleasure. "And are we not all creatures put upon this earth to learn, just as you have learned this *exquisite* medicine?"

And sometimes curiosity could not be tamed.

It was no use. Did he truly imagine he could resist her? "Well said, Miss Croft."

Unable to hold back a moment longer, Gabriel gave into temptation, lowered his head, and pressed his lips to her nape.

CHAPTER SEVEN

Calliope jolted. Sitting upright, her spine snapped into place with the suddenness of an arrow hitting a target. "Did you just...just kiss me?"

"Kiss you?" Everhart asked from behind her, his tone a combination of amusement and disbelief. "Preposterous. You know very well that I'm merely aiding in your recuperation. Nothing untoward. My fingers are here"—he thrummed them over the upper portion of her shoulders to demonstrate—"and my thumbs are here." He burrowed the tips in a circular motion directly into the aching knot at the base of her neck.

She tried not to moan, but a soft whimper *might* have escaped, nonetheless.

While he claimed this *medicinal massage* had been around for centuries, she knew nothing of it. Even so, she never wanted him to stop.

"I distinctly felt something that was neither thumb nor finger on the nape of my neck," she argued, but with no force behind the words. She found it difficult to summon any censure. Her body hummed pleasantly as if his hands massaged every inch of her, instead of *merely* her shoulders.

"This accusation comes from a wealth of knowledge on your part, does it?" He altered his grip, kneading her flesh with the heels of his hands.

She swallowed down another moan. "Well, no. But I think I would know the diff—"

"There you have it," he said succinctly. "You would not even know a kiss if it had happened, *which it did not.* Now tilt your head forward like before, or you will strain yourself again."

Oh, yes. Every rumor she'd heard about Everhart's skill with his hands was indeed warranted. Of course, she shouldn't have paid any attention to what widows whispered behind their fans at balls, but one could not simply forget what one was not supposed to overhear. Those were usually the most interesting bits of conversation.

Still, she could not allow her somewhat overactive imagination to let her lose this argument. "The flesh that brushed mine was decidedly warmer than your thumbs."

"Are you saying my hands are cold?" He did something almost wicked then, sliding his fingers along the ridge of her shoulders as his rotating thumbs slipped beneath the back of her gown.

Sweet heaven. "Not at all. Only that I'm certain what I felt was softer than the flesh of your thumbs, but not overly soft, and warmer, like the heat rising out of a brazier."

"Hmm," he murmured deep in his throat, causing her to feel the rumble of it rising up through the stair tread. "This is quite the mystery. Are you certain it was not this..." He brushed the pad of his thumb along the curve of her nape, eliciting a pleasant series of tremors through her.

Oh, please do that again. "I'm certain."

He shifted behind her. "What about this," he said, closer now. His heated breath sifted through fine strands of hair to fan out over her skin. "Perhaps you merely felt my breath on your flesh."

Everhart made the notion sound sinful and decadent. Her mouth watered.

His massage remained unhurried and thorough, delving into the deepest part of her ache, all the while creating a new one elsewhere—foreign and familiar at the same time, like a book slowly coming to life at the reader's bidding. And when his breath caressed her, she felt her pages stir.

Shortly after the beginning of their acquaintance, Everhart had been cold to her, so unlike the way he was with everyone else. She longed to discover the mystery behind his changeling behavior.

She'd been trying to make a point to him about how he could not remain cold and annoyed with her for years and then suddenly turn warm and friendly without explanation. Yet at the moment, she no longer cared. She was solely living in this moment. Her, Calliope Croft. Not a character in a story, but her.

Another breath touched her. His lips glided against her flesh once more.

"Everhart, are you kissing me now?" She knew the answer, of course, but she needed to hear him admit it.

"No, Miss Croft," he said, nipping her lightly. The fingers at her shoulders trailed down to tease the flesh beneath her lace trim, just above the curve of her breasts. "I'm offering you a frame of reference, should you accuse another man of kissing your neck in the future."

That was unlikely, but she made no comment. Shamelessly, she let him continue. *A rake should behave as a rake ought*, she reasoned. This was his basic nature at work. And she preferred the heated press of his lips far above his unwarranted coldness. The soft, teasing caress of his fingertips made her breasts tingle. Her nipples grew taut. She wanted him to touch her. She wanted to arch her back.

Surely, this solitary moment wouldn't hurt her reputation or change the fact that she would be gone from here as soon as she found the letter and... *Wait.*

The letter.

That was the reason she'd come into the map room in the first place. How could she have forgotten? *Well...* Everhart's skillful hands and lips were the likely cause. Nonetheless, now that she remembered her purpose, she could not forget it again.

Leaning forward, Calliope abruptly abandoned her spot on the pillow and clambered down the stairs. Not wanting to appear like a frightened ninny, she smoothed her hands over her gown and turned to face him. But that was a mistake.

The firelight caught the dampness of his lips, which drew her attention to the spot cooling on the back of her neck. She shivered. His blue-green eyes were cloudy and heavy lidded in a way that made her want to climb the stairs again. He offered no excuse for his behavior, but merely beseeched her with his potent, seductive charm, tempting her to return to his embrace. And *oh* she was tempted indeed.

She shook her head as if to answer his unspoken question. "You have distracted me from my purpose long enough."

A slow grin curled the corners of his mouth. "If you are ever in want of another distraction, please enter my sanctuary again. I promise to be thorough."

Her knees wobbled at the same time her suspicions went on alert. With four siblings, she understood taunting when she heard it. In addition to that, they both knew of his wager with Montwood and Danvers; therefore, he would never be so *thorough* as to compromise her. Yet apparently, that was what he wanted her to believe. "Come now, Everhart. I thought we were going to be friends, but friends do not issue threats."

"I do not think we can be friends, Miss Croft." *Another threat.* His gaze was clearly telling her something else entirely. It said, *We could be much, much more than friends.* The same way he looked at all women.

As much as it thrilled her—to be seen as a woman worthy of his seduction when all she'd earned before was his censure—somehow this felt worse than when she'd thought he hated her. Now, she was just like all the others. Not that she wanted to be different in his eyes. No, it was just that she wanted to be special to *someone*, instead of so easily forgotten.

She hid her inexplicable wound behind a tight smile. "I'm certain we could have been friends, if you weren't such a conceited, condescending prig."

Relishing his open-mouthed astonishment, she curtsied ever so sweetly and took her leave.

Gabriel fell back against the stairs, allowing the sharp edge of the tread to bite through his coat. He issued a groan that was more frustration than pain.

A familiar laugh sounded from the doorway. "Did I just hear Miss Croft call you a *condescending prig?*"

Gabriel didn't bother to look at Montwood. "You left out *conceited.*"

"Even better." From the sound of glass clinking and knowing what bottles remained on the sideboard, Montwood was now pouring a whiskey. "She left in quite the rush."

"I made sure of that." He was sure that she would never come back either. He'd already given in to temptation once—twice, if he counted the second kiss to her nape—and he would likely do so again.

He couldn't risk it. Too much was at stake. He needed to make sure she knew that he couldn't be relied upon to behave properly, no matter the circumstance.

Montwood tsked. "You're not going to make this easy, are you."

"I'm going to make this impossible." Hearing his friend's even footsteps approach, Gabriel sat upright and accepted the offered glass of whiskey. He downed it in one swallow.

"You'd deny yourself for the sake of a wager?"

It wasn't all about the wager. Not for Gabriel. His reasons had deeper roots. "Would you do any less?"

Montwood didn't answer. Instead he moved to the hearth and poked at the logs on the grate as they sizzled and popped in response. "And in a year's time, will you marry her then?"

He couldn't believe that Calliope had thought all this time that he hadn't liked her. That he disapproved of her. It was as disconcerting as it was liberating. He could easily perpetuate the lie in order to keep her away from him.

"Before she leaves Fallow Hall," Gabriel said, his mood darkening, "I'll make sure she never wants to see me again."

Chapter Eight

Gabriel opened the portal window on the far side of the attic. He closed his eyes against the blast of cold, damp morning air, perspiration cooling on his flesh. Having alternated between the use of his cane and one-legged hops, he'd managed to navigate all the stairs. He hoped the exercise would dispel the futile desires that had plagued him all night.

Typically, he enjoyed early morning hours. During travels abroad, he'd written in his journal of each sunrise and the first sounds of each new day on any given spot on the earth. Lincolnshire hosted its own sounds—the silken hush of the wind through the evergreen boughs, the quiet rush of servants' footsteps combined with the subdued murmur of their voices. It was comforting to know where one's place was on the map at any given moment. Which was hardly something that a gentleman with the reputation for being an *aimless wanderer* could admit.

By all accounts, he was supposed to roam, to revel in exploration. And he did. He loved experiencing new sights, sounds, fragrances, and flavors. But as wonderful as those experiences had been, there had been something missing.

He knew what it was, of course. A man did not advance to eight and twenty without a sense of his own mind. He'd learned firsthand how lonely traveling could be, even when among friends. For him, there had always been a certain amount of poetry to the journey home to England. Even when he had not been returning to any home in particular.

He'd never felt such acute yearning for a home until recently. It was unsettling. More than anything, he wanted to run from this feeling. Run from Lincolnshire. Run from Calliope Croft and everything she represented. But with this damnable broken leg and the restriction of his monies, he couldn't. He was trapped here.

That restlessness had woken him before dawn.

Turning away from the window, he began to rummage through crates, searching for something to alleviate one source of his distress. By the time he reached the third one, he'd found what he was looking for. "Ah. Here is something that might prove useful."

Valentine stood beside him, holding a brace of candles. "My lord?"

"Pay particular attention to this crate." Gabriel hefted the lid up from the floor and secured it once more, giving all appearances of its never having been disturbed. "There is a music box within. I believe one of our guests would find this discovery most advantageous."

Valentine's expression remained unchanged. "If there is a guest who requires a music box, then I will deliver it straightaway."

"No. The purpose of leaving it here *is* the discovery." Calliope would only start asking questions if the music box were presented to her. "*Curiosity has a voice as well…*" He couldn't endure the risk.

Gabriel drew a breath. "Should Miss Croft happen to mention a desire to free Nell from harp playing, you might wish to suggest the attic for a distraction."

In a rare display of surprise, Valentine's brow lifted slightly—more of a twitch, really—before his stoic countenance slid back into place. He inclined his head. "Very good, sir."

"That way, the maid can go about her regular duties," he said by way of explanation. He didn't want the head butler to get the wrong idea. Or the right one. He loathed revealing a side of his personality that was contrary to what he wanted everyone to believe. He didn't want to sound responsible or ready to manage an estate of his own. Thankfully, Valentine understood. The discussions regarding the running of Fallow Hall were to go no further than between them.

The truth was, he wanted to do something for Calliope— albeit anonymously—to make up for his behavior last night. And if easing her worry over the state of Nell's fingertips would help, then he was glad to offer it.

Though with that thought came another. What if "finding" a music box allowed Calliope more time to roam the manor? While he wanted her to enjoy the sights and sounds of Fallow Hall and not spend so much time in service to her cousin, he also preferred to know exactly where she was at any given moment. It set him at ease.

Of course, he would be more at ease if she were *not* at Fallow Hall at all. At least that's what he told himself. It was becoming more and more difficult to decide where he stood on the matter. The only thing he was certain of, however, was that he needed to keep her distracted. But how?

Cane in hand, Gabriel made his way back to the narrow stairs and then hesitated. "One more thing, Valentine. Notify Mrs. Merkel that she will report to Miss Croft, effective today."

This way, Calliope would be too distracted to find her way into the map room. And he wouldn't give into temptation again.

"I'm terribly glad that Milton went hunting with Mr. Danvers and Lord Lucan," Pamela said, reclining against the pillows, her head tilted toward the window. "It's good for him to get out. Sometimes I worry about how much he depends on me."

Calliope lifted the window sash and breathed in the cool, damp air, smiling at the view. Last night's rain had melted the snow in patches of mud brown and slate gray where the earth met with stone. A circle of holly bushes surrounded a Grecian folly in the distance, the columns covered in spider webs of desiccated ivy. Yet even with such a miserable sight, nothing could hamper Calliope's cheerful mood this morning. Her discovery ensured it.

"A husband and wife ought to depend upon each other, lighten each other's burdens if possible." Calliope thought of her parents and how well matched they were in that regard. Even now that her father's health was failing, he still did everything he could to bring a smile to her mother's lips, and her mother did the same for him.

"I am too cold," her cousin grumbled. Apparently, the promise of a surprise—that both Calliope and Bess were arranging on the round table near the window—did nothing to brighten *Pamela's* mood.

Calliope drew in another breath of fresh morning air before she closed the window. Finding the music box among the crates in the attic had been a stroke of pure luck. If it weren't for Valentine's suggestion, poor Nell would have doubtlessly been bleeding on the harp strings this very moment. Then, for good measure, Calliope had had two footmen remove the harp from the room, under the guise of having it restrung.

Now, after a simple wind of the key, sweet, tinkling music filled the bedchamber.

Pamela sat up, her eyes brightening. "Have you brought me a music box, cousin?"

"I am told it plays a melody for nearly half an hour," Calliope said, beaming. She'd finally managed to alleviate *one* of her worries. Nell would no longer be in danger of permanent damage to her fingers. All that was needed for Pamela's entertainment was to take turns winding the key. Between Calliope, Nell, and Bess, the task should be simple enough.

From a discreet distance down the hall, Gabriel caught a glimpse of a smiling Miss Croft. Obviously, her morning jaunt to the attic had proved fruitful. Pleased, he slipped around the corner and headed toward his chamber for a change of clothes.

Fitzroy was an accommodating valet and usually had tea waiting for him. Although currently, Gabriel needed sustenance too, or else he'd run the risk of imagining a meal of Calliope. Giving into temptation had been a grave error. The sweet flavor of her flesh still lingered on his tongue, and he craved more.

Walking into his chamber, Fitzroy indeed had a pot of tea, along with a silver dome-covered plate. His face was split in a wide grin that exposed the gradient slope of his upper teeth to the back of his jaw, giving him somewhat of a rabbit appearance. "A bright and happy morning to you, my lord," he said with a bow.

Gabriel eyed his valet with speculation. Usually, he wasn't greeted with such an excessive amount of cheer. Looking around the room for a clue, however, he saw nothing amiss. Draped over the bed was a fresh change of clothes: pressed white shirt, gold striped waistcoat, brushed hunter green coat, pristine cravat, buff breeches, wool stockings, and beside the bench at the foot of the bed, Hessians polished to a mirror shine. Even though he could only wear one currently, his valet always set out the pair.

Resting his cane against the footboard, Gabriel began to shrug out of his jacket from the previous night. He'd made a habit of late of sleeping in the map room and changing clothes in the morning. "Why the sappy grin, Fitzroy? One of the upstairs maids *accidentally* find her way into your room again last night?"

Fitzroy sprang into action and rushed around behind him to remove the coat. Then, draping the jacket over the back of a nearby chair, the man actually blushed. The valet was abundantly shy but still managed to charm the stockings off the female serving staff. "Forgive me, my lord, but the staff is buzzing about the news. May I be the first to offer my congratulations?"

"And why, precisely, are you congratulating me?"

"While there has been no formal announcement," Fitzroy said, grinning even wider, if such a thing were possible, "Mr. Valentine has made it abundantly clear that Miss Croft's status will soon be elevated, second only to yours."

"*Miss Croft?* But why the devil would Valentine—" Gabriel stopped. This morning, when he'd told Valentine to have Mrs. Merkel report directly to Miss Croft, the butler had no doubt assumed that such an honor would only go to the *lady* of the manor.

Gabriel had sabotaged himself! Why bother worrying about Montwood and Danvers conspiring against him when his own stupidity was the real enemy?

His head back, Gabriel stared at the ceiling and laughed wryly. "Hold your congratulations, Fitzroy. I was merely giving our guest an occupation to keep her from turning Fallow Hall upside down in search of a letter."

His valet looked deflated. "In regard to the letter, my lord, I've heard mention that all of Lady Brightwell's other belongings have been accounted for, save for the small ivory-handled box. The letter she desires most is still missing."

"I do not believe it is Lady Brightwell who desires the letter most of all," Gabriel murmured and then addressed Fitzroy more formally. "Should you or any of the other servants encounter this letter, bring it to me at once."

"Yes, my lord."

He opened his mouth to have Fitzroy summon Valentine. Not wanting any confusion about his motives, he would rescind his instructions to Valentine and have Mrs. Merkel report to him again.

Instead, he closed his mouth. Oddly enough, the misunderstanding wasn't entirely unappealing.

In fact, it was more appealing than he cared to admit.

Calliope slipped out of Pamela's chamber and closed the door with a quiet click. She walked down the hall, prepared to use her newfound free time in finding that letter and exposing Casanova once and for all.

Around the corner, she nearly collided with the housekeeper. "Oh! Please forgive me, Mrs. Merkel."

"I beg your pardon, Miss Croft," the housekeeper said, hastily dipping into a curtsy, which was peculiar on many levels. Not the least of which was the fact that Calliope held no title or position in society. "I was actually just coming this way so that I might speak with you, if you have a moment."

"With me?" Calliope placed a hand to her chest. Confused by the uncustomary greeting, it took a moment for her sort out a reason why the housekeeper would seek her out in particular. Then a swift rise of guilt filled her as her mind went to her recent scavenger hunt through the attic and the disturbed crates. "Oh. If this is about the crates in the attic, I have every intention of putting everything back in order."

"How kind of you, but the footmen have already seen to it." Mrs. Merkel smiled at her. "And I daresay that I am grateful for your generosity on Nell's behalf. Her return has eased many burdens."

"I wish I could take credit, but Mr. Valentine discovered the music box and directed me to it," Calliope deferred. She certainly did not expect such a response due to a music box, but now she was even happier at the serendipitous discovery. "However, I would be glad to assist in any way I can."

Mrs. Merkel's eyes brightened. "Very good. If you have a moment, I would like go over the linen schedule with you, as well as the service you'd like to use at dinner and the menu you wish prepared."

Calliope blinked, dumfounded. "While I'm honored that you would seek my counsel, I really do not wish to overstep my position here as a guest."

"Certainly not, miss. I would value your input."

Surely, if any woman in this house should be chosen, then her cousin—a baroness—should. Then again, Pamela had likely turned down the offer.

Calliope imagined it was quite taxing to be the housekeeper and manage all of Fallow Hall on her own. Her own mother and father had shown faith in her abilities to manage their townhouse in London. But to assist in running a large estate? It was such an honor that she felt rather giddy at the prospect. As a spinster, it wasn't likely she would have such an opportunity again. "That would be splendid, Mrs. Merkel."

"Shall I have a tea tray delivered to the sitting room across the hall, Miss Croft?" The housekeeper opened the door to the room in question.

Calliope agreed and made her way inside while Mrs. Merkel gave instructions to one of the housemaids. A wash of pale gray light filtered in through a row of tall narrow windows, transforming the bright green-striped upholstery into a mellow, welcoming shade. Between two tufted chairs, a low table sat. On that table was a long piece of foolscap marked in a neat, tidy script. Upon closer inspection, she noted that it was a list—a rather substantial list—itemizing everything from the linen schedule to the number of tapers in the cupboard.

It appeared that Calliope would be very busy. Too busy to spend much time with her cousin. Too busy to spend much time searching for the letter. Even so, part of her relished the new challenge.

Fallow Hall under her care? It was the highest compliment she'd ever received.

Chapter Nine

"What fine animals have you given to the cook to make inedible this evening, gentlemen?" Gabriel asked of Brightwell and Danvers as they strolled into the map room, dressed in their dinner jackets and finery.

Typically, they would meet in the drawing room before dinner. However, since Valentine tended to lavish delicacies on Gabriel—*when one has a broken leg, one must keep up one's strength, after all*—the gentlemen made this room their first stop. Unfortunately for them, Valentine's tray had been delayed.

Brightwell turned a bit green at the mention of the cook's lack of skill. "A rabbit and a grouse."

"And by dinner's end, we will believe Mrs. Swan served us a leathery mutton." Gabriel laughed, making himself more comfortable on the sofa. Beside him, Duke nudged his hand with the tip of his wet nose until Gabriel consented to scratch his head.

Danvers looked over his shoulder as he stood at the sideboard, pouring a glass of the port that Valentine had decanted a few hours ago. "*We?* Not with you hiding in here, night after night, supping on bread and cheese—and whatever delights Valentine smuggles to you from his secret pantry—leaving us to curdled soups and porkpies so salty I'd swear they were stuffed with barnacles. And you've no right to gloat either."

Right or not, Gabriel gloated, linking his hands behind his head. Indeed, Valentine had promised another hunk of blue-veined cheese.

"Why *have* you gone absent at dinner of late?" Brightwell asked.

Danvers handed Brightwell a fluted glass. "Because he's avoiding Miss Croft in an effort not to—"

"In an effort not to say something disagreeable," Gabriel interrupted, staring hard at Danvers. *Damned loose-tongued devil.* The last thing he wanted was for Brightwell to realize what Danvers had figured out. "After all, I am still cross with her for your sake, Brightwell."

Danvers did not even attempt to hide his sly smile before he laughed.

"I am always late to the party," Montwood said from the door. "Danvers is either foxed already or he's laughing at one of his own inane jokes again."

Gabriel gritted his teeth. "It must be the latter."

"You needn't come to my defense, Everhart," Brightwell said, circling the conversation back to where it had begun. "I meant what I said about leaving the past alone. There is no reason you should not get along famously with Miss Croft."

At the sideboard, Montwood looked over his shoulder and waggled his brows at Danvers, who lifted his glass in a silent toast behind Brightwell's back.

Fighting back the growl in his throat, Gabriel ignored his housemates and kept his attention on Brightwell. "Then it will be for the sake of friendship that I won't get along, *famously* or otherwise, with our guest."

"I am undeserving of such loyalty after all these years," Brightwell offered, hand to his chest. "I have married her cousin and not once has she shown me ill favor for it. She's offered her support in every way. Why, just this morning she procured a music box from the attic for her cousin's comfort. That is not the act of a young woman grown to despise the union of her former suitor and her cousin."

Montwood shared a toast with Danvers, as if they could taste victory in their glasses instead of port. "If that isn't a trump card in your hand, Everhart, then I don't know what it is."

Ha. More like a trump card in their *hands.*

"I will give it thought, Brightwell," Gabriel said, already knowing exactly what he would do instead. His avoidance tactics were working perfectly…nearly. If he decided to forget about how he'd almost devoured her neck last night. Unfortunately, he wasn't certain *he* could forget. Ever.

In the doorway, Valentine cleared his throat and then inclined his head. "Dinner is served, my lords. Sir."

Gabriel nearly sighed with relief. At last, a reprieve from the guilt of the past and the present.

Now, it was his turn to salute the others. "Be well, gentlemen."

They all grumbled and departed, one by one.

When the dog didn't follow, it was a signifier of how truly terrible the cook's food was. Gabriel reached down and gave him a solid pat. "We'll have our bread and cheese brought to us soon enough, old boy. *What* is it you have there?"

Gabriel went utterly still.

Duke held a familiar leather pouch between his teeth. A pouch that Gabriel had kept hidden in his rooms. Seeing it now reminded him of what he'd lost and made him more desperate to avoid Calliope Croft.

Unable to help himself, he unfolded the pouch and ensured the safety of the contents. They were more of a sentimental nature—a green stone that needed polishing, a red feather that had thinned in the past five years, and the bottom corner of a letter.

Relieved that the items hadn't suffered, he carefully tucked them away and tied the pouch closed.

"Are you conspiring against me as well?" he asked Duke.

The dog answered with a *woof* and a jolly tail wag.

Gabriel shook his head. "It isn't that simple for me. I cannot take what I want. And certainly not"—he shook his finger—"in the same manner that you took advantage of those Pekinese."

Duke lowered his head.

"For me, there would be dire consequences to consider."

Lucan Montwood led this evening's procession into the dining room, as his ranking decreed when Everhart was not in attendance. Brightwell and Pamela followed Montwood, while Calliope entered the room last, on the arm of Rafe Danvers. This night, however, for reasons unknown to Calliope, everything changed.

The expansive paneled room was still the same. Wall sconces gleamed brightly, reflecting against the octagonal panes of glass in the windows. The table was set for five, as was the number of their dining party. Usually Everhart's place at the high end of the table was left vacant in case he should change his mind and join them. Which he never did. Yet tonight, his place was set.

Still, there were only five in all, causing a little confusion—until Valentine stood behind the chair at the end, cleared his throat, and looked directly at Calliope. "Miss Croft, I believe you'll find this chair to your liking."

Pamela turned around to stare at her, mouth agape. Calliope shrugged.

"Is something amiss with my previous chair?" But even as she asked the question, she realized the servants would simply have rearranged the chairs, not her place at the table. Still, she could not fathom a reason why. Then, looking around at her hosts, awareness began to prickle down her spine.

Neither Montwood, Danvers, nor Brightwell looked surprised. In fact, both Montwood and Danvers appeared rather smug, as if they were privy to a secret.

It didn't take a great leap for suspicion to enter her mind. Being singled out by Mrs. Merkel to act as lady of the manor had filled Calliope with shock but also with pride. Only now, she wondered if it all had something to do with Everhart instead of with her own merit.

The more she thought about it, the more she *knew* this was Everhart's doing. It *had* to be. So then, was he merely toying with her?

As Danvers escorted her to the place at the head of the table, she started to fume. The flattery she'd felt earlier evaporated.

Oh, she was a ninny for imagining that Mrs. Merkel had reported to no one until this morning and a fool to think that Fallow Hall had needed her assistance. Of course, both the housekeeper and Valentine would report to the son of a duke. Why hadn't she put it together before? And that *son of a duke* likely had arranged tasks to keep her very busy indeed. Was this his way of teaching her a lesson about the cost of disturbing the lion in his lair?

No doubt, both Mrs. Merkel and Valentine now had the wrong idea. They believed she'd been selected out of Everhart's *preference* for her company, when the opposite was true. However, she would not make waves by explaining Everhart's game of contempt. Instead, she took her new seat and focused on how she would spoil his efforts.

Gabriel hopped down the last stair leading from the loft, grabbed his cane, and crossed the map room to settle in for a pleasant evening. He'd managed to find the journal he was looking for—Etienne de Ponte, who'd sailed with von Humboldt during his last expedition to South America.

He'd only leafed through the first few entries when a figure appeared at the outer rim of his field of vision. Believing it was one of the footmen to retrieve his dinner tray, he didn't bother looking up. He turned the page, his mind focused on the *Pizarro's* days at sea, anxious for the entry written about finding land and setting anchor. That was his favorite part—stepping on new land for the first time.

When he caught no movement, he directed an absent wave toward the table. "The tray is there, if you desire it."

"I desire no tray, Everhart."

Gabriel's head jerked up at the sound of Calliope Croft's voice. The journal slipped from his hands and fell with a thud to the floor in a good imitation of what his heart had just done.

"For that you should be thankful," she said. "Because if I had a tray in hand, I would surely knock it over your head."

By the dark gleam in her eyes, he had no doubt. "And what have I done to earn such contempt, Miss Croft?"

A smirk flitted over her lips, and her arms crossed beneath her bosom. She wore a lustrous gold evening gown, with sleeves that rested on the very edges of her shoulders, inviting a man to imagine how easily it would be to tug them down. The bodice conformed to the tantalizing swells of her breasts—though he had not been present to admire them at dinner. He frowned.

"I know what you're doing. Making a fool of me with the other houseguests and even the servants so that they now believe you and I are"—she drew a breath—"*friends*. Or perhaps more. But we both know the truth."

Gabriel swallowed down a sudden dichotomy of emotion. Seeing the raw hurt and anger on her face knotted his stomach. Yet her allusion to *more than friends* unfurled a mainsail of desire. "And what is that truth, precisely?"

"You avoid me. You refuse to take dinner in the same room with me. You must be under the misguided assumption that I'm trying to win you over." With each point, her arms had uncrossed and her hands settled on her hips. "All I want is to end the animosity between us. Can we not put the past behind us? Last night was..." Rosy color washed over her cheeks and she did not finish.

He grinned. "Enjoyable? Mutually satisfying?"

"A low attempt at distracting me from what you assumed was my purpose," she corrected, but without the vehemence necessary to convince him that was all she felt. "Then today, your tactic of using your position in this house as a means to subject me your latest amusement was reprehensible."

"You thought I was distracting you for my own amusement and because of my *supposed* animosity toward you?" Relief washed over him. She still hadn't guessed his true reasons for wanting to keep her out of arm's reach. "Ah, you have figured me out, Miss Croft. I am quite the *conceited, condescending prig.*"

Pretending to ignore her, he reached down to the floor and retrieved the book, flipping through the pages to find his place again. At the moment, however, he couldn't see a single word. The book could be upside down, and he wouldn't know. His entire being still focused solely on the woman standing only a few feet away.

She tapped the toe of her slipper over the hardwood floor at the very edge of his carpeted domain, as if an invisible wall stood between them. And then she breeched the barrier. Stepping forward, she stopped directly at his side. At once his senses were assaulted with her unique fragrance. The warmth she emanated bathed his left side, making him feel incomplete and needing to be fully immersed, fully baptized. More than anything, he wanted to reach up for her hand and tug her down on top of him.

"I wholeheartedly agree, Everhart," she said sweetly, but in a way that made him wary of the sugar.

He gave her his full attention. Lifting his gaze, he watched the firelight play against the wet-sand color of her irises. The weight of an anchor settled over his chest. If he was meant to say something in response, he could think of no reply. Instead of forming words, his tongue only had a memory of the taste of her skin, and his lips still tingled from the feel of those silken downy hairs at her nape.

"While you may enjoy certain methods of distraction, I have methods of my own," she said, reaching out and effectively stripping the book from his grasp. Tucking it behind her back, she beamed at him in triumph. Then slowly, she sauntered to the door, taunting him with a waggle of the journal. "I will be more than glad to teach you that you cannot avoid the inevitable. We will have it out, once and for all."

With those parting words, she slipped through the doorway.

"And yet *avoiding* is exactly what I plan to do," he said to himself.

CHAPTER TEN

"Hearts are trump, Miss Croft," Montwood said the following evening, smiling patiently at her from across the table.

She knew that, of course. Seeing her whist partner glance down to the table and then at her, she noticed that he'd already taken the trick with a lower card. Essentially, she'd wasted a perfectly good king. "I apologize. I don't know where my head is this evening."

"Think nothing of it," Montwood said graciously as Brightwell and Pamela pulled the fish tokens into their pot.

Both yesterday and today had gone by in a blur. Managing a house as large as Fallow Hall was more difficult than merely helping her parents when the need arose. Of course, the house had been running smoothly without her minor interference here and there, but now Calliope had something to prove.

Although she still wasn't entirely sure if she was proving a point to herself or to Everhart.

Either way, her efforts had been rewarded by an estate that now felt more like a home than a bachelor's residence. Making full use of a neglected hothouse, she had added a vase of freshly cut flowers and foliage to the most frequently used rooms. In discovering a crate full of various bolts of cloth, from silk damask to crushed velvets, she'd begun sewing simple pillow fronts to accent the sofas and chairs in the parlor and drawing room.

"Was it my imagination, or was dinner *edible* this evening?" Danvers asked while circling the table like a shark, albeit a shark that whistled merrily.

Since Calliope had spent enough time in the company of Mrs. Shortingham—her beloved cook from London—she'd picked up a thing or two about how an effective kitchen should work. The kitchen at Fallow Hall had been a disaster area, with dirty pots piled high in the sink, nearly touching the ceiling. Mrs. Swan was a dispirited cook who ran her kitchen by yelling, but over the years the kitchen and scullery maids had grown deaf to her.

Using her newfound privileges to her advantage, Calliope had requested the use of two footmen to tackle the years of filth and grime that coated the solid bank of square-cut windows along the south wall. As for the kitchen and scullery maids, they were each put on notice, and told under no circumstances was Fallow Hall a place for delinquents.

Mrs. Swan was another story. She was too proud to admit that working in a kitchen as large as this one was difficult, especially when age had crippled her hands, and she couldn't hold a knife properly any longer. Treading carefully, Calliope had suggested a plan to help Mrs. Swan with the tasks she *could* manage with ease. After a little cajoling, the cook had agreed to separate tasks for each maid, effectively giving them greater responsibility.

In the end, dinner last night had still been a disaster, but less of one. Dinner tonight had begun to show promise. The soup wasn't curdled. In fact, it was actually quite good. The bread was chewy but no longer tough. The pies were still too salty, but the puddings weren't terrible. All in all, it was a pleasant reward for her efforts.

"I believe we have Miss Croft to thank for the much improved fare," Montwood remarked, tapping the corner of his jack of clubs on the table before laying it down over Pamela's queen. Brightwell followed with a ten in the same suit, and so it was up to Calliope to win the trick. She looked at her cards.

"It's too bad Everhart wasn't present for her moment of triumph this evening," Danvers added. "Though I imagine he kept track all the same."

"I'm certain you are wrong," Calliope murmured. Everhart apparently couldn't forgive her for what she'd done to Brightwell. And the more she tried to tell herself that his dislike of her didn't matter, the more she realized it did. Which was entirely silly. It wasn't as if she'd likely see him again, or often enough to let it bother her. Then why *did* it bother her so much? Had she been this determined to make amends with Brightwell after refusing him?

Unfortunately, the sobering answer revealed a shocking lack of priorities on her part. After she'd broken it off with Brightwell, she'd never once tried to be his friend.

So why was she wasting any effort at all on Everhart?

Preoccupied, she laid down her card. Her thoughts were a jumble. Across from her, Montwood exhaled audibly. She looked at the table. Oh dear. She'd laid down a nine of clubs, when she held the ace in her hands. Where was her head?

She sent a look of apology to Montwood as another round began.

"Why doesn't Everhart join us all for dinner any longer?" Pamela asked. "He was always a consummate host before my cousin's arrival. I wonder what has changed. Is he ill, do you think?"

Clearly, Pamela did not know what she was saying—or at least, that's what Calliope chose to believe. It was her way of fending off the insult at the mention that Everhart only avoided *her* company. She tried not to feel the sting, but it might have grazed her all the same.

"I'm certain it's the splint," Danvers added. "He is forever complaining about the nuisance of it."

"Oh, look, I seem to have a trump after all," Pamela said, laying down a heart as she glanced across to Brightwell, who'd been peculiarly silent this evening.

They'd all played cards during the previous nights and shared conversation. But tonight was different. Calliope wondered at the reason. Then again, perhaps he was just as distracted as she, but for his own reasons.

When it came time for her to lay her final card, she lost another trick.

"Forgive me, Montwood. I have been a terrible partner this evening," she said and rose from her chair. "Mr. Danvers, I do hope you'll fill in for me so that our friend can win back some of his ivory fish. I believe I'll retire before I do any more damage at this table."

"*Ivory*—now, that reminds me," Brightwell said when she reached the open archway leading to the hall. His tone was more gruff than conversational. "You were looking for a patch box with an ivory handle, were you not, Miss Croft?"

Since the box in question allegedly held a letter from his wife's anonymous lover, Calliope didn't know how to respond. She imagined, however, that he wouldn't have mentioned the patch box, had he known. All the same, she bobbled her head in an uncertain gesture.

Brightwell looked down at the table and straightened the new cards he was dealt. "My valet informs me that he last saw it in the north tower. I'm certain my wife would like to have her *distractions* returned."

"Yes. That would be lovely," Pamela said cheerfully, ignorant of the tension that had settled over the card table.

Why was she always being directed to Everhart's domain? "Thank you, Lord Brightwell. Good night, everyone."

After the farewell, Calliope left the parlor with every intention of going directly to bed.

Tomorrow, she would send Nell into the map room to locate and retrieve the patch box. In the meantime, she would write to her brother and ask him to send a carriage. After all, once she read the letter, there was no need for her to remain at Fallow Hall. She would begin to sort out clues to uncover Casanova's identity either in Scotland or when she returned to London.

This time, she possessed a feeling of confidence that she was closer to solving this riddle than ever before. She didn't know what gave her this feeling, but somehow, she felt closer to making a discovery.

Distracted by her new plan, she didn't realize where she was going until she found herself staring at the map room doors.

They were closed, and with the sconces still lit in the hall, it was impossible to determine whether or not there was light coming from within the room. She wondered whether Everhart was in residence at his seemingly favorite haunt. Did she dare open the doors?

Duke loped up beside her from wherever he'd been down the hall and licked her hand. She gave his ears a scratch. "I've found myself here by mistake," she whispered to her four-legged confidant. "If Everhart is within, then I should make haste in the opposite direction. Wouldn't you agree?"

Duke gazed up at her, his tongue lolling as he panted.

Calliope took this response as complete agreement.

"But if Everhart is not within, then I couldn't very well waste this opportunity. Could I?"

Again, Duke agreed in the same manner, adding a tail wag for emphasis. Which didn't necessarily help her current conundrum. Until a fresh idea hit her…

"I imagine that you know his scent; therefore, you could tell me if he is here or not."

Even though she said the words more to herself than to the dog, Duke offered a low *woof* in response.

"Splendid." She pointed to the door. "Is Everhart in this room?"

Duke turned his head and looked behind him toward the east wing.

Calliope was stunned. Was this actually working? "Has he retired, then?"

"*Woof.*" Duke licked her hand once more.

This was almost too easy. "You are either a very smart creature, or—"

Before she could finish, Duke walked past her, nudged the door open with his nose, and slipped through the narrow opening.

Now, with one of the doors closed and the other partially ajar, she had to crane her neck to peer inside. A fire crackled in the hearth, but the sofa was vacant. Daring further exploration, she skirted sideways through the door and held her breath. Just in case Everhart was right around the corner, she forced a smile in order to pretend that she was merely dropping by to wish her bosom friend a pleasant evening. *Oh, yes.* She was certain he would believe that.

Thankfully, a quick scan of the room told her that she was alone. Well, other than Duke, who now lay boneless by the fire. Relieved, she let out a breath. At last, she could search this room in private. Bypassing the table she'd already observed on a prior visit, she walked to the sideboard in case any wayward papers or patch boxes had made their way there. Not surprisingly, they hadn't.

Surveying the rest of the space, she noted that someone must have recently cleaned. The low sofa table, which had once been littered with papers and leather-bound books, was now pristine, revealing the beautiful glossy patina beneath.

Looking up through the loft's railing, she saw rows of shelves, housing not only books but drawers large enough to hold any number of objects, ivory-handled patch boxes included. It was the obvious place to begin her search.

The clock began to chime the eleventh hour. She was nearly to the top of the curving staircase when she heard something—or rather, someone—in the loft.

"There are those, Miss Croft," Everhart said, his voice low and even, "who would find it quite forward of a young woman to constantly seek out a gentleman's company."

She'd thought she was alone. Reaching the final tread, her pulse thrummed wildly beneath the edge of her jaw. Strangely, even knowing that it was only Everhart did not seem to still the wayward drumming of her heart. *Only Everhart?* "You could have announced yourself when you first heard my slipper upon the stair, and I would have left you to your solitude."

Calliope would have preferred that. Now, however, it would be cowardly to simply turn around and descend the stairs without a word. At least, that's what she told herself.

Once in the loft, she moved toward the sound of his voice, rounding a trio of tall bookcases that kept him in seclusion. Theoretically, she could remain right here, searching the stacks and drawers without disturbing him. Yet she found herself compelled to do exactly that. She *wanted* to disturb him.

"As you are doing now, no doubt," he remarked from a dark violet-and-gray striped chaise longue. The design of it was different from a standard chaise in that it sloped gradually at one end, curving in the manner of the bow of a sleigh.

Reclining back, with his head propped on a pillow, Everhart seemed to pay little attention to her presence. Which made her want to disturb him all the more. Over the years, she'd often wondered how he'd so easily dismissed her and their friendship. Part of her resented him for it.

Because it hadn't been easy for her.

The reason for that was now becoming muddled as she stared at him. The lean length of his body took up the entire space. He crossed his splinted leg over the other. Once again, he'd abandoned his coat and cravat. Those fine golden hairs that she'd examined rather closely that first night were on display between the V of his open collar. From there, her reluctantly captivated gaze set a natural course down the buttons of his silver satin waistcoat to his dark blue breeches.

Her inner narrator looked away and advised Calliope to do the same. Yet she couldn't.

Everhart possessed a relaxed beauty that consistently drew her attention. Looking away would be like reading only half of a novel and never learning how it ended. Therefore, with his gaze fixed on the ceiling, giving every impression of ignoring her, she indulged her rampant curiosity.

She wondered if the tailor intended to make Everhart's breeches so...*perfectly* fitted. As a young woman, she'd discreetly studied paintings and statues in museums. After all, it was important to know *something* about the male form. Solely for informative purposes, of course.

Nonetheless, the outlined shape Calliope witnessed now was substantially larger than what the artists and sculptors had portrayed. The sight reminded her of the novels she read and how that part of a man's anatomy had once been described as *a blade for virtue's ruin.*

She swallowed, uncertain if this new leap of her pulse indicated fear or fascination.

Everhart lifted a glass to his lips and drained the last of the pale golden liquid. "There are those who would find your silent study as forward too. Provocative, even."

Blazing heat rushed to her cheeks. Even her ears felt hot. Embarrassed, her gaze snapped to his face, only to see that he was still looking at the ceiling. Had he caught her, or was he merely taunting her?

Hmm... If she knew anything about Everhart, she was inclined to believe the latter.

Drawing in a breath, she summoned a wealth of hauteur. "If anyone could be accused of provocation, it is you. For now, it is my every wish to be a thorn in your side. A pebble in your boot." Then, she added the absolute worst nuisance imaginable. "A worm in your book."

He feigned a gasp. "Not a *worm in my book*, Miss Croft."

His empty glass winked in the light of the single candelabra on the atlas table between them. As far as boundaries were concerned, the immense, lacquered waist-high table was quite a substantial one. In fact, it currently encompassed the South American continent.

"Perhaps you would not laugh so easily if you knew that I have discovered damage from the very creature you are laughing about within the journal you were reading the other evening." Absently, she trailed her fingertip along the intersecting longitudinal and latitudinal lines in the South Atlantic Ocean, wondering what it would be like to visit such a place. "I was just to the part where the ship had laid anchor when I noticed—"

"What? What did you see?" He sat up so abruptly that she stopped speaking and withdrew her hand from the ocean.

Candlelight stole over his furrowed brow and flashed in the depths of his blue-green irises. It was a rare moment, indeed, to see Everhart agitated.

To be the cause of it *might* give one the sense of having the upper hand.

With a grin tugging at her lips, Calliope returned her attention to the jagged coast of South America. "It could be of no interest to you. It's just a book, after all."

"It is *more* than a book," he argued. "That journal is a vital account of an exploration. Men will read such an accounting for years to come as a way of expanding their own world."

She rather liked seeing him so ruffled. Especially since Everhart was renowned for being *un*ruffled.

This was another side of him that she was certain few had ever witnessed. And while she wasn't the type to make waves—certainly not like her sisters—she wanted to know what would happen if she did.

It surprised Calliope to realize that she wanted more from Everhart than he gave to anyone else.

"I am not a man, yet I have been reading it. Ghastly business about the rats in the cook's pot, wouldn't you agree?" She smiled sweetly. "If I ever went on an expedition, I should not like rat stew."

"You on an expedition?" he scoffed. "I think not."

The muscles of her neck tightened, but she refused to reveal how he'd pricked her irritation. "When I reach my majority next year, I shall have my dowry funds released to me. I believe it is substantial enough to earn passage on a ship."

"You are an unmarried woman," he said, his tone flat. "You cannot travel alone."

Without looking at him, she clucked her tongue in disgust. "I am not a ninny, Everhart. Of course I wouldn't travel with anyone other than perfect gentlemen."

"A voyage can take months. Years." Surprisingly, he began to raise his voice. "No gentleman is *that* perfect."

Calliope feigned an absent shrug, as if she wasn't stewing over his arrogance. Running her finger across the atlas, she plotted a course on the map. The truth was, she hadn't considered an expedition until just now, when it seemed to cause a violent reaction in him. "I have a full year to consider my adventure. I imagine South America would be quite wild after that terrible battle. Perhaps I would pen my own journal, and future generations of men *and* women would read about my travels."

"You must promise me not to do something so foolish."

The harsh command drew her gaze, along with her incredulity. "Promise you? Why ever would I need to promise you anything? We are not even friends."

He sat forward as if he were about to spring, heedless of his injury. "We cannot be friends," he said, gritting his teeth as he glared at her. "However, I am still the only person of your acquaintance who has traveled extensively—"

"Brightwell has traveled," she reminded, earning another sharp glare. "In fact, he was speaking of his travels the other evening in the parlor and that he did not enjoy Indian cuisine."

Everhart released his white-knuckled grip on the edge of the cushion beneath him and swiped his hands across his thighs. His mouth curled in a condescending smirk. "With you there to hang upon his every word, no doubt."

Abandoning the atlas, she set her hands on her hips. "Brightwell married my cousin, or have you forgotten?"

"The question is, have you?"

In that moment, she wondered why she was standing here in the first place. Had insanity drawn her? "You are right, Everhart. We cannot be friends. I don't know why I continue to try." She turned to leave.

"Try? Thus far, your attempts have been to steal a book I was reading and then to goad me into an argument."

Calliope whipped around to face him. The gall of this man astounded her! "I have not *goaded* you into anything. Since my arrival, you have simply been quick to temper. Then again, I recall bringing out the worst in you years ago as well."

Had it only been a moment ago that she'd wanted to make waves and get a reaction from him? Now, with his boat capsizing, he seemed determined to take her down with him.

His smirk fell. "What do you mean? I have always been civil to you."

"Civility under duress, perhaps," she said on a huff, concealing the hurt she felt. "You do not have cause to dislike me. If Brightwell can forgive me, I do not see why you cannot."

"I do not dislike you, Miss Croft. I—" He stared at her for a moment, his lips parted, but he said nothing more. He merely released a slow exhale and looked beyond the stacks to the banister that overlooked the room below, as if he were considering jumping over the edge.

Perhaps she should give up. Her efforts were obviously in vain. Exhausted, she turned to leave, only to be startled by the sudden sound of piano music.

A fluid meandering waltz filled the chamber. Montwood was right; it rang quite clearly inside the north tower. The score was achingly familiar but for a moment, she could not fathom why—not until her gaze returned to Everhart's.

In that moment, she recalled it perfectly. This was the waltz the orchestra had played in Bath, where they'd last danced. When it had ended, the intensity of his dislike had shone in his gaze.

That same intensity was shining there now. It was volatile. Filled with such heat below the surface, she imagined he would begin to rant at her any moment.

"They played this at the Randall ball," he said without looking away from her.

Her mouth went dry. Of all the things she expected him to recall, this was the last. "Yes."

"We danced."

"I remember."

When he looked surprised by her admission, she continued. "I'm not likely to ever forget. At the end, I thought you were either going to scold me or shake me, right there in the middle of the ballroom."

"I wasn't," he said without elaborating.

"You look as if you could do the same right now."

"Do I?" His laugh sounded hollow, self-deprecating. "Perhaps I was just thinking about the dance and recalling how it felt to"—his gaze swept over her, his fists clenching around the edge of the cushion—"stand without the assistance of a cane."

Yet it seemed as though he'd meant to say something else entirely.

She kept forgetting about his injury. He always seemed so capable to her. It was difficult to imagine that he couldn't do whatever he wished, whenever he wished it. As he'd likely done all his life.

"You could lean on me." The words tumbled out unheeded, surprising her. She rationalized them away instantly, telling herself that it was only the nurturing aspect of her personality that caused her to make the offer.

Everhart arched a skeptical brow. "A dance, for pity's sake? I think not."

Not knowing what possessed her, Calliope decided to make one final attempt at friendship. Yet perhaps it wasn't friendship that compelled her but something else entirely.

She'd always hated the way things had ended years ago. So abruptly and without warning. Although she never admitted it, out of everyone from their circle of friends, she'd missed Everhart the most.

Remembering that loss keenly made walking away impossible now.

Calliope sat down beside him. The sloped portion of the chaise did not allow much room to keep a proper distance. Then again, what she was about to suggest wasn't entirely proper either. "Then a dance for friendship's sake."

"We cannot be—" He stopped as she pivoted her upper body toward his, her hand slipping onto his shoulder.

Before she could rethink her plan or accustom herself to the warmth emanating from his close proximity, she reached down and eased his grip from the cushion's edge, sliding her other hand into his.

"Friends," she finished for him.

"I have no women friends." He swallowed, his gaze drifting from her eyes to her mouth as if in a silent warning. Or perhaps it was more of an invitation.

A shiver coursed through her as his arm slipped around her waist. His hand opened against the small of her back and slowly drifted upward to rest just beneath her shoulder blades. Alone like this, it would be easy for him to nudge her closer. Perhaps that was exactly what he wanted her to imagine.

"You seduce every woman of your acquaintance, then? The same way you are seducing me now?"

"I beg to differ." He offered a mocking grin and lifted their joined hands into a less-than-formal waltzing pose. "You are the one seducing me. You are wearing me down to the point where my head is spinning as if we were actually dancing."

His gaze bore into hers, and she thought for just a moment that instead of scolding her or shaking her, he might want to kiss her. The way it had been in her dream.

"My head is spinning too," she admitted on a breath. Her gaze drifted to his mouth.

Everhart shook his head. "Don't close your eyes."

"But if I don't, then I'm likely to…" She wet her lips.

"Likely to…what?"

To kiss you, she nearly said. Thankfully, her lips didn't form the words. Yet in the same breath, her head must have misunderstood. Because before she knew it, her lips were on his.

She gasped the instant she realized what she'd done.

Yet as he'd commanded, she kept her eyes on his. They were of like mind, both holding perfectly still. The only movement he made was an exhale through his nostrils. His breath mingled with hers. He didn't even blink. But as he stared at her, his pupils grew larger, like onyx gems rimmed with aquamarine.

When she heard a low, raw rasp tear from his throat, she realized something very important. Everhart had had no intention of scolding her *or* shaking her. It was quite possible that all along, the intensity of his gaze had everything to do with kissing.

To be certain, she kissed him again. This time, she lingered and pressed her lips to his again in the only type of kiss she knew how to give. Even *she* knew it was not enough. It was too…chaste. Certainly not a kiss that a woman of four and twenty gave to a rake. Yet she'd had very little experience.

Everhart was patient, neither withdrawing nor pushing her naïve exploration. Inspired by that thought as much as the map on the table behind her did, she wondered what it would be like to *explore* Gabriel Ludlow, Viscount Everhart. She imagined that his lips were the continent rising up from the sea, awaiting her…first…step.

This was new territory. Calliope tilted her head, nuzzling the tip of her nose into the valley beside his. Her mouth slanted, silk against velvet, soft against firm. The sensations riveted her, making her wonder why she'd wasted her life on anything other than kissing expeditions. If she'd had forethought, she could've been proficient by now. As it was, with her nose pressed against his, breathing became harder. Opening her mouth seemed the only solution because she couldn't bear to draw back, even for a single breath.

Her lips parted. Against his warning, her eyes drifted closed.

Everhart shifted, tilting his chin up a fraction as his mouth opened too. He exhaled the essence of sweet whiskey. She swallowed, feeling it warm her all the way down to where her stomach seemed to have drifted, heavy, throbbing in a foreign place deep within her.

Like a dedicated cartographer, her lips pressed, brushed, and traced. Still, it was not enough. Her tongue followed the same route, earning another rasp from him. Unable to hide the pleasure that the sound gave her, she smiled against his lips. She liked kissing Everhart, more than she'd ever imagined. And she *had* imagined...

Then he moved, drawing her closer. His tongue delved beyond the boundaries of her lips and into her mouth. A sound that was neither rasp nor moan but something in between rose from her throat. Reflexively, she lifted her outer leg and turned, draping it over his. Half lying on top of him, her hands opened against his chest and closed over his waistcoat. *This is mine*, she thought. *This waistcoat. This kiss. This man. All...mine.*

The powerful need to possess him startled her. She began to pull back, only to have him follow and coax her into the kiss once again. She went willingly.

Her leg glided wantonly against his, earning a growl of approval from him. His skillful hands answered her entreaty, sliding over her back, along her sides, until they drifted up along her rib cage to map out the twin islands of her breasts. Her back arched in supplication, offering her breasts into the care of his hands.

"If you are not seducing me," she whispered against his lips, "then what are you doing with your hands?"

"I'm merely following the siren call of your body." He scraped the short nails of his thumbs across both of her nipples, eliciting a shock of pure pleasure.

A quake traversed her entire being. It pulsed in the air around her, coming out on a gasp. She let her head fall back when he did it once more. A debutante would certainly be scandalized, not only by his actions but by her own response. How many novels had warned her about the follies of a young woman taken unawares?

As for Calliope, she was neither young nor unaware. In fact, she was all too aware of everything she felt in this moment—the taut aching of her breasts, the tingles covering her heated flesh, the immodest pressure of his thigh between hers.

She never wanted it to stop. "For a man named after an angel, you have very wicked hands."

He lifted her higher, his lips against her jaw, her throat, nipping her clavicle. "Imagine what I could do with my mouth."

Hmm... "I'm certain I shouldn't."

He lowered her a fraction, sliding her body along the firmness of his thigh, and kissed her once more. "But you already have. I can see it in your gaze."

The clock below started to chime, reminding her of the person she'd been just an hour before when her foot first touched that bottom tread. "It is midnight already?"

"I don't care if it is," he said, his wicked, greedy mouth following the line of her shoulder, where he'd pulled one side of her gown free, taking with it the tapes of her stays and petticoat.

"My maid will wonder where I am." But Calliope didn't really care either. She was inside a book—her own story now. Each turn of the page brought new adventures, new sensations she'd never before experienced.

"Let her wonder."

Yes, the heroine of her own story said. *Let her wonder*. On the verge of fainting, her inner narrator fanned herself.

Still, for propriety's sake, she said, "I could not compromise you in such a manner."

His laugh vibrated against the underside of her jaw. "Compromise *me*?"

"Your wager," she said with her last noble breath. Quite honestly, she didn't know why she was trying to stop any of this. Wouldn't it be wonderful if they could live up here, shielded from everyone forever? "If we are caught then…the wrong assumptions would be made."

"Ah, yes. Quite right." He lifted his head and held her gaze. "Though wager or not, I am far from one of the heroes in your novels who would surrender to marriage in the end."

At the austere certainty in his tone, those delicious tremors abruptly stopped. The enthralling kissing haze that had settled over her began to lift. And then she remembered who she was, who he was, and the reason she was here at Fallow Hall.

With as much poise as possible, Calliope disentangled herself from his embrace and stood. She supposed it was reassuring to know exactly what to expect where Everhart was concerned. It was like knowing the end of a story. This way, she wouldn't be taken unaware again.

Still, the enormity of what had just transpired fell over her like the weight of an entire bookcase. However, under no uncertain terms would she let him see how her own book lay open, spine cracked, pages crumpled.

"Nor I, though you needn't to put it like that." She lifted her chin at an angle that didn't quite suit her, but she held the position regardless. "I wouldn't have you for a husband. Not when I'm in love with someone else."

CHAPTER ELEVEN

"**W**ho?" Gabriel leapt up from the chaise, ignoring the biting pain that knifed up his leg.

Calliope gave him a look that suggested he should know the answer.

Brightwell. His blood seethed.

"I hardly think it's any concern of yours." She angled her bare shoulder away from him and pulled up her sleeve in such a casual manner that his irritation climbed. She should be trembling and blushing like the untried virgin she was, not rearranging her clothes without a care, like a seasoned courtesan.

"It is, when you've spent the last hour kissing me." He felt compelled to drag that sleeve back down again, along with the other one and never stop undressing her until he rid her mind of any other man. Until he and he alone made her quiver in ecstasy. *Until...*

Until she was his.

"I disagree." She narrowed her eyes with that saccharine smile.

He responded similarly. "Though it is clear that you have not spent much, if any, time kissing your beloved."

She gasped at the insult, but he continued, not allowing her the chance to interject.

"You started off very green indeed. But I managed to tutor you quite effectively. I'm certain"—Gabriel gritted his teeth—"he will thank me."

She was fuming now. Livid. *Magnificent*. He wanted her with a passion that nearly consumed him.

It was madness to have kissed her at all. Now, he felt as if she'd injected him with an addictive elixir—a drug—and he had become an instant opium-eater. He wanted more. His entire body shook with need.

This wasn't wholly unfamiliar territory. He'd felt this way before. This same insanity had inspired the letter he'd written to her.

"He won't thank you. He won't even think of you. Or ever even wonder about you. Because he will know that when my lips touch his, he is the only person in my thoughts."

And then with a final blow, she added, "The only person who has *ever* been there."

Was she actually suggesting that she could have thought of anyone other than Gabriel when she kissed like that?

Not possible. "A woman does not kiss a man with complete abandon when she is in love with someone else."

He reached out, prepared to haul her back into his arms and obliterate Brightwell from her thoughts forever. But she stepped back, out of his immediate reach. It was a short distance but enough to bring him a semblance of sanity.

He could not kiss her again, or at least he should not. *Would* not.

If she still imagined herself in love with Brightwell, then why had she refused him five years ago? "After Brightwell is married, you realize you love him? Perhaps you are just as fickle as you have always been."

"Is my action from that one night all you ever think of?" Although her words came out with bite, there was something undeniably wounded in the depth of her eyes. "In regard to Brightwell, I have given you my answer. I will not repeat it again."

He felt a sharp wrenching pain at seeing that look, at being the cause of it. The need for clarity compelled him to probe further, but tender regard for what lay beneath the sandy depths of her eyes softened his tone. "You told me that you refused Brightwell those years ago because you did not love him, *not* that you were in love with someone else."

"Believe me, if I'd have come to the realization a moment sooner, we would not be having this conversation." She exhaled as if exhausted, with her hands rearranging wayward locks of hair. "Now, I feel guilty of betrayal."

"Who is he?" The air in Gabriel's lungs seized, and he felt that anchor's weight upon him again.

She gritted her teeth. "I cannot tell you."

"*Cannot?*" he scoffed. "It is more a matter of *will not.*"

"All right then. Even if I could, I would *not* tell you." Color bloomed in her cheeks. Her gaze collided with his as if she realized what she'd said.

Gabriel stilled. Her words penetrated the haze of lust, longing, and anger inside his brain. If she *couldn't* give him a name, was it because she did not know it?

He thought about the letter he'd written and wondered if it was possible. Arrogant assumption or not, he had to know. Had the letter been as altering for her as it had been for him?

His mind turned in a thousand directions as his pulse beat faster. It was far more likely that she was speaking of someone else she knew. Yet a strangely familiar sensation of yearning swept through him, like a gale wind from a cloudless sky. "How could you not be aware of loving someone?"

Her hands trembled as she lowered them to smooth the front of her gown. "It is rather easy, when you believe you hate someone for ruining your life, or the life you once thought you could have had." Tears glistened in her eyes before she turned away.

Gabriel didn't want to cause her pain. He wanted to go to her and wrap her up in his embrace. But he could not move, for fear of what else he might do. Could not speak, for fear of what he might confess.

"I regret my choices here tonight," she said quietly. "As I'm sure you do as well."

He did. He regretted every moment he'd spent with her—not only tonight but all of them. Kissing her had forced him to accept the truth: He could no longer avoid her—*avoid the inevitable*—though he would be much happier if he could.

Without waiting for a response, she wove her way past the bookcases. At the top of the stairs, she paused. "You were right, Everhart. We cannot be friends."

He wanted to agree with her and perhaps even offer a taunt for having been right.

The lie would not form on his tongue. Not any longer.

CHAPTER TWELVE

After a sleepless night, guilt churned in Calliope's stomach like Mrs. Swan's curdled soup.

It wasn't possible. She couldn't still be in love with the man who'd written her the letter. She despised him... Didn't she?

And it had taken kissing Everhart to admit it.

Worse yet, she'd enjoyed it. Far more than she should have. Especially for someone who'd realized she was in love with another man.

Was it possible to kiss one man while being in love with the other?

Well...perhaps. But could she have kissed Everhart to the point of losing herself completely and still be in love with an ink-and-paper lover?

No, she admitted.

On a sigh, her fingertips strayed to her lips as she walked down the vacant hall in the east wing the following morning. She already wondered what it would be like to kiss him again. Which was wrong, she told herself. Very wrong.

Wasn't it?

There was no future with Everhart. Just like there was no future with Casanova. But who could think about the future or anything at all when kissing Everhart?

For a while, he'd been hers. Until that moment, Calliope hadn't realized how much the heartache of the past had kept her from having a *someone* of her own. She'd been so afraid of being hurt again that she'd given up on the idea of marriage completely.

But kissing Everhart had opened her eyes to something else as well.

If she could experience that sort of passion, then perhaps she wasn't as afraid as she thought. Perhaps her heart had mended enough. Perhaps these feelings weren't solely for Casanova. And perhaps…she now ran the risk of having stronger feelings for Everhart too.

She stumbled as the last thought hit her. Reaching out, she placed her hand atop a demilune table to right herself. When a maid carrying linens appeared from around the corner, Calliope pretended to have stopped for the purpose of admiring the freshly cut amaryllis.

She drew in a breath and waited for a less romantic thought to enter her mind. Perhaps what confused her was her body's response to Everhart and the things she'd allowed him to do. Things she'd never even considered doing with Brightwell. Things she wouldn't mind if Everhart wanted to do again.

No, no, absolutely not, she scolded herself. She was not going to kiss Everhart again. She was going to avoid him and search for the letter. It would be simple. Avoid and search. That was her new plan.

But how could she search the map room when he spent most of his time there?

She would have to lure him away. Perhaps she could gain Montwood's assistance for an afternoon. It would need to happen soon, however, since she'd already written to her brother for the carriage.

Once she found Pamela's letter, all would be well, and she could leave Fallow Hall before she succumbed to temptation again.

Valentine stepped into the map room, holding a salver before him. "The post, my lord."

Gabriel took the stack and thumbed through the envelopes. There was one from his solicitor, one from his sister, one from his cousin, Rathburn—likely expounding on the bliss of matrimony—and one from…*Hullo*…his father.

"And how is Fallow Hall faring this morning, Valentine?" Gabriel asked, feeling inordinately cheerful, despite the letter in his grasp. He hadn't slept a single minute last night, and yet he felt…*revived*. The same way he felt whenever he stepped on board a ship, prepared for a journey.

"Everything is in order, my lord. Miss Croft is managing the house remarkably well."

Gabriel nodded, pleased. "I knew she would. Miss Croft isn't one to back down from a challenge." Cracking the wax seal, he wondered what reprimand he would find this time.

"No, sir."

"Admirable quality, that," he remarked absently, scanning the short missive. Surprisingly, he found no reprimand at all. *Hmm...* "It appears we are to have guests tomorrow, Valentine. If you would, instruct Mrs. Merkel to attend to the rooms in the west wing for the Duke of Heathcoat and the dowager duchess." And peculiarly, Gabriel's usual dread over such an announcement was absent as well.

"Very good, sir." The butler bowed. "However, Miss Croft is still in the Woodlark Room, which you requested for her upon her arrival. Shall I move her into a smaller chamber?"

Even having planned to avoid her at all costs when she'd first arrived, Gabriel still had wanted her to have the best room at Fallow Hall. He'd still wanted her to enjoy her stay. He'd still wanted her.

How foolish he was not to realize it until now.

A wry laugh escaped him. "No, do not disturb Miss Croft. My father and grandmother needn't know that their rooms are not the finest."

Unless Gabriel was mistaken, the slight twitching of the butler's tightly drawn cheek was a smile.

"Set a place for me at dinner this evening as well," he said, earning a twitch of an eyebrow this time.

Valentine bowed one last time before he left the room. "*Very* good, sir."

Calliope wound the music box again, continuing her odd conversation with her cousin. "Why would Aunt Augusta believe one of the gentlemen here at Fallow Hall had designs on you?"

When Pamela had said the words a moment ago, Calliope had thought the notion preposterous. Or simply a mother's attempt to spoil her child. Certainly, Montwood, Danvers, and even Everhart were reputed rakes, but they were not beyond common decency. None of the gentlemen here would think of seducing a married woman confined to a sickbed.

Yet she couldn't deny that Everhart had seemed to forget that Calliope was an innocent. Of course, she couldn't fault him for that. He was a rake, after all. She certainly hadn't behaved like an innocent last night. As for the rest of his behavior, she certainly *could* fault him for his words and accusations.

In love with Brightwell after all this time? Did Everhart imagine her world was so small that she could love no one else? That her passion had never been stirred by another? She actually felt pity for him. Obviously, he'd never felt an emotion as life altering as love—

That was a sobering thought. Especially considering the epiphany she'd had earlier, regarding her confusing mélange of emotions toward Everhart. Emotions that he was never likely to reciprocate.

"I'm not certain," Pamela responded, holding out her hands to admire her newly manicured nails that Bess had buffed to a shine. "Perhaps it was because I didn't receive the letter until after I was here. Mother didn't think anyone else would have known where to find me. But if anyone could, I'm certain *he* could."

Calliope went cold. Her cousin didn't typically make a lot of sense, but this seemed plausible. "You received the letter *after* you arrived at Fallow Hall?"

Dreamy-eyed, Pamela smiled. "As I said, I am the only married woman to have received one."

Calliope couldn't believe it, or perhaps she didn't want to believe. Now, she was even more desperate to see that letter and make sure it wasn't all a figment of her cousin's imagination. Thinking of how special she'd once felt, only to have that feeling ripped away time and again, her heart broke just a little more.

Putting her own hurt aside, she considered this new development. If the letter arrived after her cousin was invited to stay here for her recuperation, then very few people would have known where to direct the letter. There were the gentlemen in residence here, of course. While she still wasn't certain about Montwood's love-letter-writing potential, she'd removed Danvers from the list's possibilities. She'd crossed Everhart off the list years ago, shortly following the Randall ball.

As for Brightwell, well...she'd discounted him years ago too. But now she wondered if she'd been too hasty. Was there a poet lurking within him? Or a passionate nature that only revealed itself on the page? She'd never noticed any ink on his fingertips...

"Mother told me not to think about it any longer and that it was likely Milton's attempt at cheering me."

A wave of dread washed over Calliope. Could it have been Brightwell all along, and she hadn't seen it? The single chaste kiss they'd shared had stirred no passion in her. Nothing like she'd experienced last night in Everhart's arms. Surely, a man capable of writing such a letter would incite her *every* passion. Wouldn't he?

She had to find out if she'd made the biggest mistake of her life.

"It would be rather romantic if one's husband wrote passionate letters," Calliope mused.

Her cousin began to nod, her gaze drifting far away. "But he hadn't seemed pleased at all when I asked him about it."

Calliope's jaw went slack, her mouth agape. "You...you asked your husband about the letter? But Pamela, what if it wasn't from him? Surely it would cause him pain to learn that his wife was being pursued by another."

Which meant that last night at the card table, he'd known. *Oh dear.*

"I didn't think of that." Pamela blinked owlishly. "Honestly, I thought the letter was from someone far more... passionate."

It appeared her cousin had discounted Brightwell too. "You didn't tell him that as well, did you?"

"Do you suppose I shouldn't have?"

Calliope closed her eyes and dropped her chin to her chest. *Poor Brightwell.* Unless...he *was* the author. Then perhaps he'd merely wanted to conceal the other aspects of his personality. Perhaps he was simply too shy to express them.

"It would be rather thrilling to know that one's husband had written love letters to half the *ton.*"

"It wasn't half," Calliope corrected. "There were only six letters." Not counting her own.

"Seven, if you include mine."

Then make that eight, Calliope thought, her heart sinking bit by bit, like a shipwreck toward the bottom of the deepest part of the ocean. *And earlier I'd thought my heart had mended. What a joke.*

"Perhaps it would be best if we didn't discuss the letter," Calliope said. If Pamela was right, then the love-letter Casanova could very well be here, at Fallow Hall. This changed everything.

Now, all she needed to do was devise a plan to unmask him. Unfortunately, the only thing she knew about him that wasn't speculation was his distinctive handwriting.

"I need my distractions returned to me," Pamela whined. "And I am tired of cards in the parlor after dinner. Surely we could find other amusements."

"I suppose we could play a game," Calliope said absently. She was more concerned about devising a method to see all the gentlemen's handwriting. Then, inspiration struck. "We could play charades this evening and write out phrases on scraps of paper."

Her cousin wrinkled her nose. "All that flapping about and making a fool of oneself is not enjoyable."

Calliope mulled that over, and wound the music box once more. Whatever game they played, writing must be involved so that she could inspect the handwriting of each player. "How about playing Anagrams? We could take the names of important people, mix them up, and see who figures out our clues."

Pamela sighed. "I was never very good at those games."

"I will help you," Calliope offered, knowing this was the perfect game to play in order to unmask Casanova.

Because if he *was* here, then she would know the instant she saw his distinctive script.

CHAPTER THIRTEEN

Gabriel decided to make a grand entrance at dinner. His arrival caused Montwood and Danvers to lift their brows and then salute each other with their wine goblets. Pamela gasped. Brightwell offered a nod of greeting, his features inscrutable. And Calliope completely avoided his gaze.

Standing at the opposite end of the table from her, Gabriel greeted everyone in turn but saved hers for last. "Miss Croft, I have heard great things about your improvements to the dining experience here at Fallow Hall. I don't believe I've looked forward to a meal as much as this one."

His reason for joining them had nothing to do with his appetite but everything to do with the pleasure he gained from unsettling her. Oh, and she was in high color. Blushing as if he'd kissed her right here, in front of everyone.

Obligated to look at him, Calliope offered a curt nod. "I defer every accomplishment to Mrs. Swan and her kitchen."

"Well said. My grandmother would be pleased by such a remark," he offered mysteriously, saluting her with his freshly poured wine as he took his seat. "Which brings about an announcement—apparently, my father and grandmother will arrive tomorrow and stay for a short duration."

"The dowager duchess, here?" Pamela lifted a frail hand to her brow as if she might faint at any moment. "This leaves me no time to set my maid to creating a new gown, and barely enough to time to alter the ones I have. She will have to work all through the night."

Calliope gave her cousin a stern look. "Your maid took ill this afternoon, if you'll recall. Perhaps I can help you find something suitable."

"Oh, yes, that would be—"

"No," Everhart interjected, fighting a sudden rise of irritation at the thought of Calliope's feeling obligated to work endlessly for her cousin's sake. "That will not be necessary. It would pain my grandmother to know that she inconvenienced anyone."

Danvers coughed violently into his napkin. Soon enough, however, Gabriel noted his shoulders quaking in an unmistakable display of laughter. The truth was, Grandmama was infamous for being rather…particular. Thankfully, throughout Danvers's amusement, Pamela appeared to take Gabriel's response to heart and nodded in delicate acquiescence.

Begrudgingly, or so it seemed, Calliope offered him a gesture of thanks by lifting her own her glass but without saying a word. He held her gaze, stating quite clearly that he'd only made the remark to spare her. Though why he wanted her to know such a thing was a puzzle.

He'd told her last night that he had no interest in either marrying her or embarking on a friendship. And it was the truth. Last night's kiss had left his willpower in tatters. That was the reason he joined the dinner party—to be near her without any risk involved.

Yet he couldn't help but wonder if he was fooling himself.

Throughout the meal, his gaze strayed to her dozens of times. While she seemed intent on keeping all her exchanges with those closest her, it pleased Gabriel immensely that her gaze collided with his just as often. And each time, she blushed.

For the most part, the dinner fare was relatively unremarkable, which—when it came to Mrs. Swan's food—was an improvement. He gave all the credit to Calliope. Having kept track of her occupations during her stay, he found himself more and more impressed by her. She wasn't one to get overwhelmed easily, not even when faced with the abominable kitchens at Fallow Hall. Gabriel had not been able to accomplish so much in ten times the amount of time. She would have made Brightwell a very fine wife indeed.

Usually, the reminder of his own culpability at ruining a friend's happiness sobered Gabriel immediately. A swift shot of guilt had always followed. This was the first time, however, that he felt at peace with what he'd done. Happy, even. In fact, he was genuinely glad Calliope had not married Brightwell. And even gladder that Brightwell was no longer a bachelor.

After the last course, Montwood slid his chair back from the table and stood, gaining everyone's attention. "Miss Croft, I wonder if I could persuade you to postpone our game for one evening," Montwood said, all charm and politeness. "Now that Everhart has returned to the party, I believe a celebration is in order. With your permission, I would like to adjourn to the music room for our entertainment."

Gabriel watched as Calliope's shoulders stiffened ever so slightly. He wondered what game she'd hoped to play and found himself ready to come to her defense. "Surely we could enjoy both amusements this evening." The longer in her company, the better.

Calliope's gaze met his once again. "Thank you, Everhart, but that won't be necessary. We can play Anagrams some other night."

Yet Gabriel could have sworn he saw disappointment in the downward tilt of her eyes.

"Everhart will need the additional time to think of something clever," Montwood joked.

Gabriel rose from his seat, along with the others. He'd always been rather quick with anagrams. "Since I would hate to be accused of needing more time than Montwood, I shall fill out my card straightaway. I already have an idea in mind."

Although writing an anagram that transformed Miss Calliope *into* camisole slip *might not be the best idea*, he thought wryly.

To slip a camisole from her skin/the wager I would never win... There was never a truer anagram; he was certain.

Skipping the custom of men with their port while women sat in the parlor, they journeyed en masse to the music room, though Gabriel detoured to the parlor to fill out his card for the game.

Brightwell broke apart from the others and joined him down the hall, extending a scrap of foolscap. "I filled out a second anagram, Everhart. Earlier, I couldn't decide which I preferred. Now, I have this extra marvel. If you like, you can use this one."

The letters were printed with painstaking exactitude. Writing it must have caused Brightwell pain, due to an accident from his youth that had forced him to use his non-dominant hand for correspondence. When they'd traveled together, he'd usually dictated his letters to his valet.

Knowing that made Gabriel appreciate the gesture all the more. "Thank you, my friend. That saves me from trying to be clever."

The truth was, he was far too eager to join Calliope in the music room to think of anything else. He took the token and summarily handed it off to Valentine, with a request that it be added to the others.

Turning back to Brightwell, Gabriel patted him on the shoulder as they walked the hall together. "You are a good friend, far better than I deserve." The statement was truer than he cared to admit. "Though I am glad to see you well situated in your life. You are content, are you not?"

"Of course," Brightwell said, keeping his gaze on the path before him. "It is an easy exercise to move away from the past when one has the proper incentive."

"Now, you each must gather round that pedestal across the room and choose your medium of entertainment," Montwood announced when they entered the music room. "The game is to showcase that which you do best."

Calliope couldn't help but laugh. "What I do best is read, though I doubt the sight of me sitting in a chair, ensconced in a book brings much entertainment to others."

"Come now, Miss Croft. I have it under excellent authority that you sing," Montwood added with a waggle of his thick brows, his amber eyes gleaming as he looked from her to the door, which drew her attention to Everhart, who stepped across the threshold after Brightwell. "Perhaps a duet, if you are shy."

With little ceremony, Montwood began to play a jaunty tune.

"I believe I have found my perfect melody." Danvers plucked the music from the stack, whistling as he moved away from the pedestal. "Ladies and gentlemen, prepare yourselves for auditory delight."

"I do believe I would tire too easily." Pamela flipped through a few pages with disinterest and then elevated her bent wrist for Brightwell to take. "Can I be forgiven if I remain but an avid admirer in the audience?"

"Of course." They all agreed—rather convincingly too— that her health was most important.

Brightwell escorted his bride to the settee and then made his own announcement, holding up a gloved hand. "I daresay this game sounds like fun. Unfortunately, I lack the dexterity to move my hand freely. A horse stepped on it when I was a boy, and the bones never set properly."

With Brightwell and her cousin out, and with Danvers and Montwood across the room, that left Calliope alone at the ornate pedestal. Until Everhart came near.

She was all too aware of him. Even with a leg splint, he moved gracefully. She noted how he put more weight on it and relied less on his cane. A natural compulsion begged her to ask if it pained him, but after last night, she'd vowed to avoid intimacies with him as much as possible.

They hadn't parted as friends, after all.

"How is it that Montwood knows you sing, yet I have never heard you?" Everhart kept his voice low enough that his comment could not be overheard by the others. The lighthearted trill of the piano keys helped in that regard as well. Yet by all appearances, he looked more interested in leafing through the assortment of music laid out on the pedestal than in her answer.

Her sleeve brushed his, the barest contact, nothing more than a scrape of silk against wool, yet it rushed over her like a caress of his hands. "Not to worry," she said, her voice equally quiet, her throat inexplicably dry. "I do not plan to sing a duet with you. Your skill will not be tainted by my lack of one."

"I have no doubt that a...*duet* with you would be abundantly satisfying." His thumb stroked the corner of the page in a potent reminder of the night before. "A crescendo of exaltations mutually intertwined."

At a glance, she saw his lips curve into a wicked grin. The music room had suddenly grown far too hot for her tastes. Looking at the hearth to cast blame, she only saw a single log on the grate, the rest having burned to ash. The other logs must have gone up in a fiery blast simultaneously with Everhart's idea of a...duet. She resisted the urge to fan herself.

"Although that isn't why I asked," he continued. "When you are not in the map room, do you frequently find yourself in conversation with Montwood?"

His question struck an odd chord in her. Why should he care how she spent her time? He'd made his intentions, or lack thereof, perfectly clear.

And then it occurred to her. "Is this about the wager? If you are suggesting that I am able to give you a reason to win, thereby forcing Montwood into a marriage with me, then I gladly disappoint you. Your victory will not be an easy one."

"I am inclined to agree," he said, elusive in his lack of exposition.

Calliope had thumbed through more than a dozen scores but hadn't seen a one thus far. She was far too preoccupied. Everhart's nearness *and* her plan for discovering the identity of Casanova kept her head spinning. As soon as they were finished here, she would steal into the parlor and find out if *he* was truly here. "Do you play, Everhart?"

He drummed his remarkably talented fingers over the pedestal, his forearm propped over the surface as if to reduce the weight on his leg. "Not a note. You?"

"I know where all the notes are," she said, offering him the same type of ambiguity in her response. "It's putting them together that isn't my *forte*."

"I see your wit has not abandoned you after last evening."

She could hear him smile but refused to look up at him. They were supposed to be searching for this evening's entertainment. They were supposed to be avoiding each other. She'd been furious when he'd arrived at dinner, making a spectacle of both of them by sitting directly across from her. Yet now…she had to admit that she was enjoying this exchange, along with the intimacy provided by their secluded corner of the room. Far too much.

Since the other barriers she'd constructed continued to dissolve like sandcastles at high tide, she attempted to build a fresh one. "You have little influence over my wit or anything else about me, so I should not worry if I were you."

"I do so enjoy the bite of your tongue"—he paused, angling his head closer to her ear—"and your teeth, Miss Croft."

Calliope tried to ignore the tingles that tickled her spine, spreading over her like sea foam along the shore.

"You make me curious, Everhart..." She paused, allowing her words to hang suggestively between them and was rewarded by his quick intake of breath. "Curious as to why you would make such a wager with your friends. There would have to be a degree of certainty involved."

He exhaled slowly. "A great deal of certainty, indeed," he said, more to the sheet of music he lifted to study than to her. "I would never marry, if I could help it."

"*If you could help it?* Those words speak of an obligation under duress." She hid a laugh by pretending to cough. She glanced around the room; no one seemed to have noticed. Brightwell and Pamela were engrossed in conversation. And Montwood and Danvers appeared to be engaged in a pianist versus whistler battle, each one trying to outperform the other. "Though perhaps you are not yet at an age to make such a consideration by your own will. Some men stay young for a very long time."

"Why, Miss Croft, are you suggesting that I haven't grown into manhood yet? It would be my pleasure to prove otherwise," he promised. "We can take up where we left off."

It was becoming more and more difficult to ignore those tingles he caused. "Splendid. I'll simply step behind that curtain across the room so you can ravage me against the window seat." Unfortunately, the words came out with more sincerity than sarcasm. Worse, she was even imagining it.

"Be careful. You are frightening away the boy inside me and leaving your challenge in a man's hands. Or mouth, as the circumstance warrants."

Upon pain of death, she would never admit how much she enjoyed the way his rakish threats turned her brain to mush and left her body warm, malleable, and longing to be sculpted by his hands. "Is this what it is like to be your friend, then?"

"I told you before that I do not have women *friends*."

She thought about those women who were *not* his friends. Women who did not have any expectations from him other than the pleasure of his company—or pleasure *while in* his company, rather.

What would it be like to abandon the dream of a happy ending and simply live page to page?

Unable to help herself a moment longer, Calliope cast a sideways glance to his mouth. *Mmm…*"I suppose, then, that I am your first *friend*, for we are nothing more." What was meant to be a reminder to herself instead came out as if she were taunting him.

"Oh, but we have already surpassed mere friendship by leaps and bounds."

With their backs to the corner of the room, he angled his body in such a way that his arm draped behind her. His touch came as a surprise, but still she did nothing to dislodge him. This was his way of taunting her in return, a challenge to see who would be the first to concede.

Slowly, he traced a finger along the inward curve of her spine and proceeded to draw meandering shapes. They were like hieroglyphics that her mind could not comprehend. However, her body was fully capable of deciphering them.

To the rest of the room, it must appear as if they were deciding on one particular sheet of music, for they each grasped a side of it. "Friends do not seduce one another," he said, as if passing her the blame for his actions.

Her mouth watered, and she swallowed. "Then you must stop." *Oh*, please *don't stop*.

"I will, if you promise me one thing." His fingers were relentless. They moved more suggestively, stroking up and then down, rubbing in circles at the very base of her spine where it surely was indecent.

She felt a primitive desire to roll her hips against his hand. "If it involves another episode of kissing in the map room, I'm afraid our last encounter—"

"It doesn't," he said, his voice a familiar rasp. It brought to mind echoes of the previous night. Likely, his eyes were dark onyx jewels rimmed with aquamarine at that very moment. "I won't even be in the same room with you but far away on the opposite side of the manor."

"All right, then," she said, trying not to be disappointed. If he would take her hand and lead her from the music room right this instant, she didn't think she would object. "What would you have me do?"

"After you have finished reading your book by the fire in your chamber this evening—"

"How could you know that?" she asked, turning her startled gaze to him. She was right; his eyes were dark. He was so close, all she would have to do was lift up on her toes and her lips would be against his.

Grinning, he gave her a slight pinch as if he knew the direction of her thoughts. "And when you stand up to cross the room toward your bed," he continued, his voice mesmerizing, persuading her pulse to plummet down from her heart and settle between her thighs. The hand that was hidden from the rest of the room splayed over her hip, his fingertips gently molding her flesh. "You'll slip out of your night rail, letting it fall heedlessly to the floor."

She nodded, already imaging herself naked. Already picturing him there with her.

"When those wayward locks of hair brush against your shoulders," he murmured. "I want you to remember what it felt like to have my lips against your flesh."

It took a great deal of effort to turn away from him and pretend to study the music again. It took a great deal of effort to catch her breath. "Is that all?" she asked in a rather convincingly bored fashion.

Everhart chuckled. "I believe I have found our perfect duet."

She blinked in order to focus on the title. It helped when he removed his hand.

Staring down at the title, a laugh escaped her. Even though it was in German, she recognized enough to translate it. "'An Invitation to the Dance'?" *How absurdly…perfect.* Still, she shook her head. "It is a score for the piano. There are no lyrics for us to sing."

"I'm certain that inventing some will not be a problem." He turned his head to her ear once more. "Not for us."

Late that night, Calliope slipped downstairs to the parlor. The house was quiet. Montwood's soft lullabies on the piano had worked magic on the inhabitants of Fallow Hall. All except for her and, apparently, Duke.

The dog sat waiting outside the parlor, his head quirked as if he'd been expecting her.

"I couldn't sleep," she explained in a whisper. *Not with the end of my quest so near.*

Accepting her answer, he stood and wagged his tail. Thankfully, he wasn't near enough to any tables to cause damage. She scratched him behind his ears as she stepped into the room. He followed, loping along beside her.

Holding her lamp high, she searched the room for the basket of clues. Duke offered a low *woof*, drawing her attention. Paws on the table where they'd played cards the previous evenings, he sniffed the basket in the center.

Her heart beat faster. Though her steps were quick as she crossed the room, it felt like an age had passed before she finally arrived.

"You are a very good boy, Duke. I completely forgive you for misleading me last night." She rubbed his head and patted his neck, his tongue lolling off to the side. "Tomorrow, I'll ask Mrs. Swan for a special bone for you."

Setting down her taper, she took the basket in her hands and upended it. Folded scraps of foolscap skittered onto the table.

She held her breath. This was it. She would know in a single moment if the love-letter Casanova was here.

Drawing the first one from the pile, she studied the scrap carefully. The script was small and even, without a flourish. *Not a match.* The next one she'd written. The one after that had swooping, rounded letters that took up the entire space, as if it were a royal decree. *Pamela's*. The following one was nondescript, every letter formed as if it had come from a tutor of penmanship. Casanova would never write with such a lack of finesse.

Now, there were only two remaining. Reaching out, she chose the one on the right. She opened it and let out a breath, noting a very sloppy, severely slanted script. Recalling what Brightwell had said about his hand injury, she imagined this was his. *Not a match.*

She didn't allow herself to feel relief quite yet.

There was one left. *This could be it*, she told herself. She'd already found both hers and Pamela's, so this last one belonged to one of the gentlemen. The candlelight flickered, and she realized she was breathing hard.

Placing a hand on her chest to keep her heart from leaping out, she opened the last one.

Calliope closed her eyes. *Not his. Not a match.* The handwriting was too perfect and without a flourish. And so, that meant Casanova was not here at Fallow Hall. She was correct to discount Danvers and Everhart. She even crossed Montwood off her list. More important, it was *not* Brightwell.

Relief swept over her. She hadn't been wrong to refuse him after all. And yet…

Now she was back to where she'd been since the beginning. She still didn't know Casanova's identity. And the more time she spent with Everhart, the more desperate she was to find out.

Chapter Fourteen

———————————————————————

Tension gripped Gabriel by the throat. The lighthearted mood he'd carried with him yesterday had evaporated during another sleepless night.

Playing at seduction with Calliope was going to kill him. He didn't know what had come over him last night. Or the previous one, for that matter. Asking her to imagine his lips on her flesh had backfired. Because all night long, he'd known she was thinking about him as much as he'd been thinking about her.

He was taking a ridiculous risk by spending any time at all with her. With each and every encounter, he found himself more and more drawn to her. He thought of her constantly and found himself roaming about the manor simply to know where she was at any given time.

This had to stop.

"You appear inordinately preoccupied," the Duke of Heathcoat said, standing beside the chair across from him. Gabriel's father and grandmother had arrived a short time ago, along with the bespectacled family physician, who was now examining Gabriel's leg with a series of indecipherable murmurs.

Gabriel cast his father the careless shrug he'd perfected over the course of his life. "I was just thinking of an expedition to South America and hoping our good doctor would proclaim me fit enough to disembark within the month. I hear von Humboldt will be returning there soon. Perhaps he wouldn't mind a stowaway."

After all, if Gabriel had something else to occupy his thoughts, he could remove Miss Croft from *all* of them.

Alistair Ridgeway stood up from his kneeling position and removed his pince-nez with a pinch of his thumb and forefinger. "The bone has set nicely. You were fortunate that it was such a small break and just above the ankle. It has been six weeks since the accident?" At Gabriel's nod, Ridgeway continued. "Your movement will likely remain limited for a few more weeks, perhaps months, but I see no reason to resume the splint. What you need now is to strengthen the leg, but carefully. I would suggest that your valet continue to wrap it. Perhaps a shoe, but not a boot yet. You may begin to walk by using a cane."

The fact that Gabriel had been doing that for weeks went unsaid. He merely nodded, glad to finally be rid of the blasted splint.

"Thank you. That will be all, Ridgeway," the duke said, dismissing the doctor with the same severity as he spoke to everyone. After the door to the map room closed, he returned his attention to Gabriel. "You were fortunate this time."

"Yes, I—" Gabriel stopped. The instant he met his father's hard glare, he knew they were no longer speaking of the accident. No. They were speaking of the scandal surrounding it. Neither the gossips nor papers had ever breathed a word of it. Gabriel had paid to keep everything quiet. And yet, apparently his father had found out anyway. "There won't be another."

The duke issued a humorless laugh and set about wandering the room. "You have said that before."

Begrudgingly, Gabriel admitted that was the truth. It now seemed like ages ago. He felt like a completely different person, in a way that he never had before. "Yes, well...this time, I mean it."

"You're only saying that because you want me to provide the funds for your expedition."

"Not entirely." There was no point in avoiding the truth with his father. "I do feel ashamed of my actions. Otherwise, I wouldn't be here, would I?"

The carriage accident and Lady Brightwell's involvement had been a huge mistake. Nothing he would ever repeat. While he might be accustomed to letting people down with his actions, on that occasion he'd let himself down as well. He could not simply shrug off this mistake.

With a purse of his lips, the famed austerity in the duke's expression was complete. "I do give you credit for not running away this time. Then again, much of that had to do with your leg, I'm sure."

"My leg could have healed just as easily on a ship." Gabriel stood in an effort to dispel the tightness climbing along the back of his neck and stretching across his shoulders. Testing the stockinged foot, he leaned forward on it. A sensation of pins and needles climbed up from his heel.

"Your mother would not have wanted you to go on another expedition." The duke extended the cane that had been perched against the arm of the chair.

At the mere mention of her, the inescapable void she'd left behind was all the more apparent in the lines on his father's face. It was almost as if his outer husk was crumbling. There was a time, Gabriel remembered, when his father hadn't been so empty. When he was more man, husband, and father, rather than a *duke*.

Gabriel waved off the cane, earning his father's growl of disapproval. "I disagree. She was the one who sent me on small adventures, preparing me for the larger ones later in life."

"Perhaps when you were younger, but now that you are eight and twenty, I know that she would have expected you to put aside the waywardness of youth and find your rightful place." The cane fell against the low table with a clatter, rousing the dog from his lounging place by the fire, ears slanted backward.

"This isn't about Mother," Gabriel said, feeling his own hackles rise as he turned, unsteadily, to face his father. "This is about what *you* want—what you've wanted all along."

The Duke of Heathcoat released a slow breath. "Your mother and I were alike in this regard. We only desired your happiness and yes, part of that is dependent upon your assuming your rightful place as my son and heir."

The pressure to live up to expectation surrounded Gabriel, closing in bit by bit. If it wasn't his father or his grandmother, it was Montwood, Danvers, and Calliope.

Out of everyone, Calliope's assault was the worst and because she expected nothing. *Not a damned thing!*

Which—insanely enough—made him expect more from himself. He was used to the outer battles with others. But this inner war could kill him.

Gabriel felt a wave of panic rise up his throat. He wanted to run from it but couldn't. It was inside him, forcing him to face his fears. "Do you realize that every conversation we have revolves around Briar Heath?"

"Because it is where you belong!"

"I am honored that you would visit me here at Fallow Hall, Your Grace," Pamela said, smiling serenely from one of the green chairs in the sitting room across the hall from her chamber.

Calliope fought the urge to shake her head in disbelief. Her cousin did not seem to be aware that she was in the presence of one of the *ton's* elite. One could not simply speak to the Dowager Duchess of Heathcoat as if she were an equal or presume that she'd traveled all this distance to sit and chat with a baron's wife, whom she'd never met with previously.

"Undoubtedly, you are." The dowager duchess quirked her brow, incredulity in every arched wrinkle. Then, without another word, she shifted her attention to Calliope. "Miss Croft, my maid informs me that you are responsible for the fresh flowers in my rooms."

Calliope felt as if a trapdoor yawned in front of her. If she accepted responsibility, then she could easily be perceived as taking advantage of her hosts by raiding the hothouse in an effort to win favor with the dowager duchess. On the other hand, if she explained that she'd been assisting in the management of Fallow Hall, then more questions would arise, along with the likely assumption that she had an understanding with one of the gentlemen here.

She settled on a better option that completely removed her own involvement. "Mrs. Merkel is quite the capable housekeeper and ensures that all guests feel welcome, including providing the flowers for your rooms."

The dowager duchess tapped the tip of her silver-handled cane on the Turkish carpet at their feet and turned more fully in Calliope's direction, all but dismissing Pamela from the conversation. "I imagine such a *capable housekeeper* would be too busy to take me on a tour of Fallow Hall. Perhaps you would be so inclined."

Nervous, Calliope noticed that her words were not enunciated as a question. Therefore, she had no choice but to accept. "It would be my pleasure. If you are fond of flowers, we could begin with the hothouse."

"Dear cousin, you know how the flowers make me sneeze," Pamela interjected. "I would not be able to join you unless you began in the gallery. I'm certain Her Grace would enjoy the portraits far more."

Again, Calliope was both shocked and dismayed by her cousin's behavior. Pamela had spent so much of her life believing herself a queen that she'd lapsed into insensibility.

Across from her, the dowager duchess's shoulders stiffened as she rose from the chair. Calliope rose too. There was never a stonier expression than the one the dowager duchess cast down to Pamela, who remained seated. The dowager duchess did not say a single word, but instead made her way to the door.

"Miss Croft," the dowager duchess began, "I much prefer landscapes to portraits, as well as flowers of any kind. I should very much like to begin our tour in the hothouse." She held her cane as if it were more of an accessory than an aid. Or perhaps, even a device of expression.

Although wary at the moment, Calliope found herself liking that idea. It was as if they were all walking around on pages with words forming at their feet and climbing up the walls, and a single tap of the dowager duchess's cane was an exclamation mark.

Inclining her head, Calliope joined the dowager duchess, leading the way toward the garden doors at the opposite end of the house, leaving Pamela behind.

"If I may"—Calliope waited for a nod of consent from the dowager duchess—"there is a particularly lovely landscape of meadow flowers in the hall outside the drawing room. It is but a small detour and takes us past the map room, where your grandson likely is at the moment."

The dowager duchess seemed pleased by this and smiled. "I'm not surprised that Gabriel would choose to spend his time in a room that constantly reminds him of explorations. From the moment he could walk, he was always on an adventure, in search of whatever prizes his dearly departed mother had asked him to claim."

"He doesn't speak of her," Calliope remarked but was instantly astonished by her own audacity. To mention such a personal matter—and with Everhart's grandmother, no less—suggested a level of familiarity between the two of them. She desperately hoped the dowager duchess did not catch the unintentional slip.

"Gabriel was ten years old when she passed. His mother, dearest Anne, was a delight," the dowager duchess said, almost absently, though no one could ever accuse her of being lost in thought. She was as sharp as the tip of a penknife and had earned a reputation for cutting to the quick. "A more romantic person than I might say that Gabriel's father loved her to distraction and was lost without her." She released a slow breath, as if the event still pained her. "Of course, my son's current marriage is a perfectly amicable union of mutual regard. Much of society could not hope for more."

Calliope agreed without a word. She didn't want to make the error of speaking out of turn about her own parents' marriage. They, too, loved each other to distraction. Their example had set the course for her own life. She wanted life-altering love as well.

Days ago, she would have declared that her only chance at love had ended years ago. Now, more and more, she believed that her heart was ready to love again.

"Though I gather the same cannot be said of you, Miss Croft," the dowager duchess added, staring straight ahead and not seeming to notice that Calliope suddenly tripped over the hem of her own gown. "Otherwise, you would be Lady Brightwell today, in place of your cousin."

Sharp as a penknife, indeed. Calliope felt the point of it against her pulse. "A more romantic person than I might proclaim that mere friendship was not inducement enough for marriage."

The dowager duchess laughed, an unexpectedly hearty sound. "I can see why Gabriel found himself in an unlikely friendship with the reserved Milton Brightwell all those years ago."

An unlikely friendship? No, that wasn't correct. "Everhart and Brightwell always were friends. They attended school together."

"Two years apart, Miss Croft. With boys of that age, two years is quite a large expanse of time. Young men can be rather competitive at that age, or at any age." The duchess stopped suddenly in the hall. "Would these be the meadow flowers you brought me this way to see?"

Calliope looked up and blinked, orienting herself. Pre-occupied, she hadn't been aware of making the turn of the last corridor. "Umm…yes. They are lovely, are they not?"

"Indeed. You have a good eye for art," the dowager duchess mused. "You would get along well with my granddaughter-in-law, Emma Goswick, Viscountess Rathburn. She is an artist in her own right."

"Yes, we've met." Calliope cast aside the muddled line of her thoughts and wondered why it should matter to her when Everhart had become friends with Brightwell. It wasn't as if she'd played a part in it. "Lady Rathburn is a dear friend of my brother's wife. We share a common interest in needle-work, though I must admit your granddaughter-in-law has the greater skill."

The duchess turned away from the painting and regarded Calliope closely. "And where does your skill lie?"

"I am an excellent reader, Your Grace." The words spilled forth in a nervous jumble. All at once, Calliope felt like a dragonfly pinned to a board for scrutiny. She couldn't dare admit to gorging on romantic novels. "I'm nearly finished with an accounting of a French explorer's expedition to South America. It's quite fascinating."

Too late, she realized what she'd said and how closely the topic resembled Everhart's interests. The last thing she wanted to do was to give the wrong impression.

The dowager duchess angled her chin in such a way that it appeared all her attention honed in on the center of Calliope's pupils. "A woman of great confidence is allowed to fancy herself an explorer…when she is married, of course, and at her husband's side."

"Of course," Calliope agreed for agreement's sake. She was not going to have the same argument with the dowager duchess that she'd had with Everhart. "Shall we continue on toward the hothouse?"

"Yes, but perhaps we should see my grandson first. I must make certain you haven't persuaded him to embark on another expedition by your enthusiasm on the topic," the dowager duchess said with a hint of disapproval. "He is forever on the hunt for something he cannot name, or *will* not."

"Perhaps he is searching for that elusive prize of finding *himself*," Calliope blurted again, realizing far too late that it almost sounded as if she were coming to Everhart's defense. As if there were a level of familiarity between them.

"Very astute of you, Miss Croft." Surprisingly, the dowager duchess rewarded her with a wrinkled grin before she schooled her features again into a mask of cool regard. "Though for my grandson's sake, I would hope he could learn sooner rather than later that he can only find himself in the places he's already been."

Calliope held her tongue.

Then, nearing the map room, raised voices drew their attention.

"*Do you realize that every conversation we have revolves around Briar Heath?*"

"*Because it is where you belong!*" This was said with a hard edge of finality. Subject closed.

Before Calliope could offer to resume the tour of Fallow Hall, one of the French doors jerked open. Everhart's gaze collided with hers and hesitated. A vulnerability she'd never witnessed before seemed to reach out to her from those blue-green gems. Then it vanished.

He clenched his teeth hard enough to make the tendon along his jaw twitch before offering a stiff bow. "Grandmama, a pleasure. Miss Croft, as always." And without further ado, he set off down the hall at a steady limp.

"Everhart, your splint," Calliope said, alarmed to see him walking around with one booted leg while the other merely had a wool stocking exposed beneath the hem of buff breeches. He neither answered nor turned. Instead, he continued plodding down the hallway. "He should at least be carrying a cane," she huffed under her breath.

"Unfortunately, Miss Croft, we cannot save men from themselves. It would be a different world if we could," the dowager duchess said with a tsk. "Our task is to support them when they are weak and allow them to imagine that they are the stronger sex."

Calliope would have laughed at the absurdity of having such a conversation with the infamous dowager duchess, but her concern for Everhart would not abate. She stared after him, uncertain.

The dowager duchess tapped her cane. "One of us had better go after him before he injures himself again. Under the circumstances and with the distance between us growing, I feel that this task is left up to you, my dear." When Calliope looked at her in surprise, the dowager duchess made a shooing motion with her hand. "Hurry along now. We will finish our tour later this afternoon."

"I look forward to it, Your Grace." Calliope dipped into a curtsy and then rushed after Everhart. Before she turned the corner, however, she distinctly heard the dowager duchess's voice once again. Thankfully, the censure in her tone was not aimed at Calliope.

"*Clifford, you promised,*" the dowager duchess scolded. Apparently, even the estimable Duke of Heathcoat answered to a higher power.

CHAPTER FIFTEEN

Gabriel heard the quick tap of Calliope's soles against the stone tiles behind him but was in no mood to slow his pace. His leg ached. The sensation of pins and needles stabbed the bottom of his foot and climbed up his calf. More than anything, he wanted to go for a long ride. Preferably to the nearest ship. Without looking back.

"If you injure yourself again, your grandmother will blame me," Calliope said in a huff, emerging in his field of vision alongside him.

Unable to ignore her—not with her lips parted, her cheeks flushed, and with locks of honeyed hair brushing her cheeks—he stopped. "Why would my grandmother blame you?"

She blinked at him as if the answer were perfectly obvious. "She left you in my charge."

"Capable as you are, Miss Croft," he began, struggling between wanting to continue his course and wanting to reach out and tug on the tendril that drooped perilously close to her mouth, "I can manage on my own."

She shook her head. "Absolutely not. I must see you to your bedchamber." Without a by-your-leave, she took hold of his wrist, lifted his arm, and settled it over her shoulders, all the while securing herself to his side. "Come along, then."

He didn't budge and put forth a valiant effort not to enjoy the feel of her pressed against him. But who was he trying to fool? "You cannot escort me to my bedchamber."

"Of course I can." She attempted to persuade him by pushing against the lower region of his back and curling her small hand around his waist. The consequence of which was the supple pressure of her breast, the curve of her hip, and the length of her thigh, all pressed against him. "Your valet needs to tend to your limb."

"I am not an invalid, no matter what you may imagine." He could easily prove his point by turning into her embrace and allowing her to feel the part of his anatomy that desperately *did* require tending. "In addition, you must be wary of escorting any man to his bedchamber." Machinations fell so easily from the lips. Even now, there were a dozen waiting on his tongue. "And I am in a temper right now, where I would very much enjoy ravishing you. Thoroughly."

Taking a moment to digest his words, she stared, unblinking, into his eyes. Then, as if she noted sufficient evidence of his sincerity, she gestured past a dark walnut milieu table against the wall to a narrow archway. "Then I will escort you to the nearest sitting room instead. There is one not far down this corridor. Since it has begun to snow, the view should be quite lovely."

He found himself nodding in agreement. Relishing the feel of her against him, he forgot that he'd wanted no company. She had a way of making him forget quite a lot of things. The wager, for instance, which stated clearly how wrong it was to spend time alone with an unmarried, yet marriageable, young woman.

"Do you like the snow, then?" he asked, using a change of topic to dispel those worries.

"Is there anyone who doesn't enjoy the sight of an evergreen bough dusted with pristine, white snow? Or a path freshly covered and inviting one's first step?" Calliope's gaze brightened as she lifted her face to his, and in her eyes, he could see the image perfectly, even without a window near.

His heart thumped heavily, weighted down by all the secrets he kept from her and all the fears that had made him the man he was. Which really was no man at all. A man was reliable, steadfast, and never disappointed those he loved. And yet he had. All his life. He'd spent the last five years attempting to make up for that. Five years of denying himself in order to keep the worst of his crimes unknown.

"I cannot think of a single person who doesn't." His comment earned a smile that made him feel like a thief for taking it. He'd taken so much from her already. She could have had a life with Brightwell, if not for his own interference.

Calliope led him a short distance down what looked like a servant's passage. Since he'd broken his leg shortly after he'd moved in, Gabriel hadn't explored the manor completely. She assured him that it was simply an old part of the house.

Now, he found himself in the smallest room he'd ever entered. Even by closet standards, it was snug. There were only two pieces of furniture: a rosewood wine table adorned with a blue bud vase, holding a single red amaryllis; and an overstuffed yellow chair, the arms of which nearly reached both side walls. As it was, they had to turn sideways to step in to the small open area between the chair and the recessed window.

Lack of space aside, one feature made the journey worthwhile. No, make that two—the bare window, which hosted a view of the lush green forest beyond Fallow Hall; and the woman who took in all its glory, glittering with contentment like the sun against the snow.

The woman who still had her arm around his waist. The woman he wanted to kiss more than he wanted this damnable leg to cease aching. More than he wanted to plan a new expedition. In fact, he could easily imagine staying right here, kissing Calliope for all the days of his life—

He gulped a breath and blinked to clear his head. To clear those thoughts from his mind *and* his heart. But the air was filled with her scent, and a sweet, painful yearning filled his lungs.

"What is Briar Heath?" She looked up at him, her gaze filled with curiosity and concern.

The question speared through his thoughts readily enough. A cutting reminder of why he couldn't give in to temptation.

Gabriel moved apart from her, as much as he could in the snug space. "Briar Heath is my home." He exhaled, slumping into the chair. Then, leaning forward, he proceeded to massage his lower leg, though his true intention was to hide his expression from her inquisitive gaze.

"I don't understand," she said. "If you have a home, then why are you here at Fallow Hall?"

Why, indeed. "Because I once believed I could fight the Fates and outlast them."

Standing beside him, Calliope's finger absently traced the leaf pattern on the arm of the chair. "And you no longer believe that?"

Her question took him aback until he realized that he'd said *once believed*. Had a change occurred within him of which he was not aware? Instead of answering, he redirected. "Why take such an interest?"

Her fingertip stilled. "Perhaps I like stories and merely want to hear yours."

Curious, he sat up and studied her. There was an intensity about her that shimmered around her like a halo. *She could be a siren without singing a note*, he thought, knowing he would gladly dash himself upon the rocks to be with her. It was becoming more difficult to fight the urge.

The notion was as frightening as it was appealing. "And will I hear your story in return?"

"*My story?*" She traced the leaf pattern again, paying no attention to the hand he rested a mere inch from hers.

"About the man you love."

She colored. "I'm certain the tale would be of no interest to you."

Slowly, he took her hand, his fingers lightly grazing hers, gliding along the delicate ridges of her knuckles to the smooth silk of her flesh, where the faintest of blue veins marked a path, like a river on a map. "Allow me to decide."

"Very well," she said quietly, staring down at their hands without shying away. "But you will begin."

His fingers, those reckless cartographers, wanted to continue their exploration beyond the lace cuff at her wrist, but instead, he turned her hand and began a new journey over the landscape of her palm. Feeling like a gypsy fortuneteller, he wondered if he could see her future. More importantly, he wondered if he could see *his*.

"When I was a boy," he said, barely able to resist lifting her palm for a kiss, "I lived at Briar Heath with my mother and father. There was laughter and joy. Until one day there... wasn't. And that is my story."

At this, she pulled away. "That is not a story, Everhart. That was a poorly veiled warning to me. You wish to make me feel as uncomfortable and guilty as possible for asking my question. That is unfair." Calliope took a half step in retreat, pressing her hands together. "If that is the game, then I will tell you that my tale involves love and hope, only to have it ripped from me in the cruelest way imaginable. And that is my story."

He rested his head against the back of the chair and let out a breath. "Aren't we a sad pair?"

When she set her hands on her hips, her breasts jutted outward. By the narrow-eyed look she gave, he decided now was not the time to tell her how much he admired her figure when she stood like that. "I want to hear about your adventures," she said.

At the mention of adventure, the memory of his mother's voice whispered to him. *I'm going to send you on an adventure, Gabriel. A noble quest.*

He frowned and leaned forward again to massage his leg. "You've been talking to my grandmother."

"She loves you very much."

"That dragon?" Though he tried to be angry, he couldn't be. His grandmother was too dear to him, and he knew her intentions were good, albeit misguided. "Yes, I suppose she does. I spent a good portion of my life under her roof."

"Why did you not live at Briar Heath?"

One moment, he was looking at the embroidered hem of Calliope's dress, and in the next, he was looking at her face as she kneeled down before him, her face mere inches from his. In her expression, he read curiosity but also knowing. She refused to let him hide from her questions. He swallowed and found himself retreating against the back of the chair. "It held too many memories."

"But good memories—the joy and laughter you mentioned." Seemingly undeterred, she held her ground and even settled her hands, though tentatively, atop his shin and began to mimic the kneading motions he'd employed. A thick surge of lust rushed up his leg and flooded the appendage that shamelessly jolted beneath the fall of his breeches, preening for her attention as she continued her less-than-skillful but utterly seductive ministrations.

While he was capable of doing so, he leaned forward and stilled her hands. "No. Now it is your turn. Tell me about this man that you still love…even *after* kissing me senseless."

"I did no such thing." Her gaze slipped to his mouth. "You still had your wits about you."

Gabriel hadn't had his wits about him for quite some time. Proving it, he lifted both her hands, gently turned them, and then pressed a kiss to the center of each palm. Then, nudging aside the lace at her wrist, he kissed her there too. "I suggest you tell me your story before I set out to re-create the events of the other night."

Calliope didn't pull away as he expected her to do, the way a young woman in the presence of a practiced seducer ought. "Perhaps that would be preferable to suffering humiliation. I cannot bear to hear you laugh when I tell you. I wish I'd never mentioned it."

Her words surprised him. "You would rather risk ruination by me, here in this very room, than tell me your story?"

She stood, slipping her hands free of his before she turned toward the window. Exhaling deeply, her breath fogged the glass. "I have never met him, not in the traditional sense. Or any sense, really."

Gabriel stared at her, unable to look away. Unable to breathe. Was she confessing what he thought—*hoped?* "And yet, you claim to love him."

"Yes," she whispered. "He wrote me a letter that allowed me to believe there was one person for me. One person who saw the secret longings I kept hidden. One person who'd read my heart as if it were in the pages of a story."

Before Gabriel's eyes, his questions, his dreams, his fears were all answered in the journey of her fingertip in the cloudy circle of condensation.

My love, she wrote. *My siren.*

The words hovered there, trapped against the glass, as they'd been trapped within him five years ago. She loved him. She admitted it. He wanted to shout it to the world. He wanted to leap up with exultation and confess everything— that he'd been consumed by his emotion, but terrified and ultimately cowardly.

That he still couldn't marry her.

That his selfish action of writing that letter was responsible for her refusing Brightwell. And how—*bugger it all*—if it wasn't for Gabriel, she would be married now to a husband worthy of her.

Elbows propped against his knees, Gabriel leaned forward and buried his face in his hands. *My love, I am wrecked.*

Calliope stared at the words she'd written on the glass and quickly wiped them clean with the side her hand before she turned to face Everhart. The sight of him with his face in his hands caused unbidden tears to prick the backs of her eyes. Was he laughing at her? Laughing at the fool she'd been?

With a delicate clearing of her throat, she dispelled the tears. "Ah, yes. It is quite the amusing tale. A lovelorn debutante who falls in love with a Casanova letter, only to realize that the words meant nothing to him." She laughed, not wanting to give away how deeply she was wounded. "He quickly went on to write six other letters, leaving a trail of heartsick women in his wake. At least for a time. Some of the others have married."

Everhart looked up, surprising her with his severe expression. He did not look as if he found humor in her situation at all. Quite the opposite. "How could you love him after that?"

She offered an absent lift of a single shoulder, hiding the odd flutter she felt beneath her breast as she gazed back at him. "Oh, perhaps I was merely in love with the idea of him. Of what love could be like."

His brow furrowed. "Yet you would marry him if he revealed himself?"

"No." She shook her head, determined. "I would finally have revenge."

"Revenge?" He swallowed, his expression blank.

"Of course. I would expose his identity to the entire *ton* and make a mockery of him." At least, that's what she told herself. But in doing so, she would be making a mockery of herself as well. Still, she couldn't let Everhart believe that she was incapable of managing her own affairs. "That is the end of my story, and you, my friend, have a promise to keep."

"I hardly think now is the time for—"

"Everhart," she interrupted. "You may want people to believe a lot of things about you that are not true, but I know you keep your promises."

Before her eyes, he went strangely pale. "How could you know that?"

She'd all but paid the man a compliment, and he looked as if she'd threatened to whisk him off to Gretna Green and marry him. Rakes were so silly.

"The first evidence I put to you is the wager," she began. "Do you think your friends, or even mere acquaintances in society, would speak well of you if you did not uphold your honor and pay your debts? Everyone knows you are not a cheat. Montwood and Danvers certainly know it. And I know as much after our brief...*dance* in the map room, when you told me that you would not marry me." With those words, she lowered her voice and glanced over the back of the chair to ensure their conversation was still private.

"I have read many a novel where the gentleman promises marriage, when all the while he anticipates leaving the young woman to suffer ruination," she said. The wonderful thing about Everhart was that he didn't even bat an eye at her for using a novel as an example. "And need I point out that you were the one who took Brightwell on a tour of the continent after I...well, you know."

Everhart glanced away. "That was different. I owed him that much."

Owed him? What a peculiar thing to say, though she assumed he must be speaking of a gambling debt.

"You also run this house, even though you've disguised your involvement." When his gaze returned to hers, and he opened his mouth as if to form a denial, she waved a hand, shushing him. "Valentine, Mrs. Merkel, and the entire staff count on you. It will shock you to hear it, but that is a measure of a reliable man. Therefore, I know you will keep this one small promise of telling me about Briar Heath."

He stared at her as if she'd baffled him. "Be careful, Miss Croft, or I will become very jealous of the man who holds your heart."

Apparently, his humor was restored. Good. She felt as if she'd done him a service. "Even though I plan to make a mockery of him?"

"Even then." He whispered the words in a low promise that, for reasons she didn't understand, made her pulse quicken.

Now, she was certain *she'd* gone pale. Or perhaps it was quite the opposite and now all the blood was rushing to her cheeks. "I want to hear your story, Everhart."

"Since you told me a story that no one else knows, I will return the sentiment." His blue-green gaze remained fixed, holding her captive. "As you have learned from my grandmother, I began my life with an adventurer's soul that my mother indulged. Every day after my lessons, she would send me on a quest. Nothing grand—no beast slaying or mountain scaling—but more of a retrieval of treasures, like biscuits from the kitchen, and Father's snuffbox that he kept hidden at the back of his desk drawer."

Calliope smiled, already engrossed in his tale. In her mind, she could see this little bright-eyed boy accepting these tasks as if they were as important as beast slaying. She eased herself down into the window casement across from him, eager for more. "And did you have a wooden sword in case there *were* beasts along the way?"

He smiled, though less like a rake and more like boy. "A very effective tool when marching through a forest of zinnias."

"Oh dear," she said with a laugh, imagining a flower garden lay to waste at the feet of the boy he once was.

"As I recall, the gardener and my father were none too happy, but my mother accepted the carnage as the spoils of war and arranged them in a large urn…" His words drifted off, his gaze now focused on the flower in the budvase beside her.

Calliope's amusement drifted off as well. In her mind's eye, she saw those zinnias in the urn slowly wilt and die, leaving an emptiness behind. And her heart broke for that little boy.

"The last adventure she gave me was to find the feather of a phoenix, the eye of dragon, and a string of tiny white bells. I searched endlessly—or at least for what seemed like an age to a ten-year-old boy—but I could only find a red feather on the lawn and a green stone from the reflecting pool, but no white bells anywhere. So I gave up and returned with all that I had, only to find her"—he drew in an unsteady breath—"sleeping in the garden chair where I left her. But even at that age, I knew she wasn't sleeping."

"*Everhart.*" Tears rushed down her cheeks before she was even aware of crying. "I'm so sorry. I should not have made you tell the story." Until this moment, she'd had no idea how it would affect her. In such a short amount of time, she'd grown fond of that boy adventurer, yet never even knew him. She only knew the man before her. And if she wasn't mistaken, she was fond of him as well. More than fond. Much more.

Everhart stood and pulled her to her feet. "I carry no handkerchiefs, Miss Croft, and the reason is likely that I never intend to make a woman cry in my presence." He held her face in his hands and began wiping the tears away with the length of his thumbs. "Now, what am I to do with you, hmm?"

Kiss me, she thought, lifting her gaze.

He seemed to read her thoughts easily and shook his head. "I would not be the man of honor you claimed I was mere moments ago if I kissed you. Because I've quickly realized how far removed we are from where the servants tread. I know very well that we would remain undisturbed for hours on end, here in our little nook. And I could make very good use of that amount of time."

Calliope loved it when he said things like that. She had little doubt that she would enjoy all the ways he would make good use of the time. But he was right.

On a sigh of regret, she turned and faced the window again. Even before she could hope for such a thing, his arms settled around her middle and drew her back against him.

In that moment, Calliope knew—if she wasn't careful—she was in danger of losing her heart completely again. The first time, she'd been taken unawares. This time, however, it was happening so gradually that she still felt as if she could stop it at any time and survive. She only hoped she wasn't fooling herself.

"Had your mother been ill?"

He nodded, his cheek brushing against her temple. "I didn't know it at the time, but she'd lost a child a month or two before. She'd lost several over the years. Apparently, the strain had taken its toll."

"Perhaps she knew," Calliope whispered, thinking of what it must have been like. She knew from her father's weak heart that he tired easily. "Perhaps she hadn't wanted to worry you with how tired and frail she'd become. So instead, she sent you on an adventure…"

She couldn't finish. Her voice cracked and another sob threatened, but she reined it in, holding steady for that little boy she saw in her mind's eye.

"Oh, Calliope." Everhart bent his forehead to her shoulder and held her tighter. "What are you doing to me?"

"Making you forget being about angry with your father?"

He lifted his head and pressed a kiss to her cheek before releasing her. "You're making me forget a lot of things, and that is not in your best interest."

When she turned around, she watched him incline his head and gesture for her to leave the room. It was not meant as an insult, she knew, but in that instant, she realized the importance of what had changed within her. For her own sake, she left him alone in the little nook, and sincerely hoped she was not falling in love with him.

But who was she fooling?

Chapter Sixteen

The next day, Gabriel wondered how one conversation with Calliope Croft could change so much within him. Yet it wasn't just one conversation, was it? It was a collection of moments that had all started with that first glimpse of her.

Calliope had shed a different light on his life. She saw him as a man of honor. A man who kept his promises. A man who was honest and reliable. More than anything, he wanted to live up to those expectations.

The weight he carried with him suddenly lifted. Either that, or it didn't feel quite so heavy after all. It certainly didn't frighten him any longer—that much was true. In fact, shortly after he'd left the little nook they'd shared and had Fitzroy wrap his leg, he'd sought out his father. Meeting the duke's austere gaze, Gabriel had apologized and then asked about the state of Briar Heath.

For hours, he and his father settled into a comfortable exchange. They'd spoken of the place that was once a happy home and the repairs needed in order for it to be inhabitable once again. While the caretakers had done an admirable job of managing the house and grounds, there were larger issues that needed to be addressed. Gabriel had made a mental note of all that his father mentioned from his correspondence with the steward, Mr. Elliott.

Now, early this morning, Gabriel wrote to the steward with an inquiry. He also sent a missive to the caretakers, Mr. and Mrs. Wicksom, with a friendly greeting and a desire to meet in the coming weeks. He was just applying his seal when Valentine appeared in the map room doorway.

"Everything is as you requested, my lord," he said with a bow.

Eager, Gabriel pushed away from the desk. He couldn't wait to begin this day. Standing, he glanced down at the Hessian on one leg and a gardener's boot on the other. But when one wanted to venture out of doors in the snow with a healing leg, one had to improvise. "And Miss Croft?"

"Waiting in the foyer, as per your instructions." Stepping aside, Valentine waited for Gabriel to precede him down the hall.

Gabriel walked easier today, his leg less stiff but still sore above the ankle where it had been broken. In time, he knew, it would mend. "Did she ask many questions?"

"Several, my lord."

He grinned. "And she still has no idea why?"

"Miss Croft concluded that her 'errand,' as she put it, consists of venturing out of doors since she was asked to wear her coat and hat."

"No doubt she is cross with me for having her roused so early." It was only an hour past dawn, but he hadn't been able to wait a moment longer. Hopefully, she would quickly forgive him. In a few more steps, he would find out for himself.

Emerging from the hall, Gabriel saw Calliope standing at the foot of the stairs in her blue redingote with white fur trim and a bonnet to match. The annoyance he feared wasn't there at all. Instead, he witnessed bright eyes and cheeks in the high color of excitement.

"Valentine," he began, keeping his voice low as they neared, "you did tell her that it was *I* who sent the request, didn't you?"

"Of course, my lord."

Pleasure had him reeling. Last night they hadn't spoken at dinner, not with her at such an inconvenient distance down the table. And afterward in the parlor, she'd kept his grandmother company after their game of Anagrams. There hadn't been a chance to speak with her privately. That was when he'd come up with the idea of having her all to himself this morning, before anyone else awoke. He knew they would only have a short time before her brother sent a carriage for her. Gabriel was determined to make the most of each moment.

"Good morning, Miss Croft," he said when at last he reached her side. "Are you ready for an outing?"

She gifted him with a warm smile and settled her hand in the crook of his proffered arm. "Surprisingly, yes."

Taking his hat from Valentine at the open door, they crossed the threshold and headed out into the brisk winter morning air. He breathed in as if it were the first breath ever to fill his lungs. Beside him, Calliope gasped.

"Are you taking me on a sleigh ride?" She clutched his arm tighter, not taking her gaze away from the red painted sleigh awaiting them, along with a single dapple gray in the harness.

Even though he knew he was standing firmly on the ground, he felt that familiar plummeting sensation deep inside. It was like the moment when he'd first seen her at Almack's, and he'd felt the earth slip from beneath his feet. This time, however, it did not frighten him. He merely held Calliope to his side and hoped she would fall with him. "Does that please you?"

She turned to him, tilting her face in a way that made the brims of their hats touch, and drew in a breath. "It does. Very much indeed."

It took a force of will and a charging dog for Gabriel to resist kissing Calliope. Out of the corner of his eye, he saw Duke run a path around the sleigh. The dog paused to sniff the horse and earned a small kick in response before he settled himself inside the sleigh with paws draped over the helm.

Gabriel grinned down at Calliope. "It appears we have our chaperone."

"And our chaperone is as eager as I am," she said with a laugh, eyes merry.

A moment later, they were settled side by side on the snug seat, a fringed blanket draped over their knees. The intimacy of it did not escape him. He was fully aware of every place her body pressed against his, as if they wore no coats at all. Or no clothes, for that matter.

"I'm ready to embark if you are, Everhart."

He looked directly into her gaze and a rush of warmth coursed through him. "Yes. I am ready."

Another layer of fresh snow had fallen overnight. It kicked up in the wake of the sleigh like dusting sugar sent to scatter along the paths they forged. His arm brushed hers as he handled the reins, and he noted with pleasure that she didn't pull away. They neared the inner rim of the forest, farther away from the house.

Calliope slipped her hand free of the fur muff on her lap and linked her arm with his. "This is the best surprise of my life. I cannot imagine a better way to begin a morning."

He angled his head so that his lips brushed against the soft, cool shell of her ear. "Our imaginations differ in that regard. I can think of a number of pleasurable ways to begin a morning." *And each one of them with you.* "Though I am content to be right here."

"We are in view of the west wing. It will appear as though you are kissing me if you continue to tilt your head." Her attempt at scolding was undermined by the way she squeezed his arm tighter and slid closer.

"Then I will drive around to the south," he answered, with a cluck of his tongue to the horse and a snap of the reins.

She let out a laugh as the sleigh jolted. "And have the kitchen staff staring after us? I don't know about you, but I should not enjoy burnt porridge."

"Why, Miss Croft, are you attempting to lure me away from the house and prying eyes?"

"Of course not. Although aside from Duke"—she reached forward to pet their companion, who answered with a low appreciative *woof*—"we are here without a chaperone. I would not want your father or grandmother to entertain the wrong idea about my intentions toward you."

He grinned. "Do you have intentions toward me?"

"I fully *intend* to enjoy this sleigh ride with my friend, for it may be the last I have with such good company. I'm certain my brother will have sent a carriage by now and that I will be leaving in a day or two."

The reminder caused his stomach to knot. He didn't want her to go. Not ever. "And you will be glad, no doubt, to see the last of Fallow Hall?"

"Not *all* of Fallow Hall," she said with a smile. "Only the reclusive curmudgeon who holes up in the map room."

"Why, Miss Croft, you are quite deadly with your parry."

"Those who tease without mercy deserve retribution in kind." She looked straight ahead. "Surely, you must know that I will be sad to leave."

Was there a wistful gleam in her gaze just now, or had he imagined it? "Then I shall make this day one to remember."

"You already have, Everhart," she whispered.

Gabriel decided, then and there, that he needed to speak with Griffin Croft about old business. Snapping on the reins, he urged the dapple gray into a canter. Behind them, the snow plumed like waves rising from the sea, and he could easily imagine them sailing off together. "Give a wave to our little window nook as we pass."

Calliope waved merrily and then abruptly lowered her hand. "What if your grandmother is awake and believes I'm waving at her?"

"Then she will know we have nothing to hide."

"At last I feel as if you've forgiven me," she said, turning back to him, her cheeks rosy. "We are able to have fun in the same manner you do with all your friends."

He laughed at her incorrect assumptions. "I believe your only fault is your horrendous memory. Need I remind you again that I do not have women friends? And I certainly have never taken anyone on a sleigh ride first thing in the morning."

She stared at him for a moment with a grin, as if she believed this was part of a joke to make her laugh. Then she must have seen something in his expression that told her the truth. Her eyes widened.

He wondered if she would allow herself to believe what she saw.

"Are you still trying to seduce me, Everhart?"

Reaching the path beyond the Grecian folly in the east, he headed north and slowed the horse. Taking the reins in one hand, he angled toward her. "Not this time."

Calliope's breath came out in a cloud of vapor. Since yesterday, and perhaps even before that, Everhart had acted differently toward her. How was it possible for him to look at her with such intensity and somehow seem tender at the same time? The two descriptions felt oceans apart to her, and she could not reconcile them.

This close proximity kept her far too distracted to think clearly. A flurry of emotions and sensations stirred within her with such force that she could barely contain them. Restless, she shifted beside him. "Why not?"

One corner of his mouth lifted in a rakish smirk, even while he tsked at her. "That is the wrong question to ask."

Not to her. Not right now. Not with his lips mere inches from hers.

She squeezed his arm tighter and leaned into him—

Just then, the dog barked, startling her as he leapt out of the sleigh. A group of cardinals suddenly took flight, their red wings standing out in sharp contrast against the snowy landscape. Strangely, Calliope wasn't even aware that the sleigh had stopped.

Other than kissing, only one thought came to mind. "Phoenix feathers," she whispered.

"What?"

"Over there." Her gaze reconnected with his, her vision clearing enough to see that she'd surprised him. With no vapor forming in front of his nose or mouth, it appeared he was holding his breath. She wondered if she should not have mentioned anything from their private conversation. And now she was holding *her* breath. "The gardener harvested the sunflower seeds from the hothouse. The cardinals were enjoying a feast a moment ago. We could look for red feathers…if you like."

Everhart's breath came out in a whoosh. The moist warmth of it brushed her lips and then tingled, as if it turned to snowflakes. Somehow, his hand had found its way to hers inside the muff, and he squeezed it gently. "Then let's explore. Together."

Even though there was no great distance from the sleigh to the ground, he settled his hands at her waist and lifted her high so that she had to clutch his shoulders. Out of breath, she stared down into his face, which was as bright and alive as she felt. "You should worry about your limb."

"I will allow you the task of worrying about my limbs and what state they are in." Slowly, he began to lower her down in front of him. "I find that notion rather appealing."

Their coats grazed each other, gripping and pressing in places that caused her pulse to race. Even so, the friction was not enough. She wanted more. She wanted him. And she wanted…to remain here like this forever. "You are not in pain?"

He brought their faces level, their bodies flush. "In this moment, pain is the very last thing I'm feeling."

She reached up to lift his John Bull away from his head and tossed it back to the seat. Just in case kissing was the *first* thing on his mind, she wanted no barriers between them. True, they were still in view of the house but somewhere along the way, she'd stopped caring if they were seen in an embrace. This desire for him was so overwhelming that it sent a shot of alarm through her. It felt both sudden and eternal all at once.

Recognize the soul that had inexplicably crashed into yours…

Even as the words from the love letter formed in her mind, deep down, she knew that she shouldn't be thinking of them while in the arms of Everhart. She shouldn't be feeling this inexplicable connection. She shouldn't be risking her heart again. Hadn't she already learned not to fall in love with a man who had no interest in her beyond a passing fancy?

Apparently not.

Calliope wanted to live page to page, but the notion still frightened her. She tilted her face away. "You should probably put me down, regardless."

Everhart did not listen. Instead, he wrapped his arms around her waist and carried her through the snow toward a cedar tree nearby. He lowered her beneath the sparse evergreen branches, where there were more pine needles underfoot than snow.

The house was hidden from view now. When she glanced at him, she noted that his smirk had turned into a grim line.

Without a word, he untied her bonnet, lifted it away, and settled it on a branch out of her reach.

When he returned to her, his blue-green eyes swallowed up by dark onyx, he took her face in his hands. "Forget him, Calliope."

"I don't know what you—"

"Forget the letter. Forget the man who wrote it. Forget everything in the past and think of the man before you now."

Then he kissed her, cutting off her denial.

He kissed her hard, a claiming of lips and tongue, a nip of teeth.

Gabriel knew it was insane to be jealous of himself, but he felt it nonetheless. The instant he'd seen her gaze grow distant, he'd known exactly what she'd been thinking. *The letter.*

Jealousy ripped him apart inside. He didn't want her to think about the idea she had of him, of the man he'd been five years ago. He wanted her to think of him now. The man he was right here in this very moment. He refused to allow her to think of anyone else.

Drawing on her mouth, he breathed her into the deepest part of him and earned a low purr from her throat. The sound drove him mad. His mouth roamed, exploring her corners, the underside of her chin, her throat. Somewhere along the way, he'd stripped off his gloves, and now his fingers made quick work of the looped fastenings of her redingote, all the way down to her knees. On the return journey upward, he pushed the wool and fur trim wide, exposing her Nile green day dress.

Gabriel plunged forward, pressing against her, tilting his hips into hers. The breathy moan that escaped her nearly undid him, and he stilled. "Who is kissing you, Calliope?"

Eyes closed, lips parted, she arched against him. "You are, Everhart."

"*Gabriel.*" His hips rocked slowly as he tried to calm the churning sea within him. This was about pleasure, not possession, though the urge to possess her, right here against the cedar tree, was still inside him.

"*Mmm...Gabriel.*"

His lips plotted a path along her jaw to the tiny, plump lobe of her ear. "Even better. You, and you alone, will add the *mmm* before my name. Always." Yes, *always.* He liked the sound of that.

Hands splayed over her waist, they rose like the tide to her breasts. He raked his thumbs over the faint, taut peaks of each breast. The deep purring sound came again, only this time from his own throat. How long had he waited for this, years? No, centuries. Eons.

Aroused to the point of bursting, he rolled his hips against hers. His name escaped her lips on a moan. The need to touch her, to feel her flesh, to taste the ripe fruit of this uncharted territory consumed him.

His hands roamed beneath her arms and to her back, searching for a row of buttons. He found none. Instantly, he knew the fastenings were hidden in front. Grinning against her lips, he traced her modest neckline until he found the small hooks. The soft muslin front fell away. Delving beneath the thickness of her petticoat, he tugged at her stays and chemise in one motion. Then finally, he held her warm, quivering flesh in his hand.

She was perfect. Beautiful. *His.*

He panted, hard and heavy. This was the pinnacle of his journey. *The first pinnacle.* Calliope opened her eyes, slowly, drowsily. Releasing her grip on his shoulder, she settled her gloved hand over his. She whispered his name against his lips, as if declaring this terrain his. *And his alone.*

Gabriel agreed with a nod, nudging her lips apart for his kiss. Gently now, his thumb traced the small circle of ruched flesh before he brushed the peak. She trembled against him, her jagged breath filling his mouth.

"You're cold," he said, only to have her shake her head in disagreement. "*Shh…let me warm you.*" Proving his argument, he dipped his head and set his heated mouth to her breast.

Crying out, her fingers clutched the back of his head, pulling him closer. "*Gabriel. Yes.*"

He liked those words even better than *mmm…Gabriel.* Flicking his tongue over her crest, he teased and taunted it until it was firm as a pebble. Then he drew on her flesh, suckling her long and deep, taking her to the edge. She moaned his name again.

Unconscionably eager and with little finesse, he lifted the hem of her dress and petticoat and settled his hand against her silken thigh. Lightly kneading, coaxing, he drifted higher until he felt her. Soft, warm, and—*ahh*—wet. *For him.*

A whimper tore from her throat. Sweeping his tongue over her sweet flesh once more, he lifted his mouth away from her breast and took her lips again. In the narrow haven between her thighs, he cupped her. Then he shuddered, barely holding on to control.

His need for her pleasure, the longing to be inside her seeking his, overwhelmed him. He'd never felt this way before. No other woman could bring him to the brink without so much as the sounds she made.

He stroked the swollen seam of her sex, before breaching the heated folds to find her utterly drenched. Another shudder coursed through him. His hips rocked of their own volition. He didn't know if he would last. But he could not stop.

Her breathing quickened. Her teeth nipped at his lower lip. Soft wanton purrs rose from her throat. All of it told him that her need was equally as urgent. With the tip one finger, he circled her.

Instantly, she came apart in his hands, crying out. She clung to him, quaking, her hips writhing against his hand.

He yearned to be inside her. Right now. The force was so strong that he bit down on his cheek until he tasted blood.

"Hold still," he begged. Out of breath, he pressed his forehead against the bark of the tree beside her head. Releasing the hem of her dress, he settled his hand at her waist, unwilling to abstain from contact. "I'm drugged by desire...and would likely...take you...right here...in the snow."

Behind him, the dog barked, adding a growl for good measure. Soon, Gabriel felt a series of tugs at his greatcoat. Looking down to his side, he found that Duke was rather earnest in his endeavor.

A semblance of sanity returned. Gabriel thought about where they stood, what he'd done to her, *and especially* what he'd almost done. He would have changed their lives irrevocably. More than that, he'd been willing to. And if he were honest with himself, he still was.

"It appears that our chaperone is doing his duty after all." Calliope blushed as she went about arranging her clothes.

"Though, perhaps, he was not quite as vigilant as he should have been."

"Here. Allow me." On unsteady legs, Gabriel pulled away from her. Fighting the desire to remove her clothes altogether, somehow he managed to put her back to rights. Then he tipped up her chin and held her gaze. "I do not want you to have any regrets, Calliope."

She let out a breath of a laugh that brushed his lips. "At the moment, regret is the farthest thing from my mind."

"I could change that, if you like." He grinned as he leaned in to taste her lips once more. But the dog jerked the hem of Gabriel's coat hard enough to draw him back.

Calliope reached down and patted the dog's head. "You were very good to save us, Duke. Otherwise, Everhart's rakish skills would have sent me home quite altered."

"And we would be in quite the proper fix." Gabriel was not inclined to thank him but could not resist crouching down beside Calliope to pet the beast. Astonishingly, he still felt a wide grin on his face.

However, Calliope's response was quick to remove it. "Not *we*," she said. "I know you well enough not to expect your actions to be dictated by societal obligation."

"You should," he growled, annoyed that her expectations of him were so low, no matter what he'd professed in the map room the other night. "Understand that what happened between us—and what could have happened—was not simply because I am a rake."

"I like the rake in you, Everhart," she said softly. "Even more, I like knowing what to expect from you."

"You expected me to seduce you, and that is what you would've preferred?" He frowned. He should have known that the woman who read the last page of a novel first would feel this way. "Would it obliterate your expectations of me if I told you that I never intended on seducing you when I planned this outing?"

She smiled the way Eve must have when she'd offered Adam the first bite of apple. "Didn't you?"

Damn. She was right. He was always thinking of seducing her.

He scrubbed a hand over his knitted brow. Out of the corner of his eye, a flash of color drew his attention to a lone red feather lying atop the snow. Reaching out, he picked it up and twirled it between the tip of his thumb and forefinger.

"Oh, look!" Calliope exclaimed.

Thinking she was going to comment on the feather, he held it out for her. Instead, he saw her gaze on the ground at Duke's feet. Before Gabriel could blink or draw in a breath, she reached down and lifted a speckled green stone resting above a sparse bed of needles. "The eye of a dragon." Her eyes widened when she looked at the feather in his grasp. "And a phoenix feather."

"I often find them not too far apart from each other."

"What about the white bells?"

He thought of what he kept in the leather pouch, remembering that day five years ago when he had finally found all three together, but he did not tell her. Not yet. "There has only been one time when I have found all three on one single quest."

And that moment had changed him forever.

Gabriel pressed the feather into her glove as a token. A promise. He was ready to confess everything.

"Perhaps we will find them yet this morning," she said and then gasped. She straightened and immediately started fastening her coat. "*Morning! Oh dear*—I nearly forgot. Your grandmother asked me to have tea with her in the morning room. Do you suppose I'm too late?"

His confession would have to wait for now. "It is early yet," he assured her but wasn't entirely certain.

Gabriel retrieved her hat and led her back to the sleigh. On his mind was his plan to court her and give her back all of the years that he'd stolen from both of them. Of course, this was assuming that she felt the same way toward him. Right now, however, she was in a rush. It was not the time for such questions.

Yet there was one way he could find out if they were of like minds.

"Just so you know, my grandmother prefers lemon in her tea and tends to approve of anyone whom shares her taste." And if Calliope cared for him at all—and not the man who wrote the letter—then her choice would be simple.

Sitting beside him, Calliope quirked her well-kissed lips. "Does she? Well, it so happens that I prefer mint in mine."

That was not the response he'd hoped for.

Frowning, Gabriel snapped the reins. "I'm relieved to know you're not interested in making a favorable impression. We rakes enjoy knowing we are safe from marriage-minded young women."

Chapter Seventeen

Calliope rushed to the morning room. After the outing with Gabriel, she'd barely had time to don a less wrinkled dress. Her hair was still unkempt, however, but there was no more she could do. Tardiness showed an unforgiveable lack of respect—even more so than arriving disheveled—and contrary to what Everhart thought, she *did* want to make a favorable impression on the dowager duchess.

Why?

Calliope wondered the same thing. Already she knew her reason was something more than simply wanting to please one of the *ton*'s most formidable dragons. Much more.

Reaching the doorway, she gulped in air and released it slowly before stepping into the room. She expected her cousin to be in attendance already, but the dowager duchess and an upstairs maid were the only occupants of the pale blue sitting room.

Gabriel's grandmother looked over to the clock on the mantel and then to Calliope. She was one minute late. Only one; that wasn't too terrible. "Forgive me, Your Grace," she said, dipping into a curtsy.

Making no comment, the dowager duchess gestured to the chair directly across the low table from her place on the gold silk settee. "I trust you enjoyed your outing this morning, Miss Croft."

Calliope felt a rush of panic. Had the dowager duchess seen them together and without a chaperone? "Very much, though it is the only time such an outing has occurred. I have spent the majority of my time indoors. With my cousin." Who was not here to corroborate her story.

The dowager duchess looked to the empty seat and then summoned the maid to pour the tea. "Your cousin sent her regrets this morning. She is...unwell. I do hope your high color does not mean you are becoming ill too."

Calliope lifted her hands to her face, trying to cool her cheeks. Absently, she wondered if her lips were swollen as well. "I don't believe so, Your Grace."

"Good. I've always found that those who come from larger families have heartier constitutions."

Calliope glanced at the dowager duchess, who had an air of careless disregard as she folded her hands in her lap, waiting patiently. On the tray was an assortment of small dishes filled with sugar, milk, lemon slices, and even mint leaves. After what Gabriel had mentioned a few moments ago, she knew this was a test.

Did Gabriel care whether or not his grandmother approved of her?

Her heart quickened. Calliope was no longer the young debutante who'd been so easily swept off her feet. The truth was, she never would have allowed Gabriel—or wanted him—to seduce her if she didn't love him already.

Love him.

But wait…wasn't she still falling? Surely, it was like stumbling after tripping over a hem. She still had the chance to right herself. Didn't she?

Shaken, she already knew the answer.

Love.

It had taken her unaware again. This time, it was different. Real. Tangible.

Reaching forward, Calliope picked up the tongs. She made her choice, her hand surprisingly steady.

The lemon slid into the dark liquid without a ripple. Yet she felt as if a great wave had risen out of her cup and washed over her. In this one simple act, a profound realization took hold. By choosing a slice of lemon, she was declaring her love for Gabriel.

She'd had no idea that tea with the dowager duchess would be such a monumental occurrence in her life.

"Your family is moderately sized, with you the second eldest, beneath your brother and above your three sisters," the dowager duchess continued, adding a slice of lemon to her own tea as if nothing of great importance had transpired. Or as if she'd expected nothing less. "Do twins run in your family?"

Calliope was still reeling. It took a moment for her to catch up to the dowager duchess's question. It surprised her that the dowager duchess knew so much about the Crofts, including the fact that Phoebe and Asteria were twins.

Had she passed the test, she wondered, or was this another part of it?

Calliope nodded. "On my mother's side, my uncle has two sets of twins among his seven children."

"*Seven*. Good heavens, what a number." The dowager duchess's eyes widened, her cup paused in midair. Then she pursed her lips and tilted her head, as if in contemplation, before she returned the cup to the saucer. "The important news is that you are used to large families. As you know, until his father remarried, Gabriel was an only child. Though he dotes on his siblings, the years between them are too great to have offered him much companionship. I've always thought that he is of a nature that would do well with a large family."

Suddenly, Calliope remembered the wager. The light fluttering of her heart stopped.

How could she have forgotten? The three gentlemen living here had declared not to marry for a year. Or perhaps, not to marry at all. What if she was the only one suffering from this affliction? After all, Gabriel had made no declaration.

The dark liquid in her teacup had turned sour. And now, her fleeting hope wavered, like the slice of lemon on the surface.

To her companion, Calliope nodded in agreement but did not say a word. It was not her place to inform the dowager duchess that Gabriel had no intention of marrying or of starting a family, large or small.

She recognized her own pang of remorse. These days with Gabriel had opened her heart to love once more. Unfortunately, she had a peculiar tendency to fall in love with men who only pretended an interest in her.

From the window in the north tower, Gabriel stared out at the cedar tree across the expanse of snow, and smiled. The sleigh tracks nearby were still visible, even though it had been hours since he'd had Calliope in his arms. He wanted those marks to remain there forever.

"I'm disappointed, Everhart," a voice said from a distance behind him. "You're making it far too easy for your friends to win the wager."

Gabriel glanced over his shoulder to see that Brightwell had entered the map room. His friend wore no easy grin or teasing expression, and the lack of it caused apprehension to settle like a vise at the back of his neck. "I don't know what you mean."

Brightwell picked up a spyglass from a nearby table and peered through it toward the window over Gabriel's shoulder. "Or perhaps you'll be saved—*once again*—and she will leave Fallow Hall."

The mocking tone singed his ears. Gabriel had never heard such spite from Brightwell. "If you are concerned for your new cousin-in-law's reputation, you needn't be."

"I've seen the way you look at her." Brightwell lowered the telescope and replaced it on the table. "The way you've always looked at her."

He'd known all these years? Did Brightwell still have feelings for Calliope, even though he'd married Pamela? The idea left him uneasy and wary.

Gabriel's pulse accelerated, as if preparing for a physical attack. Yet he knew Brightwell would never cross the distance to challenge him. That hard glare was the only blow he would strike. "There is no point in speaking of the past. We are friends. That is all that matters."

Brightwell scoffed. "Yes, and I have been most fortunate to have your friendship."

If Brightwell knew everything—even about the letter—then Gabriel supposed he'd earned such censure. He had to admit that their friendship had been more about Gabriel's needs and then his guilt, than about any true bond. "The truth is, you deserved a better friend in the beginning, but I have tried to make amends." If everything progressed as Gabriel imagined, they would become family.

Brightwell gave a stiff nod.

Valentine cleared his throat from the doorway. "My lord, Miss Croft's carriage and driver have arrived."

Her carriage? Damn! It was here too soon. He had much to tell Calliope before she left. First, he needed to confess to her about the letters. "Make the driver comfortable for the remainder of the day."

The butler inclined his head. "In addition, my lord, when the tea concluded, there were two slices of lemon missing from the dish and nothing more."

A breath rushed out of Gabriel's lungs. "Thank you, Valentine. That will be all."

When the butler departed, Gabriel turned back toward the window so that Brightwell would not see the undoubtedly sappy grin spreading across his face.

"Two slices of lemon missing," Brightwell said, his curiosity evident. "What an odd event to report."

Gabriel shrugged. "Who knows why Valentine says the things he does? Perhaps there is madness at Fallow Hall."

Right that instant, Gabriel felt a fierce sort of madness swimming in his veins at the thought of Calliope's choosing lemon for her tea. That simple choice meant a great deal.

It meant that she was choosing *him*.

CHAPTER EIGHTEEN

The carriage had arrived.

Calliope spent the afternoon discussing her gown for the evening and her traveling clothes for tomorrow with Meg, while everything else being was packed away. She visited with Mrs. Merkel, who professed a desire for Calliope to return to Fallow Hall very soon. Mrs. Swan said that she was preparing a special syllabub for Calliope's last dinner here. And since the cold weather in Lincolnshire did not agree with the dowager duchess, she wanted to enjoy one more tour of the hothouse. Unfortunately, she did not want to stop by the map room on her way.

During the tour, nothing of great import was mentioned. There was no more talk of the dowager duchess's desire for Everhart to have a large family. Instead, they spoke at length of flowers and the differences of native species in England as opposed to those of South America.

At dinner, the dowager rearranged the seating so that Calliope was to her right, while Gabriel sat at the opposite end beside his father. Not wanting to appear rude, Calliope tried not to let her gaze drift down the table any more than six or eight times. Certainly no more than a dozen glances in all. And he looked down the table at her just as often.

She wanted to speak with him. Privately. Not having the chance to do so filled her with anxiety. She wasn't about to reveal her epiphany at tea with the dowager duchess and proclaim her love for him. However, she would like to know if she would see him again. Perhaps in one year, when the wager was over.

Shortly after dinner, everyone gathered in the parlor. Everhart, his father, and his grandmother sat among the chairs and sofa, facing one another. Montwood and Danvers were at a smaller table, playing cards. Pamela and Brightwell had retired immediately after dinner, as had Alistair Ridgeway.

Calliope hoped to steal away for a moment to speak with Everhart, but the dowager duchess requested that she read passages from the journal she'd mentioned during the tour of Fallow Hall.

"I should like to understand the appeal of such explorations," the dowager duchess said.

It wasn't long before a discussion ensued, and even the Duke of Heathcoat had an opinion on South America. Throughout this, whenever Calliope's gaze met Gabriel's—which she had to admit was quite often—he appeared equally frustrated.

They hadn't had a single moment alone to say good-bye. Or to shed light on what was happening between them.

"Miss Croft," Everhart said abruptly when she paused to turn the page. "I have heard that you are leaving on the morrow."

At his uncharacteristically earnest expression, she swallowed. "So it would seem, Lord Everhart." Had it really only been hours ago that she was whispering his name in ecstasy? She blushed at the thought and hoped no one noticed. "Preparing for the journey has been quite the whirlwind."

"I can well imagine." His lips quirked in a grin, as if he'd read her *every* thought. "So much can change in so short a time. Wouldn't you agree?"

She searched his face, wondering if there was a chance that he reciprocated her feelings. "I would."

He offered an imperceptible nod and was about to speak again, but instead his grandmother interrupted.

"You must forgive me, Miss Croft. I have kept you up late to read for my enjoyment." She rose from her chair, and everyone in the room followed suit.

"It has been my pleasure, Your Grace," Calliope said.

"I must lay the blame at your feet, however, because of your exceedingly pleasant tone. It brings to mind your namesake, the muse that inspired Homer." The dowager duchess tapped her cane once on the floor. "Wouldn't you agree that our Calliope is a veritable muse, Gabriel?"

Our Calliope. She could scarcely breathe. Had the Dowager Duchess of Heathcoat just granted her approval?

A veritable muse? Gabriel studied his grandmother carefully before responding. "I would."

How much did she know?

"You have nearly completed your own odyssey, I'd say." A gleam flashed in the dowager duchess's eyes. "And many years away from home."

Without a doubt, the dear old dragon knew everything. Gabriel grinned. Then he leaned forward and bussed his grandmother's cheek. "You still manage to surprise me."

"Age brings with it certain advantages, young man. Not to mention a sense of urgency." She patted his cheek. "Since you are fond of early mornings, I expect you to be ready to see off your guests. Your father and I will be leaving in the morning as well."

Gabriel looked from the dowager to his father before resting on Calliope. "Perhaps I would prefer a large snowfall overnight that would keep all the guests here. If a blizzard fell over Fallow Hall tonight, it would be most welcome."

Calliope blushed.

"What nonsense," the dowager duchess said, her gruff tone belied by the fact that she wore a grin. "Miss Croft, we would do well to leave this charmer's company before he has each of us wishing for snow."

Later that night, Calliope stood alone in her room. Staring out her bedchamber window, she did indeed wish for snow. Unfortunately, not a single flake appeared in the sky. In fact, this close to spring, there wouldn't likely be another snowfall.

Before dinner, she'd told Meg to retire early and that she would ready herself for bed. They had a long day ahead of them tomorrow. However, instead of preparing for bed as she ought, her restless thoughts took her to the writing desk. She couldn't leave without telling Gabriel how she felt.

Unfortunately, the first letter she wrote did not convey the depth of feeling she intended. The second letter contained too much. And the third was entirely too stilted and forced. While it was easy for her to write a list of characteristics of the gentlemen she'd studied, putting an overwhelming sea of emotions on the page proved impossible.

Frustrated, she stood and walked to the hearth to warm her hands. The mantel clock read midnight.

Instantly, the memory of kissing Everhart in the map room warmed more than her hands. She glanced at the crumpled pages on the desk and then to the door. The others would be abed by now. In Lincolnshire, people did not keep London hours. Therefore, it was entirely possible that she could speak directly to Everhart with no one the wiser.

Calliope was ashamed at how quickly her hand found the doorknob.

Then, like her first night here, Duke was there in the hallway. This time, instead of ignoring her, he began to wag his tail immediately, as if he'd been expecting her. Without delay, he led her down the hall to the stairs. At the bottom, he stopped and turned, as if to make sure she followed.

"Why, you sly matchmaker. You know exactly what you're doing, don't you?"

Duke gave a *woof* in answer.

She quickly bent down to scratch him behind the ears. "Shh…We mustn't draw attention."

He licked her hand, his tail wagging with exuberance. So much so, in fact, that he bumped a guéridon table and sent it tilting onto two of its three legs. Reaching out, she saved it just in time, catching the silver salver on top of it as well.

Unfortunately, a stack of letters yet to be posted scattered to the floor.

After a quick peek over her shoulder to make sure none of the servants had heard, she kneeled down and picked up the letters. Duke's enormous paws covered two of them. She tried to shoo him away, but his tongue lolled to the side, and his tail started wagging again as if this were a game.

Calliope couldn't budge his paw. "If you could just"—she tried to lift it—"step off to the side." She grunted and received a cold, wet nose to her ear as he sniffed her. With a huff, she sat back and shook her finger at him. Finally, his paw lifted, and she picked up the first letter and then the second.

However, just as she was prepared to return them to the salver with the others, something familiar caught her gaze. She looked closely at the letter addressed to Kinross. *Kinross…*

"*The K,*" she whispered, staring down at the script. The slant. The flourish on the top. The tail on the bottom. She'd seen this K hundreds of times. Perhaps thousands.

Only one person wrote a K like this. Casanova was here after all. But how could that be? She'd read the Anagram clues in the parlor, and none of them had matched.

Slowly, as if she feared waking from a dream, she turned the letter over to examine the seal on the back.

In that same instant, it fell from her fingertips.

CHAPTER NINETEEN

From the loft in the map room, Gabriel stared out the window. The moon shone so brightly that the stars were all but blotted from the sky. There was nothing in that dark expanse other than the bright white orb, hovering above the tree line.

Right now, he was waiting out the moon, listening to the low melody Montwood played, rooms away, on the piano and counting the hours until dawn.

He needed to see Calliope. A need that tempted him to traverse the darkened halls. There was so much to say. He needed to tell her about the letter and...

An unmistakable click of the map-room doors closing downstairs pulled him away from his thoughts. He was certain he'd closed the doors already before venturing up to the loft.

Stocking-footed, he made his way past the shelves and to the railing. The fire in the hearth burned brightly, illuminating the empty room below. The doors were still closed. Yet there was an unmistakable shadow rising along the wall, undulating in the light of the crackling fire. Someone was coming up the stairs.

Before he could call out to question who it was, his answer emerged from the circular staircase, beneath a fall of dark honey tresses.

His heart gave a jolt of longing. "Calliope, what are you doing here?"

"I needed to speak to you." Without a glance, she skirted past him, making her way to the open room beyond the bookcases.

"I need to speak to you as well, but perhaps we should wait until morning." Even he knew the temptation of having her here alone with him was too great. His gaze lingered on the tendrils spilling from her combs to brush against her bare shoulders and on those six pearl buttons. She had not changed after dinner and still wore her burgundy evening gown with white trim.

Still with her back to him, she shook her head. "This cannot wait."

Her cool tone pricked an alarm within him.

"You don't know my parents, Everhart," she began, her voice barely above a whisper, "but they have this connection with each other that's as elusive as it is tangible. I spent all of my life hoping to be as fortunate. I feared I'd never find it. The closest thing I came to feeling anything that powerful was when I immersed myself in a book. In those pages, I felt everything—love, fear, anguish, joy. It was all there. Only there. Until one day, I received a letter."

It wasn't until he heard the unmistakable crinkle of paper that he looked down to her hands. Every ounce of blood in his veins froze.

Turning slowly, she faced him. Her eyes reflected the shifting firelight from below, making them unreadable. She lifted a well-worn, yellowed page with a familiar tear at the bottom corner. "*This* letter."

"Calliope, I—"

"When I read it," she continued as if she hadn't heard him, "something inside me altered. I felt as if the cover of *my* book had opened for the first time and the story of my heart was exposed. I read the longing in each word—a yearning so potent that it seemed to mirror my own. I thought I'd found the one who felt the same burgeoning passion that I did." Her voice trembled. "I thought I'd found my soul mate."

The firelight in her eyes turned liquid. The sight held Gabriel immobile. Seeing her pain, and knowing that he was the sole cause, was utter agony. Regret and anguish tore through him, ripping into his heart. "I was going to tell you."

She lowered her chin, and her brows lifted in doubt. "And confess that it was only a lark for you?"

Gabriel shook his head, the only part of him he seemed able to command. "It wasn't a lark."

"Do you know what it felt like when the next letter was revealed?" She closed her eyes briefly as if she couldn't bear to look at him. "Of course, no one knew it was the *next* letter, because I'd never revealed the first. Oh, but I knew. My only consolation was that her letter didn't stir any souls. It was a simple rhyme that had no depth of feeling. At least"—her breathing hitched—"that's what I'd told myself. Until the next letter arrived, and then the next. Six in all. Six chances for my heart to break a little more."

He reached for her, but she shrank back two—*three*—steps. "I'm sorry, Calliope."

A single tear caught the light as it swept down her cheek. "The worst part of all was the fact that I gave up on that dream. I decided love and marriage weren't worth the pain. I didn't need to marry. I would just read my books and take care of my parents and that would be my life."

"No," he commanded, but she went on, not hearing him.

"Then I grew bitter. I set about getting revenge. I was determined to unmask the love-letter Casanova and expose him to ridicule for playing with my heart. I kept a journal on every gentleman who showed possibility. I'd even had a few pages about you. I'm certain they would entertain you."

When he shook his head again, she issued a short laugh, the sound hollow and dark.

"As time went on, and my anger gave way to disbelief, I convinced myself that the letter meant nothing. And I would do better to forget all about it. So, I gave my journal to my younger sisters and thought that my heart would mend."

She searched his face, as if seeking an answer for the cruelty he'd wrought on her heart. "What I learned instead— what *you* helped me understand—is that a person might be able to mend the spine of a book, but a broken heart never heals. It remains splintered around the edges and breaks a little easier after the first time. I have proof of that in my hand. I never got rid of the letter. I've read it thousands of times until it's worn and nearly transparent. I know every word, every letter, every flourish."

"Calliope, I never intended to—"

"That's why, when I saw this, I stopped in my tracks." She held the sealed missive aloft in front of the letter in the same hand. "A letter to Kinross. A perfectly innocent letter, and yet there was a single thing that stood out." The tip of her index finger traced the address. "You pen a very distinct *K*, Lord Everhart. A flourish on the top and a tail on the bottom."

He'd hurt her. He'd let her down. It was killing him. He'd gone over every possible way to confess to her but had come up with nothing, time and again. For him, revealing her brother's threat would be unconscionable. Croft had only been protecting his sister, after all. Gabriel should have protected Calliope too. He should have risked everything for her. He should have been worthy of her love from the beginning. Instead, he'd broken her heart.

He was going to lose her forever if he didn't say something. "I love you."

Her eyes narrowed. "*That* is how you choose to explain your actions?" She released an exhale, her shoulders sagging as the letters drifted to the floor. "Forgive me if I choose not to believe any more of your lies."

"I've always loved you. Since that first night we met at Almack's." He stepped forward and took her hands before she could leave. "You've told me your story, and now it is my turn."

"Wouldn't you rather run away? Plan your next expedition?" She jerked her hands free. Even though her words came out harsh, her eyes told him how weary she felt. "We need not see each other again."

She swept past him.

No. He couldn't lose her. Not now. Not when he finally had the courage to go after what he wanted most. "I don't want to run from the truth any longer, and there is no reason for you to start."

He managed to stop her at the top of the stairs but felt powerless, knowing that he couldn't force her to stay. Yet she surprised him by lingering, her hand gripping the rail, her knuckles turning white.

This was his last chance. "I've already told you about the phoenix feather and dragon's eye and how I've found them together over the years. I found them the evening we first met as well. They were lying side by side, directly outside Almack's. Just waiting in the corner of one of the steps, as if I was meant to find them together. As if I was meant to be reminded of the missing string of white bells." He took a breath. "But that night, I found those too."

Still, she kept her back to him, prepared to bolt.

He quickly continued. "I tucked the feather and the stone in my pocket and climbed the stairs. Inside, not two steps from the ballroom doors, I saw those bells. A sprig of lilies of the valley. A simple adornment that stole the breath from my body."

Gabriel took a step closer, his throat raw with a sudden wave of emotion at the memory. "Your head was turned. All the candlelight in the room focused on your face. And suddenly I knew. *I knew.*"

On a sharp intake of breath, her hand slipped from the rail. She didn't say a word, but he sensed something shift inside her.

"I didn't want to believe in love at first sight. I fought it for months." Stepping close enough to feel the silk of her gown brush his legs, he dared to take her hand. This time, she didn't pull free. "But I could never stay away from you. I'd hoped that being among the circle of friends around you and Brightwell would give me the opportunity to catalog your flaws. I'd wanted to convince myself that I was wrong. Instead, I ended up liking you in spite of my efforts. Your wit, your brightness, those absurd little things you say that seem to come directly from a novel—I loved them all." He loved them still.

Turning her head, she searched his gaze, her brow furrowed in confusion. "What about the others? Would you be having the same conversation if any of them had discovered your secret?"

He shook his head. "I wrote those other letters—those terrible lines of drivel—out of guilt and fear. The guilt because of what I'd done to Brightwell, and the fear because you were getting too close, asking too many questions. You even wanted to know if I'd had ink on my fingertips."

"I remember," she whispered, her expression tender yet wary.

"I was afraid of discovery." He drew in a breath, preparing to reveal the truth. "I was afraid of loving you."

Calliope drew in a breath, startled by Gabriel's admission. All of it.

He loves me? When he'd first said it, she thought it was another of his tactics of distraction. But hearing his voice crack just now, seeing the vulnerability in his eyes, made her want to believe him more than she'd ever wanted anything in her life.

However, she knew better than to trust this feeling. "You hurt me. More than I care to admit. You could be saying anything to ease your own guilt, or to keep me from exposing your secret."

"And now, my secret *and* my fate lie in your hands." As he spoke, he slowly started to walk backward through the row of shelves, pulling her along with him, his grip light enough that she could let go at any time. "Come away from the stairs, please. I know I don't deserve it, but I'd like one more chance to explain."

Frustrated that she couldn't will herself to leave, she lashed out at him. "*One* more? You've had five years."

Her accusation hit the target. He winced. "You have every right to despise me."

She should turn, walk down the stairs, and take her broken heart with her. But she wanted answers first. "Why would you be afraid of loving me?"

Gabriel drew her closer in nearly imperceptible movements. A subtle turn. A breath. A touch. His fingers threaded through hers, his thumb gliding along the sensitive inner curve between her thumb and forefinger. Before she knew it, they were less than a half step apart.

"Because I knew my life would end if I loved you completely and then lost you." The low intensity of his voice held her captive.

One after the other, he lifted her hands to his shoulders and then slid his own around her waist. "I watched it happen to my father—the life draining out of him. He merely exists now. Yes, he's made a life with Agnes, and they are cordial to each other, but I remember what he was like when he loved my mother. She was the light of his world—his sun in the morning sky; his moon and starlight in the evening. She was everything to him. Growing up, I feared that kind of love as much as I longed for it."

Gabriel brushed her cheek. Only then did Calliope realize that tears were falling. "And she was his friend too."

"Yes." Which was why Gabriel never had any women friends.

Finally, she understood. To witness such a loss as a boy, all the while feeling his own, had changed him. On the outside, Gabriel appeared as if he hadn't a care in the world. Yet on the inside lived a man afraid of the misery that only losing someone you love could cause.

Tenderly, he kissed her brow, her temple, the bridge of her nose. "When I first saw you, I suddenly knew that love would be the same for me. That's why I tried so hard to deny it."

It felt so natural to be in his arms that it didn't feel like self-betrayal. It felt like she'd always belonged here.

But why did it have to take him so long to come to this realization? "Five years, Everhart. Five *very* long years. And you'd turned so cold to me before you disappeared from my life."

"After I'd written those other letters to keep you from discovering my identity, a...*friend* helped me understand how deeply I'd wronged you." He closed his eyes and pressed his forehead against hers. "At the time, I'd made a choice to stay away from you. I thought you would marry a man more deserving. Yet even then, the thought of not seeing you for six weeks had driven me mad. So I followed your family to Bath. I had to be near you. Now, five years later, those feelings are just as strong. No—*stronger.*"

Calliope felt as if the earth had suddenly slipped from beneath her feet. Instinctively, she gripped his shoulders. "How can I believe you?"

"Trust your heart." Gabriel brushed a kiss over her lips.

Unable to help herself, she kissed him in return, sliding her hands to the back of his neck. "A fanciful notion, to be sure."

He took her face in his hands, beseeching her forgiveness with his earnest gaze. "I regret not coming forward back then. I regret not saving you from heartache *before* I caused it. Most of all, I regret not marrying you that very first day."

Her breath rushed past her lips. "Married on that first day? I've heard it takes at least four to travel to Gretna Greene."

"Then we would have been married on the fourth day, but no later."

He said it with such certainty that it was impossible not to believe him.

"Do you know how many novels I've read, trying to forget the words you placed inside my heart?" Her attempt at scolding him was likely undermined by the way she fitted her body against his. "Enough to fill a very large library."

"I will build you the grandest library you've ever seen." He seemed to be holding his breath, waiting for her next response.

It suddenly occurred to her that her life was about to change. "Be warned, Everhart, I will hold you to that."

He kissed her suddenly, deeply, binding their agreement. The long-denied passion surged through her, washing away all doubt and filling her with a ravenous, consuming need.

Wanting more of him, she slid her tongue against his, tasting the tang of whiskey. The kiss turned urgent.

Breathless, she didn't want it to end. Rising up on her toes, she moved against him to ease the sudden ache in her breasts. His hands drifted over her back, tugging. In the next instant, she felt her gown loosen and hang on her shoulders.

On a gasp, she lifted her gaze to his.

He grinned in response. His skillful hands splayed out, touching the bare flesh between her shoulders, and then slipped downward. Drawing her hips flush with his, his thick arousal was evident, his intention clear. He meant to make love to her. Here. Now. "As you said, it's been five *very* long years. I cannot leave you with a modicum of doubt."

"What about the wager?"

Gabriel held her gaze. "I will risk everything for you, Calliope."

Five long years. And the waiting was over. She answered him with another kiss, drawing his lower lip in her mouth. He growled deep in his throat.

Her hips arched against his, sliding against the hard ridge of his erection. Through the layers of her clothing, Gabriel's hands brushed, stroked, and kneaded in ways that not even her vivid imagination could have conjured. Her hands clenched fistfuls of his linen shirt. A tiny cry escaped her—half pleasure, half need. Pure, wanton hunger. The kind that led innocent characters into ruin.

At last, she understood why.

Impatient, she lowered her arms to her sides so that her dress slipped free. The heavy brocade collapsed to the floor.

Wasting no time, Gabriel unfastened the buttons of her petticoat, and before she could draw another breath, it too was on the floor. Her stays were next, followed by her chemise, until she stood before him in nothing more than her stockings and slippers.

Strangely, she didn't feel bare at all. Instead, she was blanketed by the desire in his gaze. Her body responded in kind, her skin drawing taut over her breasts, an urgent heat pulsing deep within her.

"My love, you are indeed a siren." He drew her forward, his hands stroking and kneading without any layers between them. *Sweet heaven.*

Quivering, her bones turned liquid. She didn't think she'd be able to stand for long. Not surprisingly, Gabriel seemed to sense this and gently coaxed her down onto the curved chaise. Bending over her, he kissed her tenderly and removed the combs from her hair.

"I have one more confession to make," he whispered, distracting her with the brush of his lips across her jaw, her throat, and to the curve of her shoulder. "My fascination with an expedition to South America is solely because of this."

She tilted her head, watching him trace the rosy blemish near the outside corner of her breast. "My birthmark?"

Dipping his head, he traced the imperfection with his tongue. "*Mmm.* It is shaped like the South American continent and, as I always suspected, tastes exotic on your flesh. It sets my mind to exploration, my love."

Before she could respond, he drew her taut nipple into his mouth. On a gasp, she arched off the chaise, her spine bowing in supplication.

Gabriel hauled her to him, lifting her, feasting on her flesh. The back of her neck lay over the upper curve of the chaise, her body positioned for his appetite. Burrowing her fingers through the thick layers of his hair, she held him to her breast; she held him as his exploration ventured down the valley between her ribs; she held him as his tongue dipped into her navel; and she held him when he set his mouth to her most intimate recesses.

Calliope's lips parted, but no sound emerged. She was lost. Gabriel was her guide on this journey, and she trusted him to know the way. Raising her arms, she gripped the curve of the chaise above her head with both hands, holding on as her body began to tremble. Her eyes drifted closed. He nudged her legs wider with his shoulders. His hands slid beneath her, lifting her hips, laving her. Like the sea in a storm, an overwhelming pressure built within her, rising.

Relentless, his tongue swirled inside her and then slowly licked upward, flicking over the tight nub of flesh. A string of gasps and moans poured from her lips and throat as he devoured her. Waves crashed over her. She cried out. Her body spasmed, hips jolting, arching, quaking...while the sound of her ecstasy echoed down around her.

Gabriel lifted his gaze and gave her one last slow lick. Through the window, moonlight glanced off the wetness glistening on his lips and chin. With a rakish grin, he wiped his hand across his mouth and then licked his fingers. "You taste like an exotic fruit, my love. Luscious, ripe, and delectably wet."

It was impossible not to blush. And in the next moment, she had even more of a reason to do. Her Casanova stood and stripped out of his shirt, before bending over to strip out of his stockings. Then he stood before her, unbuttoning the fall of his breeches, inviting her to look her fill.

And she did.

"You're"—*beautiful, exquisite, godlike*—"naked," she said on a breath.

Gabriel flashed a grin. Her gaze roamed over his finely chiseled form, from the breadth of his shoulders to the expanse of golden hair dusting his chest. Those golden hairs narrowed into a line over the ridges of his stomach and down past his navel. From there, the color darkened and...

She swallowed, her gaze riveted to the most masculine part of him jutting forth proudly. It was less a *blade of ruination*, and more a *broadsword of destruction*.

Good heavens! She gulped down a bubble of nervous laughter at the turn of her thoughts. For the first time, a wave of trepidation washed over her. Looking down at herself, she realized she was still wantonly draped before him, legs apart, feet dangling off either side of the chaise.

Gabriel knelt between her thighs and moved over her, slowly, as if he sensed her wariness. The heat of his body covered her. The hair on his chest and abdomen brushed her stomach and breasts, teasing her sensitive nipples into tiny aching points.

"My love," he murmured against her lips. "Open your eyes."

When had she closed them? *Likely when you saw his broadsword*, her inner narrator taunted with an uncharacteristically saucy laugh.

Calliope opened her eyes and was instantly captivated by the intensity in his blue-green depths. Only now did she truly recognize what she'd seen all along. He loved her. Completely.

Lifting her hands to his face, she pressed a tender kiss to his lips and then held his gaze. "I have something I need to confess."

"Right now?"

Under different circumstances, she would have laughed at his look of total bewilderment. But this was too important to leave unsaid. "I look over the last page of every book before I decide to read it."

Gabriel smiled down at her, brushing a wayward lock of hair from her forehead. "I know. You like to know what to expect. And right now…you are uncertain of the next page."

"Yes," she admitted.

He pressed his lips to hers and shifted so that she could feel the heated length of him against her stomach. "If you like, I will tell you everything that is about to happen in detail."

She nodded, and he settled his mouth next to her ear. His warm breath teased while he proceeded to tell her everything he would do, in extremely vivid detail, until she was writhing beneath him.

"Please," she begged, breathless, unable to take the torment.

Positioned on the chaise, they were flush, with nothing between them. Bracing his foot on the floor beside, Gabriel lifted her leg to his hip. The searing heat of him settled against her dampness. Her body pulsed in anticipation. Then slowly, he nudged inside and then stilled.

His staggered breath fanned her lips. "For five years, I've imagined you like this."

He moved again. Another nudge, deeper this time. And when he stilled again, she marveled at the rapid pulse of his body inside her. It matched the beat of his heart.

Cupping her hands to his face and overwhelmed by the love she felt, she kissed him. Gabriel groaned into her mouth as if in surrender. He drove forward, filling her, stretching her. She gasped, more startled than in pain. Her body strained to accommodate him, burning at her core. She wanted to welcome him, but instead felt too full.

But then Gabriel kissed her again. Sweetly. Tenderly. Whispering endearments against her lips. His hands caressed her legs, her hips, her breasts. Gradually, her body stretched to embrace him.

He moved against her. Inside her. Withdrawing only to sheath himself again. And this time it was different. With each slow thrust, the utter fullness elicited wondrous sensations. Tingles rushed through her. Entranced by this change, she lifted her other leg to his hip and circled his waist.

Gabriel smiled, but his gaze was feral and dark onyx. Intense. Determined. He shifted over her, devouring her mouth as he drove deeper, faster. "You are *mine*, Calliope. Always."

She agreed. Opening her mouth, she prepared to amend his declaration by stating the same about him, but her breath caught in her lungs. A fierce tide of pleasure crashed over her. Her breasts tightened, firmed. The hair on his chest grazed her nipples, making them ache. Her body clenched around him, seizing. At any moment, she feared she would splinter.

And then she did. She broke apart like a ship against the rocks. Her body quaked, rising up against his. A cry tore from her throat. Her hips jerked against his, shuddering. Another tide washed over her. Pleasure. Love. Ecstasy. Gabriel pushed forward once more, his hips jolting as a harsh, soul-deep groan ripped through him.

Shortly before dawn, Calliope collapsed over Gabriel. Her face nestled into the curve of his neck as she panted for air. "I believe we could write a very naughty book about pleasure after last night."

Gabriel barely had the energy to chuckle. His arms lay at his side on their makeshift bed on the loft floor. He was utterly spent and had never realized such bliss was possible. Even *he* felt as if they'd invented the art of making love, in ways that no one could have imagined before. It was all so new and unexpected. "Were we to travel to India, I could show you that such a book already exists and contains even more than what were able to accomplish."

She lifted her face, her cheeks flushed, her eyes bright. "There's more?"

"I will show you, but you must allow me time to recuperate. The day, at least," he said with a kiss. "As for later this morning, I will arrange for my carriage to follow yours to Scotland. There, I will speak with your brother for his consent, travel to Bath for your father's consent, and then return so we can be married in Gretna Green."

She clasped her hands over his chest and rested her chin on them, a smirk toying with her well-kissed lips. "What if I don't want to marry the love-letter Casanova?"

"It is too late for that." He kissed her impertinent smirk. "You've already given your consent in the many different ways you pleasured me."

"Hmm," she mused, pursing her lips as if she needed a moment to consider her options. "I suppose I did thoroughly ruin you."

"Completely," he agreed, grinning like a half-wit.

CHAPTER TWENTY

———————————————————————

Hours later, Calliope donned the same traveling costume she'd worn the day she'd arrived at Fallow Hall, but she never could have imagined how drastically her life would change during these past weeks. Abundant proof was in the telltale, albeit delicious, aches inside her body.

Gabriel indeed possessed a poet's soul and a passionate nature. He was the perfect man for her. The *only* man for her. This was not a whim for him, after all. He'd declared his love for her. And they were getting married!

How strange would her brother think it of her marrying Everhart within a fortnight? As for own thoughts, she could hardly believe it. Yet her heart told her that the past five years had been nothing more than a trial to be borne in order to earn her happily ever after with Gabriel. Beaming from the top of her head to the tips of her toes, she drummed her fingertips over the door to Pamela's bedchamber. "Cousin, are you awake? It is time for me to leave."

Much to Calliope's surprise, her cousin answered the door. Even more surprising, she was not in her morning dress but in traveling clothes, her hair arranged in an elegant coiffure.

"Pamela, you are looking remarkably well this morning."

With a glance into the mirror, her cousin agreed. "Yes. It is time for us to leave Fallow Hall as well. Milton reminded me this morning that it has been nearly six weeks since the accident."

Good for Brightwell, Calliope mused. She supposed there was a limit to how much cosseting anyone could give. And Brightwell had indulged his wife a great deal already.

"I suppose it was silly to have stayed for so long," Pamela said, turning to walk to the opposite end of the room. "But I so wanted to be near Lord Everhart."

Calliope stiffened in shock. Gabriel was hers and hers alone. She felt compelled to explain this fact to her cousin. "I don't see why *you* would want to be near Everhart."

"I'm sure many a young woman, married or not, finds herself in love with him. Then again, I'm certain there aren't many who can say they'd planned to run away with him," she said on a sigh as she stood gazing out the window.

A prickle of unease draped over Calliope's shoulders like a horsehair shawl. She stared at her cousin's back, unable to speak. Surely, she didn't know what she was saying.

"Oh, but that was before the accident," Pamela continued. "It was my fault that he broke his leg. If I hadn't leapt across the carriage to kiss him just as the driver turned a corner, we never would have tipped over."

Unease gave way to the heavy weight of dread. Still, Calliope tried to convince herself that she'd misunderstood. Her cousin didn't always make sense. "The accident...you were with Everhart?"

Until now, Calliope had never connected Gabriel's broken leg and Pamela's carriage accident.

Pamela looked over her shoulder with a dreamy smile on her lips. "He was always so attentive, asking me all sorts of questions about my family. Milton never asks. I don't even think he likes my family. Lately, he's been very cross with me, especially since I received the letter."

The letter—the one that Pamela claimed to have received not long after she arrived here at Fallow Hall. Calliope had nearly forgotten. It had been her sole purpose for extending her stay here, yet the urgency she'd felt about finding it seemed so far removed from where she was today.

Gabriel had never explained about Pamela's letter. Was it a love letter as well or full of drivel?

Yet drivel or not, the letter obviously meant a great deal to her cousin. And if it meant nothing to Gabriel, then why would he keep it a secret?

None of the answers that came to her eased her worries.

Dizzy, she reached out and braced herself against a corner post of the bed. "You and Everhart were planning to run away together? You were going to leave Brightwell?" All the sudden, she recalled what the dowager duchess had said about Everhart's convenient friendship with Brightwell and how competitive young men at that age were. *No...*

She shook her head, refusing to believe everything that had happened in the past few hours had been nothing more than a lie. *Or a competition that had begun five years ago.*

"Of course, Lord Everhart wasn't nearly as friendly after you arrived." Pamela pouted, and her words sparked a memory. *"Why doesn't Everhart join us all for dinner any longer?*

He was always a consummate host before my cousin's arrival. I wonder what has changed."

"With my letter gone as well, I was left to languish," her cousin continued. "Milton hardly smiled at all...until this morning, when he came into my room, having found my ivory patch box. He said it must have been in his own chamber all this time." She gestured to the table beside her, where the box lay open, covered with a piece of unfolded parchment. "Can you believe the luck? Now I have my letter back, and every word speaks to my heart. I will cherish it whenever the diversions of *town* do not fulfill me."

Calliope couldn't stop staring at the table. "Is that your letter?"

"Oh, yes." Her cousin picked it up and pressed it to her bosom on a sigh. Then, she crossed the room and held it out for Calliope. "Please read it and tell me if your heart does not fairly fly from your breast."

Her hand shook as she reached for the letter. She turned away from Pamela, pretending to study it closely. In actuality, she feared her emotions would reveal themselves in her expression.

> *My dearest Pamela,*
>> *My heart yearns for the siren who captured it...*

Siren? Calliope could read no more. Her vision blurred. A sea of tears washed down her cheeks. This letter was not rhyming romantic drivel, like Gabriel's others had been. These words were too similar to her own letter.

I am a fool. A blind, overly romantic fool.

Then, one alarming truth struck her with crippling force—she had never been special to Gabriel. Not when he'd written the love letter. Not when he'd taken her on a sleigh ride. And not even last night when they'd...

"What do you think?" Pamela asked, her voice ebullient with excitement. "Is it not the most romantic letter you've ever read?"

Surreptitiously, Calliope wiped her cheeks and, without turning around, passed the letter back to Pamela. "It's lovely, cousin. I wish I could stay and admire it more, but my carriage is waiting."

Before she gave herself away, she rushed out of the room, down the hall—and directly into Everhart.

"*Oof!*" Gabriel caught Calliope by the shoulders as she barreled into him from around the corner. "What's this? Are you so anxious to see me that you've taken to running through the halls?"

He didn't see the dampness of her cheeks or her red-rimmed eyes until she lifted her chin and stared straight at him.

"It was never me, was it?" She sniffed and lifted the back of her hand to swipe at the tip of her nose. "All those things you said last night, I...I was merely a diversion like all the others. A whim."

Panic set Gabriel's pulse racing. She'd just come from the direction of her cousin's room. He could only guess what she'd heard. "You don't believe that. You can't, not after... We've made plans, Calliope. My carriage is waiting."

"And when I arrive at my brother's house, how many days, weeks, months, *years* will I wait for you?" She shook her head and took a step back.

He'd proposed in the letter and again this morning. He *was* going to marry her! Nothing else mattered. Couldn't she see that? "You still have the letter. That is your proof, a binding contract, no matter what you may have heard."

"The letter." she scoffed. "I've been fooling myself for too long. I thought mine was special. I thought that *I* was—" She broke off and gave an angry shrug to dislodge his hands.

He released her, dropping his arms to his sides. Pamela's missing letter must have been found. He should have told Calliope and explained everything last night. "You are special to me. You are everything to me. The letter I sent to your cousin was merely a chance to—"

"Don't you mean a *second* chance?" she spat. "I believe your first chance was right before the carriage accident, when you were planning to run away with her. Your second chance of luring her away from her husband was in the guise of the letter."

Bugger it all. "I was not running away with your cousin. She misunderstood my friendship." He'd been trying to explain that very thing to Pamela Brightwell that day.

"Friendship?" Calliope's brows lifted, her mouth set in a grim line. "I seem to recall that you have no women friends."

"I used the word in an effort to be polite to a member of your family. I couldn't very well tell you that she was too bird-witted to understand that the sole reason I spoke with her was to glean information about you."

Gabriel had thought Calliope was able to see past his façade to the real man beneath in a way that no one else had. Hadn't she said as much when they were alone in the nook?

"Perhaps I was merely in love with the idea of him. Of what love could be like."

His breath caught. Was she in love with the idea of the man who'd written that letter, or was she in love with *him*? Recalling every moment with her, he realized she'd never once told him that she loved him.

He had always been afraid of loving someone so completely that he was lost without her, that he would drift through the remainder of his days as a mere shell.

"Were you not alone in the carriage with my cousin moments before you broke your leg?" Calliope asked.

He gritted his teeth. "Yes."

"And did you kiss my *married* cousin?"

"No." But he could see that she did not believe him. Although it was ungentlemanly to explain, he said, "But she attempted to kiss me."

"I've always been a romantic person. Too romantic." She exhaled, her breath catching ever so slightly. "I should have expected this outcome."

He was battling the Fates again. And losing. "You were right to expect more from me. You deserve everything." Was he destined to lose her?

No. He refused to believe that, and yet...

He couldn't force her to love him.

Calliope walked past him but paused. "I wish there had been a way to read the last page, Everhart. I never would have chosen this story."

CHAPTER TWENTY-ONE

For the next week in Scotland, Calliope pretended that she was the same person Griffin and Delaney had left at Fallow Hall. She went on walks with her sister-in-law and visited shops in the village. She wrote to her parents and to each of her sisters, telling them all about the wonders of Brannaleigh Hall. Yet she did not mention a single day from her two weeks in Lincolnshire.

Those days were hers, and hers alone. Her mistakes. And if her brother caught her daydreaming, he did not think it unusual for her.

When a letter arrived from Fallow Hall, however, she could no longer pretend that she was the same. Everything had changed. She'd left her heart in shreds on the stone floors of Fallow Hall. Receiving the letter from that address was only a reminder. She stared at it for several minutes, her hand shaking.

"Are you unwell, Calliope?" Delaney asked from across the table in the cozy breakfast room.

Standing at the buffet, Griffin looked over his shoulder. His brow furrowed instantly in concern. "You've gone pale."

"All the better for my complexion." Calliope attempted a laugh, but even to her own ears it sounded a trifle *off*. Her brother and sister-in-law stared back at her with mirrored expressions of concern. "I suppose you could say that I'm homesick. As lovely as it is here, I miss the Temple of Muses on Finsbury Square." Her favorite bookshop. Though the truth was, she no longer had the desire to read. Happy endings were mere fables, better left to children who'd never experience heartbreak.

In response, Griffin nodded and went back to filling his plate, and Delaney smiled warmly. This answer seemed to ease their worry.

"I feel the same about Haversham's," Delaney said. "With the Season beginning, there will be many new ribbon colors to choose."

"And last Season's ribbons?" Griffin crossed the room to his chair, pressing a kiss atop his wife's head as he passed. "Did they all dissolve into nothing, or are they still bulging from drawers in your dressing chamber?"

"I've sent them to Mr. Harrison in preparation for the new school. I've spoken with the headmistress, and she and I both agree that every girl deserves a selection of ribbons." Delaney beamed, deservedly pleased by her efforts at establishing a school for less fortunate girls. "With that said, I think we should make plans to return to London by week's end."

"Well, if it is a matter of ribbons, then *of course* we shall." Griffin winked at Delaney.

"Only if you've settled your business here," Delaney said. "I must say, you have been somewhat distracted since your last meeting, though you never gave a reason."

"It was nothing. Some local half-wit spouting Homeric nonsense about being caught between Scylla and Charybdis." Griffin glanced over to Calliope, his expression turning serious. "I hope that once your appetite for new novels is fed, then your appetite for food will improve as well."

"I'm sure it will." She looked down at her uneaten slice of toast. It still looked as unappetizing as it had when she'd first put it on her plate. Nothing appealed to her. She wasn't ill. She was simply…*numb*. After all, one could not feel anything— not even hunger—without a heart.

The letter in her hand challenged that statement by terrifying her. Mustering the courage, she turned it to check the seal on the back—to see whether she should toss it directly into the fire or not. Yet surprisingly, it was from Mrs. Merkel.

Calliope released a breath. Was it possible to feel relief *and* disappointment at the same time?

Upon reading the short missive, she learned that her presence at Fallow Hall was missed by the entire staff and even two of the gentleman. Mrs. Merkel professed to believe that Calliope would also be missed by a third gentleman but he was—at the time of the letter—no longer in residence and was instead now at his family estate, Briar Heath. She also said, peculiarly, that she had found red feathers in the map room each time she cleaned. Blaming the dog, she worried about the cardinal population in Lincolnshire.

As Calliope stared down at the letter, a drop of water fell onto the paper, blurring the ink.

Not water, you foolish girl.

Another green stone. Gabriel reached down, snatched the little bugger, and hurled it off in the direction of the reflecting pool. The same way he had done with the hordes of others he'd found in the past two weeks. When Gabriel was a boy, his father had had green aventurine shipped here from India, solely for the purpose of filling the reflecting pool. Over time, the stones seemed to have multiplied.

"Have I come at a bad time?" a familiar voice asked.

Gabriel turned to see Montwood striding across the garden at Briar Heath.

Wiping the dirt from his hands onto his trousers, Gabriel stepped over to greet his friend. "It's never a bad time." He hoped the practiced smile he wore was convincing.

"You appeared angry at whatever object you just threw." Montwood's amber eyes were razor sharp, as usual. "I wondered if I dare approach."

Gabriel shrugged. "Merely tired of finding stones everywhere I turn."

Montwood looked down and picked up another stone near the toe of his boot and tossed it up in the air before catching it. "Then you shouldn't spend so much of your time in the garden."

"Perhaps you are right."

"How are you finding Briar Heath?" Montwood asked as they walked the short distance to the terrace. Half a bottle of whiskey waited in the center of a small table.

Sliding into one of the chairs, Gabriel looked at the brick façade with the white stone casements around the windows and doors. Memories of laughter were so distant now that they seemed like specters, staring at him from the reflective glass. "Much unchanged," he said, exhaustion creeping over him. "After all, there has been no one here to make alterations for years."

"And yet," Montwood said, "I suspect that you anticipated a difference."

His friend was too perceptive for his own good. The difference Gabriel had wanted was to have Calliope here with him. Always.

"Nothing of the sort." And before his friend could scrutinize him further, Gabriel continued. "So tell me of Fallow Hall. Is Valentine looking for a new post since I left him with you and Danvers?"

"Danvers and I left little more than a week after you. He wanted to be in town for the happy arrival of his new niece or nephew—and your new cousin—though as of yet, I have heard no news regarding Rathbun's child. Although we were quite surprised to run into Croft at Gentleman Jackson's."

Gabriel made sure to relax his jaw in case his friend would read anything into his clenched teeth. The mere mention of the name caused him to recall his recent meeting with Croft in Scotland.

Gabriel had followed Calliope, just as he'd promised. When he'd spoken with her brother in the study at Brannaleigh Hall, however, he'd gained no more ground than he had with her.

"I intend to marry your sister."

Croft scrutinized him. "I find it strange that my sister has said nothing about this. And certainly nothing in regards to having decided to marry the love-letter Casanova."

"If this is your method of asking whether I told her about the letter—or letters, rather—I have." But he'd botched it in the end.

"You confessed all?"

"All except your part," Gabriel said. "I did not see a reason to make excuses for my actions. I take full responsibility for my own choice, and I mean to give her back all the years she's lost through my carelessness."

"How am I to believe you? Perhaps seeing her merely brought your guilt to the surface, and this is how you mean to remedy that inconvenient emotion."

"Five years ago, I had to choose between Scylla and Charybdis— or more aptly, between disgracing my family and keeping my distance from the woman I loved. And I am here to tell you that I still love Calliope. I always have. Brand me with an iron; I care not. She will be my wife."

Croft crossed his arms over his chest. "Then tell me, Everhart, if this love of yours is so apparent, then why hasn't Calliope mentioned your intentions or your name even once?"

Gabriel's last conversation with Calliope at Fallow Hall only confirmed that she and her brother were of like minds.

She hadn't believed him or given him the chance to explain. Of course, a lifetime of imprudent choices had worked against him. He could have resolved it by forcing her to hear him, but he'd feared the same result. And her lack of faith in him—after she'd been his champion—had wounded him far more than he wanted to reveal. Still, he knew he was to blame for all of his own misery and hers.

"I thought Croft would have remained in Scotland for a few more weeks," he said to Montwood, feigning a lack of interest.

"Apparently his wife and his sister were eager to return." His friend tossed the stone up in the air again. "Oh, and he might have mentioned a concern for Miss Croft's health."

"*Calliope is ill?*"

As if indifferent, Montwood continued to toy with the stone. "No need to concern yourself. She seemed in fine health when Danvers and I dropped by for a visit at her family's townhouse."

"And what did you speak of?" Gabriel reached forward and snatched the rock from midair.

"Oddly enough, the wager," the amber-eyed serpent said with a laugh. "Miss Croft said—in no uncertain terms—that the wager was yours to win. Essentially, she told Danvers and I that we were fools to bet against someone so determined never to marry."

Gabriel bit back an oath. Hadn't he proved how wrong such a statement was? He'd wanted to marry her all along. He still did. Even now, he was devising a plan to win her back. But instead of answers to his conundrum, he found only these buggering green stones!

"No. I was the fool," Gabriel said. "I never should have made that wager. And if Miss Croft so chooses, she holds the key to humiliate and ruin me. The key, I might add, for you and Danvers to reap the rewards by year's end."

"Do you mean with this?" Montwood reached inside his coat and withdrew a familiar letter. "She asked me to give it to you. Of course, it had been folded into a blank page and sealed, but—wouldn't you know it—the seal broke, and this old letter simply popped out. Damndest thing."

No. Gabriel stared at the familiar page as if it were about to catch fire. This wasn't right. Calliope couldn't return the letter. She'd kept it for five years. By her own admission, she was in love with the man who'd written that letter. That was all Gabriel had to cling to at the moment. He refused to believe she was letting him go.

He swallowed. "You read it, I suppose."

Montwood grinned, revealing a dimple in his cheek.

Bugger it all! Gabriel snatched the letter. "So then you know."

His friend lifted one shoulder in a careless shrug as he settled back into the chair, crossing one leg over the other. "I've known for years that you loved her. I was there watching you make calf's eyes after her when Brightwell was courting her. Although I never realized you were so poetic." He waggled his brows. "You know, together we could write the most maudlin of love songs. I say we leave our gentlemen's cloaks behind, become *the Traveling Casanovas*, and take the *ton* by storm. What say you?"

"The wager." Gabriel threw the rock at him. "You set me up to fail, all along."

"Actually, I was *planning* to set you up, but as it turned out, serendipity was my bosom companion. I didn't have to do anything other than play a waltz when I knew you were together. You, my friend, sabotaged yourself."

Montwood picked up the rock and resumed tossing it, but this time it slipped out of his hand and onto the stone terrace floor. Looking down, he started. "You are utterly surrounded by green stones. I don't recall seeing them here a moment ago. How strange. It reminds me of all those red feathers we started finding around Fallow Hall before we left. There were positively hundreds of them."

Red feathers? And now the green stones? There was only one thing missing.

Gabriel shook his head and started to laugh. "You have the right of it, my friend. The only thing I seem to do well is sabotage myself. It's time I did so again."

Chapter Twenty-Two

In Calliope's bedchamber on Upper Brook Street, Meg finished buttoning the back of Calliope's blue striped day dress and let out a long, slow breath. In the mirror, the edges of a ruffled cap shimmied as the maid shook her head.

"What has put a worrier's mark on your brow, Meg?"

Another exhale followed as her maid slowly met her gaze in the glass. "Your monthly bandages are still in the wardrobe, untouched."

Calliope gulped and moved away from the mirror. Surely her courses weren't due yet. She counted the days in her head…"I'm certain traveling for so many days in a carriage has altered my schedule."

Traveling had never altered her courses before, but the notion *seemed* plausible. The thought was better than panicking over the unexpected. And for someone who liked knowing exactly what to expect, her lack of dread was quite novel.

"*Altered*," Meg murmured. "Though I wonder why your sisters' didn't change too, and they only just returned from their trip to Bath. You and your sisters all have your courses on the new moon. Only this time…"

"It's only been a week since then." Three weeks since she'd made love to Gabriel. Calliope's stomach clenched, and her pulse quickened. Perhaps she felt *a little* panicked. She turned on her heel. "Oh, Meg. Do you think anyone else has noticed? Though I'm sure it's nothing more than travel weariness."

"Mrs. Hatchet in the laundry didn't say anything." Meg held Calliope's gaze. "And you know I would never."

"I know," she said with a nod. Both were a relief. One good thing about living in a house full of women was that a few missing bandages during such a week would hardly be noticed. Had it been different, Mrs. Hatchet would have gone directly to Octavia Croft, and Calliope's mother would have gone directly to Father. The last thing Calliope wanted was to disappoint her parents.

"What will you do?" There was no getting anything by Meg. They were the same age and had been together for the past ten years. The bond between them was more akin to friendship than to servant and mistress.

Calliope's courses had never been late before. Not once. Not even when she'd suffered an illness. A more romantic-minded person might try to convince herself that they were merely delayed. A more romantic-minded person might believe there was little cause for worry, because it usually took months to conceive a child. Her sister-in-law was proof of that, wasn't she? It couldn't have happened in one night. No matter how life-altering that night had been.

But Calliope had given up being romantic-minded.

She looked at her reflection once more, securing a comb in her hair. So much in her had altered and not only her innocence. She knew that holding onto foolish dreams was pointless. Life was not about dreams and hoping to turn the page for a happy ending. Life was about stepping outside of her own novel and seeing the truth of what she had before her.

A baby. A child of her own. Would he be a bright-eyed boy, full of adventure? Or would she be…a bright-eyed girl full of adventure. Either way, Calliope had a feeling that she would be traveling a great deal in order to hide her new secret.

"I might ask Griffin if I can watch over Brannaleigh Hall while he and Delaney are in town," Calliope said, releasing a breath. Beyond that, she couldn't guess.

Yet surprisingly, the notion of carrying Gabriel's child had softened her heart toward him. Of course, she still loved him. That hadn't changed. It never could. Losing him—and losing the dream of what she'd seen in him—didn't hurt quite so much with this realization. Because in that one single night they'd shared, she had believed herself in love and loved in return, with a passion that rivaled any novel she'd ever read. Hadn't that been what she'd wanted all along?

No matter how foolish she'd been for wanting it.

Therefore, when Montwood and Danvers had come to see her last week, she'd decided to return the Casanova letter. She wasn't going to unmask Gabriel. There was no spite in her. Just an ache that she hoped would mend someday.

Meg had just finished making the bed when someone knocked at the bedchamber door. The sound roused Calliope from a daydream enough to notice that she was standing in front of the mirror again, her hands splayed over her middle.

As Meg crossed the room, Calliope dropped her arms to her sides. A flush of guilt tinged her cheeks.

"You have a caller, miss."

"At this hour?" To be certain she hadn't been daydreaming overly long, she glanced to the clock on the mantel. Indeed, it was too early for callers. The family was not roused yet for breakfast. "Who is it?"

Calliope descended the stairs and crossed the hall to the parlor. In the midst of the vibrant colors of the room, Brightwell stood, hat in hand, wearing somber gray attire. She hadn't realized until this moment how he never would've fit in her world. All along, she thought it was the other way around. But where was Pamela?

He inclined his head. "Miss Croft, I apologize for arriving at such an unseemly hour."

"I admit it is rather alarming, and for you to arrive without my cousin." Her mind flew into dozens of different directions, and none of them eased the unsettled pall that fell over her heart. *Perhaps Pamela has run off with Gabriel after all.* "Was my cousin well when you left her this morning?"

"Yes, your cousin is well and, I might add," he said, pausing to clear his throat, "still residing in our home."

In other words, she hadn't run off with Gabriel. Calliope sagged onto the arm of the sofa with relief. "That is good news."

A look of understanding passed between them.

"Which brings me directly to the purpose of my visit." Brightwell placed a hand over his heart. "I have wronged you, Miss Croft. I have had knowledge of a certain matter that would have spared you grief, had it not been for my own jealousy."

Jealousy, indeed. And rightfully so when it concerned his wife and Everhart.

He continued before she could form her response. "I have always known about the Casanova letter that Everhart wrote to you all those years ago." His mouth pressed into a firm line. "I also know about the letter that he wrote to my wife…*not* so long ago."

"Brightwell, I'm so sorry."

He shook his head. "No, Miss Croft. It is my place to apologize. You see, I must also confess that…when I proposed to you, I knew that you were never going to marry me."

Calliope felt her brow furrow. "How could you have known such a thing?"

Brightwell cleared his throat and glanced at the hat he held before him. "I'd realized it the moment that Everhart joined our circle. For lack of a better word, you *glowed* whenever he was near. Why he pretended not to like you when it was patently clear to anyone who saw the two of you dancing, I'll never fully understand. All I can say is that when he didn't step forward, I did."

And they both knew how that had turned out. "I am sorry, Brightwell, for so many things." One of them being that she'd never loved him. The thing about Brightwell was that he never would have broken her heart. But that was because she never would have given it to him.

"You made the right choice," he reassured her. "Had it not been for my jealousy, I would have encouraged Everhart to pursue you. Instead, while he was taking me on a tour of the continent, I incited his guilt."

"Not very noble of you." She wondered why she felt compelled to come to Everhart's defense. But knowing that Brightwell had abused him irritated her.

"Very true, Miss Croft. And now to the main point of my visit. I must admit to the most recent of my crimes." He tucked his hat behind him and drew in a deep breath. "I wrote out two anagrams for your game at Fallow Hall, to purposely thwart your discovery of Everhart's secret."

At first she was confused. *Two anagrams?* Then swiftly, she was appalled. Her mouth dropped open. "That was why I hadn't recognized Everhart's handwriting. Why would you do such a thing?"

"I am ashamed to tell you." His gaze lowered, and he shuffled his feet on the edge of the carpet. "When Pamela told me of your conversation with her about the letter and about the questions you posed to her, I was struck by an overwhelming sense of... *vanity*. I'd never once been accused of writing that letter, and I should have been. So after I heard of your sudden interest in a game where handwritten clues were required, I took a leap of logic and determined that you were hoping to identify the handwriting. I wanted the mystery of Casanova's identity to continue. Because with the mystery, I couldn't be discounted."

Guilty of his accusation, Calliope flushed. "Brightwell, I—"

He lifted a hand to stop her and shook his head. "Please don't, Miss Croft. There is no need to explain. Besides, it is my place to apologize. Likely, I'll add many more to the list before I am finished."

Seeing him color in what she perceived was embarrassment, she accepted this with a nod. It could not be easy for him.

"And to the next," he continued, forging ahead, as if eager to put it all behind him, "I knew that your cousin fancied herself in love with Everhart. When it first began, I was actually relieved that she'd stopped mooning over the gardener. At least I knew I could trust Everhart alone with her. Yes, Miss Croft, that's correct. I trust Everhart."

That surprised Calliope. "Even now?"

Brightwell nodded. "The only types of conversations he had with my wife were about her family. I believe it was in the hopes of discovering whatever he could about you. Over the years, Everhart frequently steered conversations toward your family and your father's health, and to your brother and his recent marriage. He'd even taken to speaking of those who live on Upper Brook Street, Miss Croft." He offered an uncharacteristic shrug. "So you see, he never would have run away with Pamela. In fact, I'm the one who asked him to drive her to the country to see her mother on the day of the accident. Looking back, I should have warned him about her nature."

At the mention of the accident, and the fact that her cousin had thrown herself at Everhart, Calliope was not inclined to feel much forgiveness. "That does not explain why Everhart wrote Pamela a love letter."

"Doesn't it?" Brightwell's pale brows lifted. He blinked. "Forgive me, but I thought you'd read it. From my understanding, even though the address is to my wife, I believe the contents were written to you."

"No. You are wrong." Wasn't he? She couldn't have made such a mistake.

Reaching into his coat, he withdrew the letter and unfolded it. "*My dearest Pamela, My heart yearns for the siren who captured it. For years, I have waited for her to find me—waiting endlessly for one word that would draw me to her shore. I crave the sight of dark honey tresses spilling over*"—he cleared his throat and kept his gaze on the letter—"*the bare shoulders I never touched. I long for the brush of those*"—he paused again—"*lips I dared not taste. And my arms ache from the weight they do not hold. I am wrecked without her, and I would never allow Brightwell to endure such a fate. Your friend…etcetera.*"

Calliope could barely breathe. She hadn't read the full letter at Fallow Hall. After reading *siren* on the first line, it had been too painful to imagine that he was using the same words to woo her cousin. And yet, Pamela did not have *dark honey tresses*. Her hair was pale, like corn silk.

I am wrecked…

Could it be true? She didn't want to allow her overly romantic notions to cloud her judgment any longer. She wanted to see things for exactly what they were. Knitting her fingers she walked from the sofa to the window and back again. "I'm not certain what to think."

Brightwell folded the letter and returned it to his pocket. Then, as if he thought better of it, he placed it on the sofa table, leaving it in Calliope's possession. "With what's in the *Post* this morning, I thought it high time you had the full story."

"The *Post*?" She stepped out into the hall and saw a freshly pressed copy waiting on the rosewood table. Carrying it to the table near the window in the parlor, she quickly skimmed the first page, the second... Then, halfway down the third, her breath caught in her throat.

<u>CASANOVA UNMASKED</u>

I, formerly known as the love-letter Casanova, do hereby confess to cowardice.

I fell in love with a young woman years ago and subsequently wrote a letter expressing this sentiment. Yet before I posted the letter, I removed my signature from the bottom of the page. Even so, this undeniably clever siren nearly discovered my true identity. In fear, I wrote a series of other letters—for which I must apologize—in order to keep her from finding me. In doing so, I broke my beloved's heart, in addition to others.

With this confession, I hope that her precious heart will begin to mend. I love her still. I will love her always.

> *Hers irrevocably,*
> *Gabriel Ludlow*
> *Viscount Everhart*

Turning around to face Brightwell, she felt her lips, her cheeks, and even her eyes tilted upward into a smile. Unable to suppress her happiness, she crossed the room, fully prepared to embrace him. He, however, held his hat in front of him like a shield, and she dared not.

"Brightwell, you've made me the happiest of women. If you weren't married to my cousin, I'd kiss you."

The sound of a low growl from the parlor doorway drew her attention.

"And if you so much as return the sentiment, Brightwell," Everhart growled again, "I will kill you in a field of honor this very morning."

CHAPTER TWENTY-THREE

Gabriel's hand squeezed the fragile stems in his grasp. Before he realized it, the bouquet of lilies of the valley collapsed over his fist, lifeless. The remains of a red ribbon dangled over his fingers. Unfortunately, he'd left his walking stick—along with his hat, coat, and gloves—with the butler, or else he'd have been armed with a silver-tipped spear and fully capable of wielding it directly through Brightwell's heart.

"Everhart, there's hardly a need for threats," Calliope stated. She set her hands on her hips—which was fine with him, as long as her hands stayed far from Brightwell. "And just look at the violence you wreaked on those poor flowers. I certainly hope they weren't meant to be an offering of any kind."

Gabriel's gaze sharpened on her. How dare she sound so merry and cheeky when his every moment apart from her had been utter misery!

Her eyes were bright, her cheeks glowing…and a moment ago, she'd nearly been in Brightwell's embrace. Fortunately for Brightwell, Gabriel noticed that the chap had sense enough to keep his hands clutching the brim of the gray top hat. That hat may have saved Brightwell's life. But not the flowers.

Glancing at the sad bouquet, he looked for a place to set it down. That was when he noticed that the parlor was filled with lilies of the valley. Small clay pots and colorful vases adorned every table. The room was fairly bursting with tiny white bells.

When his gaze met hers, a shared memory passed between them.

"As you can see," Calliope said softly, "we've had an abundance of lilies of the valley in the past week. The gardener has never seen the like."

She skirted past the sofa and stopped in front of him, standing on one side of the threshold with him on the other. Her gaze flitted across his, uncertain. Then, with tender care, she reached for the blossoms, her bare fingertips brushing his, lingering.

"Do you think you can salvage some of them?" he asked for her ears alone, his voice gruff with longing. It had been three weeks since he'd seen her. Since he'd held her. Since she'd told him that she never would have chosen their story.

She lifted her lashes, her expression a mystery to him. "I hope so."

"Well, all this talk of murder for the sake of honor has made me realize I haven't broken my fast," Brightwell announced, donning his hat. "Everhart, should you still require a meeting this morning, you know where I live. Just please don't kill me before I've had a proper cup of tea."

"Noted." Gabriel inclined his head, not fully convinced that murder wasn't necessary. "We are gentlemen, after all."

Brightwell paused in the foyer. "Did you know…with that tone of voice, you sound remarkably like your father?" With a laugh, he tipped his hat, bid them good day, and left.

Gabriel was no longer bothered by such attempts to rile him. When the front door closed, he refocused all his attention on Calliope. "Tell me, does Brightwell often visit you before calling hours?"

"That depends on what you consider often." She smirked as she walked to a table near the window and laid down the bouquet. Next to her was a copy of the *Post*.

He noted that it was open to reveal his confession. Stepping inside the room, he took in his surroundings. The exotic blend of colors reminded him of his travels. The flowers reminded him of his home.

Home. With the thought, he automatically moved toward Calliope, who busied herself with untying the ribbon and sorting through the stems.

Beside her, he leaned in and set his hand on the newspaper. Absently, he trailed his index finger over the words. "Read anything interesting?"

She kept to her task, offering an indifferent lift of her shoulders. "There's a new exhibit at the museum."

"Hmm…Is that all?" His face was only inches from hers. The morning light loved her skin. She truly did have a glow about her. It was remarkable. Captivating.

She looked up, not at him but at the paper. Her hands were still busy with those tiny white bells, pinching off broken stems and saving the rest. "There was one thing that drew my interest. A confession. I can only imagine what the author's family would think. He is a viscount, after all."

He imagined his grandmother would laugh—only in private, of course. To the rest of the *ton*, Grandmama's severe expression would challenge anyone to speak on the matter. As for the estimable Duke of Heathcoat, Gabriel liked to imagine that he would feel a sense of kinship. He'd once been a man of great passions, after all.

Though none of that truly mattered. "It's my guess that the author doesn't care about what his family thinks," Gabriel said. "He only cares about her."

"You may be right." She pursed her lips. "However, there was one very large error in the letter."

"What error?" He slid the page toward him and read over the words carefully. When he didn't see anything amiss the first time through, he read it again. The confession was put in exactly as he'd intended.

"It's dreadful," she said with a tsk. "Now that he's admitted to writing all those other letters, he will be forced to marry one of the women he wooed with his prose."

Gabriel's attention returned to Calliope's profile. He caught sight of a faint line above the ridge of her brow. If he didn't know any better, he'd guess that beyond the teasing there was actual concern that he would be forced to marry another. "I do believe he only proposed to one woman."

"Without proof, there's really no way of knowing for certain," she said, her shoulders stiff. "Now that he's revealed himself, any of the unmarried women could lay claim to him."

"But there is only one who has his proposal in writing."

She let out a breath and a smile tugged at the corner of her mouth. "Oh, but from what I heard, the letter was never signed."

"Hmm…" He reached into his pocket, withdrew the letter in question, and unfolded it. Nudging the lilies aside, he laid it on the table.

Calliope's fingertips brushed his as she pointed to the missing bottom corner. "See? No signature."

Gabriel reached into his pocket again and withdrew a slender leather pouch. He had her attention now. Slipping his hand inside, he first withdrew a rather scraggily red feather and set it on the table. Then he withdrew a polished green stone and placed it beside the feather. And then, carefully, he withdrew a small scrap of paper with a crescent-shaped edge. Like a puzzle piece, he fitted it to the bottom corner, complete with his signature.

Calliope's hands flew to her mouth. Wide-eyed, she stared at the letter and then at him. "You've kept it, all this time?"

He nodded. "And this is the feather and the stone I found on the steps at Almack's." Refusing to wait a moment longer, he drew her into his embrace. "So you see, there really *isn't* another woman who can lay claim to my heart. It's only you. And it always has been."

"I ought to write you a letter in return," she said.

He pulled her closer. "And keep me waiting longer? No. Absolutely not."

"Then I will tell you what I would write." She rose up on her toes, linked her hands around his neck and kissed him. "My dearest Gabriel, I love you in more ways than I can ever express. Even before you wrote that beautiful letter, I was drawn to you. I want no sea to separate us. I want no more rocks between us—unless they are green. Please anchor your heart inside mine, where I will keep it safe. Always. Your siren, Calliope."

Unable to contain his joy, he clutched her tightly to him and spun her around in a circle. "I will give you back each day of all the years we've lost because of my stupidity. You deserve a long courtship."

"Perhaps not a *very* long courtship." She laughed, her eyes shining, before she whispered into his ear…

Hours later, Gabriel returned to the townhouse on Upper Brook Street.

Garnering a special license from the archbishop of Canterbury had been easier than he'd imagined. Of course, having the Duke of Heathcoat's support had helped. And while his father may not have approved of the confession in the *Post*, or the need for a hasty wedding, he hadn't been surprised either.

Gabriel had thought that confronting his father would have been the hardest part. Only now, standing in the Croft study, did he realize that the Duke of Heathcoat could take lessons in intimidation from Calliope's father and brother.

"I should like your blessings, of course." Gabriel swallowed. "But we will be married tomorrow morning."

"A special license?" Griffin Croft bellowed. It was likely heard throughout all of London.

Gabriel held up a hand to ward off Griffin's blow. He'd hoped that the reception would be less violent, but considering the circumstances, he understood. "Remember that day at Gentleman Jackson's, when you'd said you owed me one?"

Croft hesitated. Then, begrudgingly, he lowered his hand. "One, Everhart. But she is my sister."

"And *my* daughter." George Croft's hard fist collided with Gabriel's jaw.

Gabriel landed, sprawled out on the floor. Looking up, George Croft stood over him. Only a moment ago, the man had been seated in his chair, looking frail. Now, he appeared larger than life.

Gabriel shook his head to clear it. Much to his regret, both father and son knew how to land a solid blow. Bending his leg, he rested his arm on his knee and worked his jaw back and forth. He deserved this, he knew. If a man had approached him with a special license for his daughter, then there would be hell to pay.

His daughter... Right this very instant, Calliope could be carrying his child.

Suddenly, he was far too content to feel pain. "My apologies, sir. I will do everything to keep your daughter happy all the days of her life."

George Croft gave a sharp nod and then held out his hand to assist Gabriel off the floor. "Welcome to the family, son."

Church bells rang merrily the following morning as Calliope and Gabriel settled into the carriage. She wore lilies of the valley in her hair. And he had a red feather and a green stone tucked into his pocket.

Her husband. Calliope smiled, beaming. She could not imagine greater happiness than what she felt in this moment.

Once the driver set off, Gabriel pulled her close and kissed her. "You are mine at last, *siren*."

"I would argue the fact and state that, quite clearly, it is the other way around," she teased. "However, I *have* cost you a pretty penny, indeed. You have lost the wager. Danvers's and Montwood's grins could not have been more smug."

He tugged on a wayward lock of hair. "On the contrary, I have lost nothing. In fact, I've gained the only prize I've ever desired."

"As much as I love you for saying that"—she placed her hand over his heart and pressed her lips to his—"I'm certain that your friends will not be satisfied with your reasons. They will want their winnings."

"But who is to say that they will win? There are many months left in this year, and I now have you to help me." Gabriel settled his hands at her waist and lifted her onto his lap.

She laughed and slipped her arms around his neck. "Nothing underhanded. I would prefer to *help* them find their perfect matches."

"Whatever you say, my love." He kissed her again, his mouth drifting below her jaw, along her throat, and then to the ribbon trim of her pale gold dress. "It is a good thing I ordered a closed carriage."

She arched her neck, allowing him better access. "But we will arrive at our wedding breakfast in a minute or two."

"I've asked the driver to take a tour of the park first. Unless you'd rather begin with breakfast." He nudged her sleeve off one shoulder and...

Calliope gasped. "No, you are right. *This* is the perfect beginning."

ACKNOWLEDGMENTS

Thank you to my Facebook peeps—April Shafer, Cara Ross, Kim Castillo, Lori Worthington, and Lynne Ernst—for helping give the "matchmaker" of this series his name.

Thank you to Chelsey and the spectacular Avon Impulse team for all your hard work, dedication, *and* a swoon-worthy cover.

Thank you to the romance community and the fans of historical romance, for all your love and support.

Vivienne Lorret's steamy new series continues!

Keep reading for a sneak peek at the next book in her

Rakes of Fallow Hall series

The Devilish Mr. Danvers

Coming April 2015 from Avon Impulse.

An Excerpt From

THE DEVILISH MR. DANVERS

When Hedley Sinclair inherits Greyson Park, she finally has a chance at a real life. The only person standing in her way is Rafe Danvers, her handsome neighbor who also claims ownership over the crumbling estate. Rafe is determined to take back what's his—even it means being a bit devilish. Knowing the stipulations of her inheritance, he decides to find her a husband. The only problem is, he can't seem to stop seducing her. In fact, he can't seem to stop falling in love with her.

"A young woman in society usually flirts when given the opportunity."

How was she supposed to flirt when she could barely think? Rafe stood close enough that she could feel the alluring heat rising from his body. Hedley drew in a breath in an effort to think of a response. When she did, however, her nostrils filled with a pleasant scent that only made her want to draw in another breath. It was *his* fragrance. From their previous encounter, she recognized the woodsy essence and a trace of sweet smoke.

Hedley caught herself rocking onto the balls of her feet to get closer, but then quickly rocked back to her heels. She swallowed, her throat suddenly dry. "I am not in society. Nor am I likely to be. Therefore, I have no reason to flirt."

"You don't need a reason." He leaned in, his voice low. The angular cut of his side-whiskers seemed to direct her gaze toward his mouth. "Flirting is a skill. You use it to get what you want."

Hedley forgot why she'd come here. *To get what you want…*

The more she stared at Rafe's mouth, the heavier her eyelids seemed to weigh. Why was she suddenly so tired? Perhaps it *was* too early to pay a call. Or perhaps it was because he stood so close that his warmth blanketed her. It would only take a single step to rest her head against his shoulder. "Like a type of currency used in society?"

"An astute observation." He grinned.

She was definitely out of her element. The least she could do was *try* to keep her wits about her. "Then, I should assume that you want something from me."

He moved closer, but she dared not imagine that he was under the same trance. No, he was far too skilled in the ways of society for that.

Even so, the curve of his knuckles brushed her cheek. "What shade of pink do you suppose this is?"

"And that was a terrible change of topic." Believing that he was speaking of one of the colored glass vases in the cabinet, she looked them over. She found deep red, the color of merlot; a blue vase, bright and clear as a summer sky; daffodil yellow, among other hues. Turning away from the cabinet, she lifted her gaze to his. "Besides, I see no pink."

"No, this color. Here." His thumb caressed her cheek, his fingers settling beneath her jaw.

Was it possible for a man to have eyelashes that looked as if they were smudged with soot, all soft and curled up at the ends? It didn't seem possible to her. Yet that's exactly what she saw as he studied her. Knowing that her skin had betrayed her thoughts in a blush should make her want to shy away. Yet she'd gone too long without being noticed to feel an ounce of shame. Instead, she reveled in the attentiveness of his gaze, the nearness and warmth of his body, and the contact of his flesh to hers—even if it was a false show for him.

While not entirely certain that he expected her to answer, she indulged him. "Some roses are pink."

"True." He tilted her chin. Four thin, horizontal lines appeared above the bridge of his nose, as if he truly were studying her. "Though when I think of rosy pink, it is darker, redder than this."

She tasted his breath on her lips. Other than their clumsy spill on the ice, this was the closest she'd ever been to a man. Heat poured from his body, sweeping over her, compelling her to draw nearer to the source. She couldn't help it.

"Berries are sometimes pink," she whispered, wondering if he could feel her breath as well.

He licked his lips. "Only *unripe* berries are pink, and you are a most decidedly ripe fruit, sweeting."

The tone of his voice changed ever so slightly. The silky timbre turned deeper, indulgent, like slipping into a pair of warm velvet slippers.

She wanted to sink into that sound. "Pink carnations."

"Yes. That's it." Abruptly, his hand slipped away. "A carnation pink blush, and berry-stained lips."

Missing the contact, her chin tilted of its own accord. His gaze slowly dipped to her mouth. Whatever this game was, she wanted it to continue. "Was this a lesson in flirting, or is the color of actual importance?"

Abruptly, he stepped away from her and headed toward a tasseled bell-pull on the far wall. It was almost as if he suddenly wanted to put as much distance between them as possible.

She had her answer. He was only using flirting in order to gain something. The only thing she possessed that Rafe Danvers wanted, however, was not for sale. No matter how tempting the currency, she would not give him Greyson Park.

USA Today best-selling author **VIVIENNE LORRET** loves romance novels, her pink laptop, her husband, and her two sons (not necessarily in that order...but there are days). Transforming copious amounts of tea into words, she is proud to be an Avon Impulse author of works including *Tempting Mr. Weatherstone*, the Wallflower Wedding Series, and the Rakes of Fallow Hall series.

Discover great authors, exclusive offers, and more at hc.com.

Give in to your impulses . . .
Read on for a sneak peek at six brand-new
e-book original tales of romance
from HarperCollins.
Available now wherever e-books are sold.

WHEN GOOD EARLS GO BAD
A Victorian Valentine's Day Novella
By Megan Frampton

THE WEDDING BAND
A Save the Date Novel
By Cara Connelly

RIOT
By Jamie Shaw

ONLY IN MY DREAMS
Ribbon Ridge Book One
By Darcy Burke

SINFUL REWARDS 1
A Billionaires and Bikers Novella
By Cynthia Sax

TEMPT THE NIGHT
A Trust No One Novel
By Dixie Lee Brown

An Excerpt from

WHEN GOOD EARLS GO BAD
A Victorian Valentine's Day Novella
by Megan Frampton

Megan Frampton's *Dukes Behaving Badly* series
continues, but this time it's an earl who's meeting
his match in a delightfully fun and sexy novella!

"While it's not precisely true that nobody is here, because I am, in fact, here, the truth is that there is no one here who can accommodate the request."

The man standing in the main area of the Quality Employment Agency didn't leave. She'd have to keep on, then.

"If I weren't here, then it would be even more in question, since you wouldn't know the answer to the question one way or the other, would you? So I am here, but I am not the proper person for what you need."

The man fidgeted with the hat he held in his hand. But still did not take her hint. She would have to persevere.

"I suggest you leave the information, and we will endeavor to fill the position when there is someone here who is not me." Annabelle gave a short nod of her head as she finished speaking, knowing she had been absolutely clear in what she'd said. If repetitive. So it was a surprise that the man to whom she was speaking was staring back at her, his mouth slightly opened, his eyes blinking behind his owlish spectacles. His hat now held very tightly in his hand.

Perhaps she should speak more slowly.

"We do not have a housekeeper for hire," she said, pausing

between each word. "I am the owner, not one of the employees for hire."

Now the man's mouth had closed, but it still seemed as though he did not understand.

"I do not understand," he said, confirming her very suspicion. "This is an employment agency, and I have an employer who wishes to find an employee. And if I do not find a suitable person within . . ." and at this he withdrew a pocket watch from his waistcoat and frowned at it, as though it was its fault it was already past tea time, and *goodness, wasn't she hungry and had Caroline left any milk in the jug? Because if not, well,* "twenty-four hours, my employer, the Earl of Selkirk, will be most displeased, and we will ensure your agency will no longer receive our patronage."

That last part drew her attention away from the issue of the milk and whether or not there was any.

"The Earl of . . . ?" she said, feeling that flutter in her stomach that signaled there was nobility present or being mentioned—or she wished there were, at least. Rather like the milk, actually.

"Selkirk," the man replied in a firm tone. He had no comment on the milk. And why would he? He didn't even know it was a possibility that they didn't have any, and if she did have to serve him tea, what would she say? Besides which, she had no clue to the man's name; he had just come in and been all brusque and demanded a housekeeper when there was none.

"Selkirk," Annabelle repeated, her mind rifling through all the nobles she'd ever heard mentioned.

"A Scottish earl," the man said.

Annabelle beamed and clapped her hands. "Oh, Scottish! Small wonder I did not recognize the title, I've only ever been in London and once to the seaside when I was five years old, but I wouldn't have known if that was Scotland, but I am fairly certain it was not because it would have been cold and it was quite warm in the water. Unless the weather was unseasonable, I can safely say I have never been to Scotland, nor do I know of any Scottish earls."

An Excerpt from

THE WEDDING BAND
A Save the Date Novel
by Cara Connelly

In the latest *Save the Date* novel from Cara
Connelly, journalist Christina Case crashes a
celebrity wedding, and sparks fly when she comes
face-to-face with A-list movie star Dakota Rain . . .

Dakota Rain took a good hard look in the bathroom mirror and inventoried the assets.

Piercing blue eyes? Check.

Sexy stubble? Check.

Sun-streaked blond hair? Check.

Movie-star smile?

Uh-oh.

In the doorway, his assistant rolled her eyes and hit speed dial. "Emily Fazzone here," she said. "Mr. Rain needs to see Dr. Spade this morning. Another cap." She listened a moment, then snorted a laugh. "You're telling me. Might as well cap them all and be done with it."

In the mirror Dakota gave her his hit man squint. "No extra caps."

"Weenie," she said, pocketing her phone. "You don't have time today, anyway. Spade's squeezing you in, as usual. Then you're due at the studio at eleven for the voice-over. It'll be tight, so step on it."

Deliberately, Dakota turned to his reflection again. Tilted his head. Pulled at his cheeks like he was contemplating a shave.

Emily did another eye roll. Muttering something that

might have been either "Get to work" or "What a jerk," she disappeared into his closet, emerging a minute later with jeans, T-shirt, and boxer briefs. She stacked them on the granite vanity, then pulled out her phone again and scrolled through the calendar.

"You've got a twelve o'clock with Peter at his office about the Levi's endorsement, then a one-thirty fitting for your tux. Mercer's coming here at two-thirty to talk about security for the wedding . . ."

Dakota tuned her out. His schedule didn't worry him. Emily would get him where he needed to be. If he ran a little late and a few people had to cool their heels, well, they were used to dealing with movie stars. Hell, they'd be disappointed if he behaved like regular folk.

Taking his sweet time, he shucked yesterday's briefs and meandered naked to the shower without thinking twice. He knew Emily wouldn't bat an eye. After ten years nursing him through injuries and illness, puking and pain, she'd seen all there was to see. Broad shoulders? Tight buns? She was immune.

And besides, she was gay.

Jacking the water temp to scalding, he stuck his head under the spray, wincing when it found the goose egg on the back of his skull. He measured it with his fingers, two inches around.

The same right hook that had chipped his tooth had bounced his head off a concrete wall.

Emily rapped on the glass. He rubbed a clear spot in the steam and gave her the hard eye for pestering him in the shower.

She was immune to that too. "I asked you if we're looking at a lawsuit."

"Damn straight." He was all indignation. "We're suing The Combat Zone. Tubby busted my tooth and gave me a concussion to boot."

She sighed. "I meant, are *we* getting sued? Tubby's a good bouncer. If he popped you, you gave him a reason."

Dakota put a world of aggrievement into his Western drawl. "Why do you always take everybody else's side? You weren't there. You don't know what happened."

"Sure I do. It's October, isn't it? The month you start howling at the moon and throwing punches at bystanders. It's an annual event. The lawyers are on standby. I just want to know if I should call them."

He did the snarl that sent villains and virgins running for their mamas.

An Excerpt from

RIOT

by Jamie Shaw

Jamie Shaw's rock stars are back, and this time
wild, unpredictable Dee and sexy, mohawked
guitarist Joel have explosive chemistry—but will
jealousy and painful memories keep them apart?

"Kiss me," I order the luckiest guy in Mayhem tonight. When he sat next to me at the bar earlier with his "Leave It to Beaver" haircut, I made sure to avoid eye contact and cross my legs in the opposite direction. I didn't think I'd end up making out with him, but now I have no choice.

A dumb expression washes over his face. He might be cute if he didn't look so. freaking. dumb. "Huh?"

"Oh for God's sake."

I curl my fingers behind his neck and yank him to my mouth, tilting my head to the side and hoping he's a quick learner. My lips part, my tongue comes out to play, and after a moment, he finally catches on. His greedy fingers bury themselves in my chocolate brown curls—which I spent *hours* on this morning.

Peeking out of the corner of my eye, I spot Joel Gibbon stroll past me, a bleach-blonde groupie tucked under his arm. He's too busy whispering in her ear to notice me, and my fingers itch to punch him in the back of his stupid mohawked head to get his attention.

I'm preparing to push Leave It to Beaver off me when Joel's gaze finally lifts to meet mine. I bite Beaver's bottom lip between my teeth and give it a little tug, and the corner of

Joel's mouth lifts up into an infuriating smirk that is *so* not the reaction I wanted. He continues walking, and when he's finally out of sight, I break my lips from Beaver's and nudge him back toward his own stool, immediately spinning in the opposite direction to scowl at my giggling best friend.

"I can't BELIEVE him!" I shout at a far-too-amused-looking Rowan. How does she not recognize the gravity of this situation?!

I'm about to shake some sense into her when Beaver taps me on the shoulder. "Um—"

"You're welcome," I say with a flick of my wrist, not wanting to waste another minute on a guy who can't appreciate how long it took me to get my hair to curl like this—or at least make messing it up worth my while.

Rowan gives him an apologetic half smile, and I let out a deep sigh.

I don't feel bad about Beaver. I feel bad about the dickhead bass guitarist for the Last Ones to Know.

"That boy is making me insane," I growl.

Rowan turns a bright smile on me, her blue eyes sparkling with humor. "You were already insane."

"He's making me homicidal," I clarify, and she laughs.

"Why don't you just tell him you like him?" She twirls two tiny straws in her cocktail, her eyes periodically flitting up to the stage. She's waiting for Adam, and I'd probably be jealous of her if those two weren't so disgustingly perfect for each other.

Last semester, I nearly got kicked out of my dorm when I let Rowan move in with me and my roommate. But Rowan's asshole live-in boyfriend had cheated on her, and she had nowhere to go, and she's been my *best* friend since kindergarten. I ignored the written warnings from my RA, and Rowan ultimately ended up moving in with Adam before I got kicked out. Fast forward to one too many "overnight visitors" later, I still ended up getting reported, and Rowan and I got a two-bedroom in an apartment complex near campus. Her name is on the lease right next to mine, but really, the apartment is just a decoy she uses to avoid telling her parents that she's actually living with three ungodly hot rock stars. She sleeps in Adam's bed, his bandmate Shawn is in the second bedroom, and Joel sleeps on their couch most nights because he's a hot, stupid, infuriating freaking nomad.

"Because I *don't* like him," I answer. When I realize my drink is gone, I steal Rowan's, down the last of it, and flag the bartender.

"Then why is he making you insane?"

"Because *he* doesn't like *me*."

Rowan lifts a sandy blonde eyebrow at me, but I don't expect her to understand. Hell, *I* don't understand. I've never wanted a boy to like me so badly in my entire life.

An Excerpt from

ONLY IN MY DREAMS
Ribbon Ridge Book One
by Darcy Burke

From a *USA Today* bestselling author
comes the first installment in a sexy and
emotional family saga about seven siblings
who reunite in a small Oregon town to
fulfill their brother's dying wish . . .

Sara Archer took a deep breath and dialed her assistant and close friend, Craig Walker. He was going to laugh his butt off when she told him why she was calling, which almost made her hang up, but she forced herself to go through with it.

"Sara! Your call can only mean one thing: you're totally doing it."

She envisioned his blue eyes alight with laughter, his dimples creasing, and rolled her eyes. "I guess so."

He whooped into the phone, causing Sara to pull it back from her ear. "Awesome! You won't regret it. It's been waaaaay too long since you got out there. What, four years?"

"You're exaggerating." More like three. She hadn't been out with a guy since Jude. Easy, breezy, coffee barista Jude. He'd been a welcome breath of fresh air after her cheating college boyfriend. Come to think of it, she'd taken three years to get back in the game then too.

"Am I? I've known you for almost three years, and you've never had even a casual date in all that time."

Because after she and Jude had ended their fling, she'd decided to focus on her business, and she'd hired Craig a couple of months later. "Enough with the history lesson. Let's talk about tonight before I lose my nerve."

"Got it. I'm really proud of you for doing this. You need a social life beyond our rom-com movie nights."

Sara suspected he was pushing her to go out because he'd started dating someone. They seemed serious even though it had been only a couple of weeks, and when you fell in love, you wanted the whole world to fall in love too. Not that Sara planned on doing that again—if she could even count her college boyfriend as falling in love. She really didn't know anymore.

"I was thinking I might go line dancing." She glanced through her clothing, pondering what to wear.

"Line dancing?" Craig's tone made it sound as if he were asking whether she was going to the garbage dump. He wouldn't have been caught dead in a country-western bar. "If you want to get your groove on, Taylor and I will come get you and take you downtown. Much better scene."

No, the nearby suburban country-western bar would suit her needs just fine. She wouldn't be comfortable at a chic Portland club—totally out of her league. "I'll stick with Side-winders, thanks."

"We wouldn't take you to a gay bar," Craig said with a touch of exasperation that made her smile.

"I know. I just don't want company. You'd try to set me up with every guy in the place."

"I'm not that bad! Taylor keeps me in line."

Yeah, she'd noticed. She'd been out with them once and was surprised at the difference in Craig. He was still his ener-getic self, but it was like everything he had was focused on his new boyfriend. She supposed that was natural when a relationship was shiny and new. "Well, I'm good going by myself. I'm just going to dance a little, maybe sip a lemon drop, see what happens."

Craig made a noise of disgust. "Don't ass out, Sara. You need to get laid."

An Excerpt from

SINFUL REWARDS 1
A Billionaires and Bikers Novella
by Cynthia Sax

Belinda "Bee" Carter is a good girl; at least, that's
what she tells herself. And a good girl deserves
a nice guy—just like the gorgeous and moody
billionaire Nicolas Rainer. Or so she thinks,
until she takes a look through her telescope
and sees a naked, tattooed man on the balcony
across the courtyard. He has been watching
her, and that makes him all the more enticing.
But when a mysterious and anonymous text
message dares her to do something bad, she
must decide if she is really the good girl she has
always claimed to be, or if she's willing to risk
everything for her secret fantasy of being watched.

An Avon Red Impulse Novella

I'd told Cyndi I'd never use it, that it was an instrument purchased by perverts to spy on their neighbors. She'd laughed and called me a prude, not knowing that I was one of those perverts, that I secretly yearned to watch and be watched, to care and be cared for.

If I'm cautious, and I'm always cautious, she'll never realize I used her telescope this morning. I swing the tube toward the bench and adjust the knob, bringing the mysterious object into focus.

It's a phone. Nicolas's phone. I bounce on the balls of my feet. This is a sign, another declaration from fate that we belong together. I'll return Nicolas's much-needed device to him. As a thank you, he'll invite me to dinner. We'll talk. He'll realize how perfect I am for him, fall in love with me, marry me.

Cyndi will find a fiancé also—everyone loves her—and we'll have a double wedding, as sisters of the heart often do. It'll be the first wedding my family has had in generations.

Everyone will watch us as we walk down the aisle. I'll wear a strapless white Vera Wang mermaid gown with organza and lace details, crystal and pearl embroidery accents, the bodice fitted, and the skirt hemmed for my shorter height. My hair will be swept up. My shoes—

Voices murmur outside the condo's door, the sound piercing my delightful daydream. I swing the telescope upward, not wanting to be caught using it. The snippets of conversation drift away.

I don't relax. If the telescope isn't positioned in the same way as it was last night, Cyndi will realize I've been using it. She'll tease me about being a fellow pervert, sharing the story, embellished for dramatic effect, with her stern, serious dad—or, worse, with Angel, that snobby friend of hers.

I'll die. It'll be worse than being the butt of jokes in high school because that ridicule was about my clothes and this will center on the part of my soul I've always kept hidden. It'll also be the truth, and I won't be able to deny it. I am a pervert.

I have to return the telescope to its original position. This is the only acceptable solution. I tap the metal tube.

Last night, my man-crazy roommate was giggling over the new guy in three-eleven north. The previous occupant was a gray-haired, bowtie-wearing tax auditor, his luxurious accommodations supplied by Nicolas. The most exciting thing he ever did was drink his tea on the balcony.

According to Cyndi, the new occupant is a delicious piece of man candy—tattooed, buff, and head-to-toe lickable. He was completing armcurls outside, and she enthusiastically counted his reps, oohing and aahing over his bulging biceps, calling to me to take a look.

I resisted that temptation, focusing on making macaroni and cheese for the two of us, the recipe snagged from the diner my mom works in. After we scarfed down dinner, Cyndi licking her plate clean, she left for the club and hasn't returned.

Three-eleven north is the mirror condo to ours. I straighten the telescope. That position looks about right, but then, the imitation UGGs I bought in my second year of college looked about right also. The first time I wore the boots in the rain, the sheepskin fell apart, leaving me barefoot in Economics 201.

Unwilling to risk Cyndi's friendship on "about right," I gaze through the eyepiece. The view consists of rippling golden planes, almost like . . .

Tanned skin pulled over defined abs.

I blink. It can't be. I take another look. A perfect pearl of perspiration clings to a puckered scar. The drop elongates more and more, stretching, snapping. It trickles downward, navigating the swells and valleys of a man's honed torso.

No. I straighten. This is wrong. I shouldn't watch our sexy neighbor as he stands on his balcony. If anyone catches me . . .

Parts 1 – 8 available now!

An Excerpt from

TEMPT THE NIGHT
A Save the Date Novel
by Dixie Lee Brown

Dixie Lee Brown concludes her thrilling
Trust No One series with the fast-paced
tale of a damaged hero and the sexy
fugitive he can't help falling for.

She pursed her lips and studied him. "That's deep, Brady." A crooked grin gradually appeared, erasing the worry wrinkles from her forehead. Then, without any encouragement from him, Mac took a step closer and leaned into his chest, sliding her arms around his waist.

He hesitated only a second before wrapping her in his arms and pulling her close. A groan escaped him.

She shifted her head to glance up. "Do you mind?"

A soft chuckle vibrated through him. "Sugar, I'll hold you anytime, anywhere."

Mac snuggled closer, and he tipped her head with his fingers, slowly covering her mouth with his, giving her plenty of time to change her mind. When she didn't, he drank of her sweetness like a man dying of thirst. Again and again he kissed her, his tongue pushing into her mouth, swirling and dancing with hers. He couldn't get enough of her full, soft lips, her sweet taste, and the bold way she pressed against him.

Brady couldn't say which of the day's events was responsible for her change in temperature where he was concerned, but it wasn't important. They were taking steps in the right direction, and he wasn't going to do anything to screw that up. He wanted her warm and willing in his hands, but he also wanted her there for the right reasons. The decision was hers to make.

When he lifted his head, there were tears on her eyelashes, but her smile made his heart grab an extra beat. He let his fingers trail across the satin skin of her cheek as he kissed her neck tenderly and breathed in her sweet scent.

"God, you smell good." He kissed each of her closed eyes, then leaned his forehead on hers and took a deep breath. "I'd love for this to go on all night. Unfortunately, Joe wants us to meet with Maria." He steadied her as she straightened and took a step back.

Mac's gaze was uncertain. "We could meet later . . . if you want to . . ."

"Aw, sugar. If *I* want to? That's like asking if I want to keep breathing." He threaded his fingers through her hair and brushed his lips over hers. "I've wanted you since the first time you lied to me." Brady chuckled as her eyes lit up.

She punched his chest with a fisted hand. "Hey! That was the only time I lied, and I had a darn good reason. Some big galoot knocks me down, pounces on me, and then expects me to be truthful. Nuh uh. I don't think so." Her eyes sparkled with challenge.

"*Galoot*, huh? No more John Wayne movies for you, sugar."

She sucked in a big breath, and he could tell by the mischief in her eyes that she was getting ready to let him have it. He touched his fingers to her lips to silence her. "Let me say this, okay? There's a good chance we'll go in and meet with Maria, and sometime before, after, or during, you'll think about us—about me—and decide we're not a good idea. I want you to know two things. First . . . it's the best idea I've had in a long time. Second . . . if you decide it's a mistake or that you're not ready to get any closer, that's okay. No pressure."

He stepped back and gave her some room. It struck him that he'd just lied to her. What he said would have been true for any other woman he'd ever known, but he damn sure wasn't going to give up on Mac that easily.

A grin made the sparkle in her eyes dance as she slipped her hand into his. "Obviously you're confusing me with some other woman, because I don't usually change my mind once it's made up, and I'm a big girl, so you can stop worrying that your charm, good looks, and sex appeal will bowl me over. As for thinking about you—yeah." She stepped closer and lowered her voice to a silky whisper. "You might cross my mind once or twice . . . so let's get this meeting over with."

"You got it, sugar." Brady couldn't remember when he'd been so contented—or when he'd ever used that word to describe himself before. Whether or not tonight ended with him in bed with this amazingly beautiful and brave woman didn't really matter. The last few minutes had made it clear that his interest in her went way beyond just the prospect of sex. He wanted everything she had to give. *Shit!* She'd turned him upside down and inside out until he doubted his own ability to walk away . . . or even if he wanted to.